THE LOST SON

THE LOST SON

A NOVEL BY

BRENT SPENCER

ARCADE PUBLISHING · NEW YORK

FIRST EDITION

Lines from "The Lost Son" and "Infirmity" by Theodore Roethke. "The
Lost Son" copyright 1947 by Theodore Roethke. "Infirmity" copyright
© 1963 by Beatrice Roethke, Administratix of the Estate of Theodore
Roethke. From *The Collected Poems of Theodore Roethke* by Theodore
Roethke. Reprinted with permission of Doubleday, a division of Ban-
tam, Doubleday Dell Publishing Group, Inc.

The italicized passages on pages 205–218 are from *Handbook for Boys*.
Copyright © 1948 by Boy Scouts of America. Used by permission.

The characters and events in this book are fictitious. Any similarity
to real persons, living or dead, is coincidental and not intended
by the author.

Library of Congress Cataloging-in-Publication Data
Spencer, Brent.
The lost son / Brent Spencer. — 1st ed.
p.   cm.
ISBN 1-55970-266-4
1. Mothers and sons — Pennsylvania — Fiction.   2. Man-woman
relationships — Pennsylvania — Fiction.   I. Title.
PS3569.P4458L67   1995
813'.54 — dc20   94-31906

Published in the United States by Arcade Publishing, Inc., New York
Distributed by Little, Brown and Company

10   9   8   7   6   5   4   3   2

BP

Designed by API

PRINTED IN THE UNITED STATES OF AMERICA

I'm grateful to James Michener and the Copernicus Society for a generous grant during the early stages of writing this novel. For giving me time and space to grow, I thank the Iowa Writers' Workshop and the Stanford Program in Creative Writing. I owe so much to so many writers and friends that I can't list them all here. But special thanks go to Nancy Packer and her unerring good sense and to John L'Heureux for his tireless and brilliant guidance. And I'm grateful for the keen eyes and big wit of Timothy Bent, my editor. Thanks also to Brad Owens and Leslee Becker for much good criticism and many soul-restoring trips to flea markets. Lynne McFall has never failed to give me the truest words she knows. I'm glad you stood in my way. And when I thought I was lost forever, Rosemary Catacalos found me — *gracias, mija.*

Nora

Tell me:
Which is the way I take;
Out of what door do I go,
Where and to whom?

　　　　　"The Lost Son"

Things without hands take hands: there is no choice.

　　　　　"Infirmity"

　　　　　— Theodore Roethke

THE LOST SON

Lloyd is so small he can't say his name without making it sound like something's caught in his throat. He and his parents live in the country. In a white, white house.

But he's not in the house now. He's running naked through the spiky green yard and into the cornfield, afraid of something, lost. The ground between the rows is hard and bare. The roots of the cornstalks are green fingers clutching the ground. Hot summer shines through the green leaves. Wind scuttles through the green leaves. He stops.

Down the row, a raccoon has shimmied up a cornstalk, hugging the top tightly. Its weight bends the stalk slowly to the ground. The raccoon and her two cubs carefully strip the stalk bare, small black hands tugging fiercely at the knobs of corn. He wants to pet the babies — their soft, black, gray, and brown fur — the babies no more than balls of fluff.

But he hears the chortle and hiss, the thin growl. He's afraid the raccoon wants to claw out his eyes. But she hears it too. She raises her mysterious face, sniffs the air. She noses her cubs and nips at them. They scurry down the row ahead of her and out of sight, leaving the corn behind, leaving him behind.

The growling and hissing grow louder. He's running now. Running between the thick green pillars — to the growl, away from the growl, he can't tell where. He feels his father's bare feet pounding against the hard ground. Closer now, pounding, the corn trembling. He's crying for his mother but doesn't know where she is. And now his father's on him, catches him up in his big hands. "Do I have to show you what happens to dirty little things that can't keep a secret?" His father shakes him hard. "You don't run away from me, boy. You don't never run away from me." Bright sunlight burns his eyes. The day's on fire.

1

LLOYD REDMOND WAS THE KING OF TOMATOES. The king. Nobody knew more than he knew about tomatoes. He could tell you all about their secrets — from seed to set, from the pale-green knuckles of the first fruit to the knobby tentacles he ground into mulch at the end of summer.

That afternoon was meant for tomatoes. It was spring. It was time. He'd staked out a half-acre garden in the paddock below the barn, and a good bit of it would soon be thick with tomatoes. But first the electric fence needed fixing.

He and the kid made their way down the field, Redmond wrestling a wheelbarrow piled high with tools over the uneven ground, Nick drifting placidly beside him. They stopped at the power box attached to the potting shed. Redmond pulled the switch, making sure Nick was watching. "When the fence is fixed, I'll wave and you reconnect it. OK?"

"Yeah," Nick sighed. "Sure." It was Saturday and he had mall plans. He was a tall, muscular sixteen-year-old with a well-cultivated look of boredom. Something in the way his gaze settled on you, lightly and from a long way off.

Redmond shoved the wheelbarrow ahead of him, slogging through the long grass toward the pasture below. There wasn't much to the fence — a strand of wire running along a line of aluminum stakes, held up by an insulated curl at the top of each stake. The thing barely stood upright. He parked the barrow and walked the perimeter, running his hand along the wire, looking for the short. The yearlings, all big-boned Charolais the color of heavily creamed coffee, were huddled at the lower end of the field, their fat dull eyes buzzing with flies, their mouths bristling with swatches of new grass.

He found the problem right away, a clump of weeds leaning against the wire. Why were weeds always the first crop of the season? The fence was guaranteed hot enough to cut through anything it touched. "Some weed burner," he said, making a face.

"I found it!" he yelled. With one hand he held the wire aside, with the other he chopped at the roots with the hoe.

That's when Nick juiced him, threw the switch, sent all that voltage along the wire and into him. Fire shot up his arm, his teeth snapped shut, the ropes in his neck jumped, the ground seemed to swell under him. When he pulled his hand free, he didn't let himself cry out, wouldn't even touch the arm, though his hand felt peeled to the bone. He closed his eyes tight, tighter, until white flames danced on the backs of his eyelids.

When he opened them again, the pain had faded, but his arm hung dead from the shoulder. Nick was wandering down to him, brushing his blond hair back over his ears with the palms of his hands, stepping carefully over the cow flop, trying not to sully his new black sweatpants, trying not to sweat.

Redmond picked up the hoe he had dropped, chopping at the ground, working it one-handed. He held his jaw so tight his teeth hurt.

By the time Nick reached him, he had finished hacking out the weeds. He threw the hoe on top of the other tools in the wheelbarrow — hatchet, wire cutters, saw, wrenches, baling wire, hammer — everything he needed for a day's work. He swung the heavy wheelbarrow about, forcing his dead muscles to work.

Nick turned right around and followed him uphill, acting as if nothing had happened, and that was the greater indignity. The feeling still hadn't come back to Redmond's arm, not really, not completely. He bulled the wheelbarrow uphill toward the barn, but he couldn't bounce it over the rough ground the way he usually could. Every time he hit a rock or furrow, the wheelbarrow stopped dead and tipped so suddenly he could barely right it. The muscles in his arm had turned to mush. And walking beside him — thick-muscled, straight-backed, nothing in the empty hands of his two good arms — the kid picked his way gingerly through the weeds, trying not to get grass stains on his eighty-dollar running shoes.

They were coming up to the chicken run. Two years ago, Redmond decided to raise some Rocks, Reds, even a few Anacondas with shimmery blue-green spats. He read books, talked to the county agent, knocked together a coop from old lumber he found stacked against the barn. He did everything you were supposed to do. But now half his flock were diseased. They spent the days huddling in the dirt or chasing each other in crazy circles or pecking at each other, pulling out each other's feathers, right down to the obscenely pink skin. The chicken run was scattered with loose feathers, the fence clotted with them. When the wind blew, small white pinfeathers rose up in clouds, like dandelion puffs, and clung to the branches of the shaggy willows that surrounded the run.

The coop was already falling apart, brittle gray planks rotting off their nails. That morning he'd asked Nick to tack some of them down. All it took was a hammer, but now Redmond saw that he'd used the power nailer, Redmond's toy, the gift he bought himself when they moved to the farm. There it was, lying in the wet grass, still plugged in, its orange extension cord coiling through the open doorway.

As they walked past the coop, Nick said, "You think I could have ten dollars to go out for a soda and a burger with some people?"

And that was all it took. Redmond heaved the wheelbarrow over, dumping his tools onto the ground. With his good hand he grabbed Nick by the back of his shirt and shoved him into the coop. He slammed the door so hard dust flew from every crack, loose boards rattled, and the air was thick with the cries of outraged chickens. He grabbed up the power nailer and pegged the door with a dozen nails, toenailed them good and sharp so they'd run deep into the jamb. He pumped nails into the door until the machine went dead, until there was nothing but a dry click when he pulled the trigger.

Only when the kid was safely shut inside, only then did Redmond allow himself to shake the arm out, to flex the dead fingers of his dead hand.

He reloaded the wheelbarrow and struggled uphill, shoving it into the paddock garden. Nothing was going to keep him from getting those tomatoes in the ground. The coop was boiling over with chickens, cackling and flapping out the hole, falling down the ramp. The kid made no sound.

Redmond came from farm stock. Maybe he'd never really farmed, but his grandparents had, and his parents grew up on farms. They'd lived on a farm when he was young. He didn't remember much about it, didn't want to remember. Corn. He remembered corn. And anyway, he didn't have to remember. Farming was in his genes, his blood.

The feeling was starting to come back to his arm. He worked the blade of the shovel into the hard ground, beginning his yearly ritual. First the hole, three feet deep. Then a shovelful of ripe, wet cow manure. But it was hard to keep his mind on tomatoes, now that Nick had started yelling.

"You fuck! I'll kill you!"

You wish, Redmond thought as he filled each hole with the dark loam he had screened so carefully, adding extra sand to help the roots along. Close but not too close. That was one of the secrets. The roots would reach down to the pocket of manure, would grow rich with it, but if they grew too close, the manure would burn the roots, and all your work for nothing. People think the secrets of tomatoes are pruning, weeding, watering. But none of these is the big secret. The big secret is controlling the growth of the roots.

Again the sound of cracking wood as Nick jumped against the door. But Redmond wasn't worried. At sixteen, the kid was tall and strong, but the coop was small. No room to get a nice run at the door. What good was all his karate now? The only things breaking in there were his bones.

Ellen, Nick's mother, had been gone six months now. Hard to get used to. Redmond was the one who usually did the leaving. Probably found herself a new life. New house, new job, new man. Let her. But why stick him with the kid? Her kid. If you're going, go, but do it clean. Don't leave loose ends lying around.

Twelve years ago at The Hourglass, the night they met, he knew as soon as he laid eyes on her that she'd leave him someday. Hell, he knew it before he ever laid eyes on her. He had a kind of radar for rejection. That's why he left so many times. Do it to her before she did it to him. So she was really gone. Six months is pretty goddamn gone. So what.

But he couldn't get her out of his mind. When she made love to him, he wept, he trembled. She'd look down at him and say, "Was it a good one?" And he'd lie there breathless, his heart galloping, too weak to answer.

He went to the potting shed just below the paddock and brought back two flats of tomato sets, sets he'd forced from seeds, seeds he'd collected from last year's plants. He didn't trust mail order seeds or the spindly, dried-out sets they sold at Kinsey's Feed and Supply. Anyway, it was cheaper using his own seeds, even with the employee discount Mrs. Kinsey gave him. His plants had a lineage. He knew where his plants came from. Six years, six seasons of tomatoes — all grown from the same handful of seeds.

The chickens had slowly gathered around the coop again, making low mournful noises. But when Nick yelled and charged the door, they ran shrieking to the other end of the run.

Redmond pried a set out of a flat. With the blade of his hand, he cut a hole in a low mound of soft loam, then tamped the plant carefully into place. He drove a ten-foot stake into the ground next to it. Ridiculous, the giant stake next to the slender shoot, but it wouldn't be long before the shoots grew tall — first lanky as the legs of roses, then taller, until each towering stalk was as thick as a child's wrist, each creaking with a hundred pounds of tomatoes, the dependable mystery of flower and fruit.

It was late afternoon by the time he finished planting the last of them. Twenty plants in all. He gave them each a drink of water, then gathered his tools — the shovel, the empty flats, the rake — piling everything into the battered blue wheelbarrow.

One quick look at the coop. The chickens were crowded together at the far end of the run, pecking each other nervously, chasing each other. Off by herself, Fatima the turkey stood watching everything through one cocked eye.

Nick was so surprised he hadn't even had a chance to react. One minute he was walking up the hillside, the next he was being shoved into the coop, the nailer coughing long chisel points through the door at him. Most of them went into the frame, but some shot through the middle of the door. Redmond wanted to hit him, wanted his blood. That's when Nick saw the thick orange power cord clamped between the door and the jamb. He grabbed it, yanked the plug out of the socket, and listened to Redmond finger the useless trigger.

He thought he was big enough and strong enough to break down the door, but there wasn't room, only a narrow work space between the door and the cage.

The wire cage inside was filled with wooden perches, nesting boxes, a metal feeding trough, and a twenty-gallon watering can. The whole thing was built a foot off the floor so the droppings fell through. Easier to clean, easier to keep the chickens healthy. Still, the flooring wire was gummy with gray-green shreds of chicken shit and loose feathers. The air was sharp with the smell of ammonia.

There was one other way out, on the far side of the coop, a small square chicken hole. But he'd have to tear the cage apart to get at it. And anyway, he would not let Redmond do that to him, make him crawl across the shitty wire like some animal. Besides, the hole didn't look large enough.

He leaned his forehead against the cage and grabbed it with both hands. He stood there with his eyes closed, hissing threats, the sharp wire digging into his skin.

When he heard Redmond push the wheelbarrow away, he felt calmer. The man was crazy, completely crazy. *This* was the guy his mother — but he wouldn't let himself think of her, would not even think her name. He didn't want to blame her. She was all he had, the only good voice in his head.

He unhooked his hands from the wire and turned around. Dust hung thick and yellow. Knives of sunlight came through the cracks, glinting off the nails in the door. He picked a bare spot, held his left arm across his stomach, crouched, and rammed the door. Loose boards rattled and hardware clattered. Dust flew everywhere. But the door held tight. The thing had started falling apart, like all Redmond's projects, the minute they'd built it. Now, of course, it would take a sledgehammer to get him out.

He stood there, nursing his crushed shoulder, breathing in the sharp, rank smell of chicken shit. This time Redmond had gone too far. This time something had to be done.

When he finished planting the tomatoes, Redmond headed back to the house, leaving his power nailer behind. He had no choice. Its cord was clamped in the closed door. He could already feel the damp evening air beginning to rise from the woods below the farm. By morning the nailer would be a pile of rust. It bothered him. He was the kind of man who took care of his tools. He'd get it later, when he let the kid out, after they both had a chance to cool down.

He'd worked hard and he was hungry. His black hair was stiff with dust and dried sweat. Dirt lined the crease of his neck, the folds of his elbows. He washed up at the cellar sink, then went to the kitchen and microwaved the last of the frozen burritos, the only dinner Nick would eat these days. He emptied a half jar of salsa over it, though he knew it would kick a hole in his insides. He sat down in front of the local news and started to eat. The burrito tasted of the freezer, and part of it was cold. He'd followed the directions exactly, but there it was, a spine of frost running along the bottom. He ate it anyway.

He watched a story about a guy who had killed his neighbor by dropping a commode on him from a second-story window. The neighbor never knew what hit him. Redmond's sympathies were instantly and completely with the man who wrenched that commode off its mooring, wrestled it up onto the windowsill, and waited — how long? — for that son-of-a-bitch to walk below. The rest of the news bored him, so he took his dirty plate to the kitchen and wedged it among the others stacked in the sink. He stood there for a while, looking out the kitchen window, watching the coop.

By now it was getting dark. The yelling had stopped long ago. He heard an occasional halfhearted kick at the door, but that was all. Maybe the kid had learned his lesson.

He slipped out of the house quietly and snuck down there, standing among the willows, watching. The chickens, about thirty of them, were huddled outside the coop. A sickly bunch, crazy. Most of them had stopped laying long ago. Too nervous. They fought all the time, tearing out each other's feathers. The backs of some were plucked clean. It was just a matter of time before the bald ones caught pneumonia. Did everything he touched fail, fall apart, or die?

Some of them were sleeping in shallow holes in the dirt, heads sucked in, making themselves small. A few strutted nervously back and forth near the ramp to the chicken hole, uttering low moans of despair. The only sound from inside the coop was the tinny hum of the space heater. He had to let the kid out, if he could only think what to say to him.

As he stood there, one of the Reds strutted stupidly up the ramp and slipped its cocked head through the hole. And then Nick's voice, hollow, booming — "No!" — followed by an explosion of noise — banging, crashing metal, breaking wood. The hen fled back down the ramp in a panic of flapping and squawking. The others woke up, snapping their wings, squawking, running into each other. Only Fatima the turkey stayed calm, a huge dark shadow at the far end of the run. I should kill the fat thing, Redmond thought, but she's too old and sick to eat.

He'd let the kid out. In a little while. He would. Ten dollars for a soda and a hamburger. What kind of fool did he take him for?

He went back to the house and ate the last two bags of corn chips he'd bought for Nick's lunch. They were too salty, but he ate them anyway. Then he filled a glass with ice and took a fifth of Bushmills and what was left of a two-liter bottle of Coke back to the living room.

He watched TV, mixing the Coke and whiskey until the Coke was gone, then drinking the whiskey by itself. He flipped through the channels so often he got the stories and characters all mixed up. He listened carefully to evidence for crimes he had not seen committed. He heard confessions and revelations that made no sense to him, that didn't satisfy him the way they seemed to satisfy the characters.

But that was nothing new. Sometimes, if he wasn't careful, his own name didn't make sense to him. He'd be paying bills, signing check after check — Lloyd Redmond, Lloyd Redmond, Lloyd Redmond — and soon something about the name would strike him as wrong. He'd stare at his signature until it seemed so strange he'd think he must have misspelled it, until it looked not like a name at all but like a phrase from a language he didn't understand.

By now it was after eleven. He remembered seeing a half gallon of ice cream in the freezer. He wasn't hungry, and besides, it had been in there so long it had probably turned to paste. But that wasn't the point. When he pulled the box out of the freezer, he found it empty, nothing left but a sickly yellow scum icing the sides. He pressed the box into the overflowing garbage can under the sink.

When he straightened up, he let himself glance out the window, down the hill, at the darkened coop. The orange glow of the space heater bled from its cracks. At least the kid was warm. One more drink and he'd go down there, pry open the door. But then he remembered the way his arm had burned, how for one long moment the hot wire wouldn't let him go.

He went to the refrigerator for ice, saw the nearly full gallon of milk, and poured it into the sink, splashing it over the mound of dirty dishes. Then he put the empty jug back in the refrigerator.

Six months ago, on the morning after Ellen left, Nick hung in front of the open refrigerator, looking for breakfast, and said, "Where's Mom?"

After trying to think of a lie, an excuse, anything that made sense, Redmond said, "Gone."

Nick straightened up, turned slowly to him. "Gone?" The voice mocking but frightened.

That's right, Redmond thought, blame me. Go ahead. He stared straight back at Nick. "You got it." They stood there in silence for a while. Then, quietly, they began to get breakfast, carefully setting out the cereal, the milk, the bowls and spoons. They moved so quietly someone might have been lying asleep under the kitchen table. They ate in silence. When they were finished, he caught Nick's eye. "She'll be back."

That's what he'd said to Ellen the night before, while she yanked clothes off hangers and grabbed up the few things she'd wanted — her boots, her photo album, her coffee mug — and carried the whole heap to the car, dumping it into the backseat.

"You'll be back," he said as he followed her to the car.

"The hell," she said, turning on him.

"You think I care if you leave?" he said. "You think I don't know you've been planning this moment since the day we met? Besides, that shitbox'll break down before you're even out of the neighborhood."

She had the door open now, and she was looking off into the night, at a future she couldn't yet imagine. "You know what you were to me?" She shook her head slowly, her eyes wet. "A wide spot in the road." Then she climbed into the car and was gone.

The morning after she left, Nick just sat there at the kitchen table looking blank, waiting for an explanation. Redmond said it again: "She'll be back." But he knew he was only talking to himself.

It was getting late. He poured himself a good strong whiskey with ice and went upstairs. He switched on the television that sat on his dresser and crawled into bed. He'd lie down for a few minutes. Then he'd know how to face Nick.

The TV was an old black-and-white with a coat hanger for an antenna and no sound, but he didn't care. He didn't need the talk. It was the shifting light he liked, its wash and swirl. He thought it made him sleep better. He took another sip of his drink and watched a man talking so fast he seemed to be chewing a tough piece of meat. He was selling something or preaching or explaining. Hard to tell which.

That was another thing she didn't like about him, the way he left the TV on all night. He'd wake up sometimes and see her lying next to him in the dark, eyes shining, staring at the ceiling, probably already planning her getaway. He didn't want to think about her, but how could he stop his head?

He arranged the pillows so he could sit up. Why was he worried about the kid? The coop was so rotten he could get out of it anytime. One swift kick and he'd be free, but no, he wanted Redmond to suffer.

A phone number flashed across the bottom of the screen. The camera pulled back to reveal another man, listening to the first with maniacal intensity. Redmond put his drink on the nightstand and pulled the phone and the Pennsylvania road map onto his lap. The map was folded to the northeastern corner of the state. For three inches in every direction from the town of Esther it was covered with black check marks. He'd been trying to track her down for months, calling town after town without luck. She seemed to have dropped off the planet.

He picked a new town and dialed information. Electronic windows were unfurling on the TV screen. A fluffy, smiling couple appeared inside each one, making testimonials, confessions, special pleas, whatever.

"Wyalusing," he said into the mouthpiece. "The number for Loomis, Ellen Loomis. That's L-o-o-" He called a half-dozen towns, without luck, checking off each one on the map.

He was so tired. He had to sleep a little. It felt like someone was pushing his head under water. He gave in to it, wanted it. The map slid off the bed. As he turned in his sleep, he knocked the receiver off its perch but didn't hear the mechanical voice asking if he'd like to make a call. He slept through the phone's shrill bleating, and now the line was dead. His drink sat untouched on the nightstand. There was no sound in the room but the small music of ice cubes melting and resettling against each other.

Much later, in a distant corner of his mind, he was aware of someone else in the room, a shadow passing in front of the throbbing light of the TV, a displacement of air, the heat of another life. Whatever it was, he did not wake up.

THE SWEET SMELL OF HIM, MOONLIGHT AND SHADOWS. Was that why she was going back?

At first Ellen thought it would clear her head to return by bus, all those miles covered honestly, inch by inch. When it was over, you'd know you'd arrived somewhere. No, she knew why she was going back. There were things she'd forgotten to say to him. The break couldn't be complete, she told herself, until she rubbed his nose in a little reality. But sometimes she remembered how he held her so close she forgot what she was afraid of. He was all over her, inside her.

He said, Does this hurt or does it feel good?

Yes, she said. Yes.

And then there was Nick. She never even said goodbye. She owed him an explanation. At least that. But now, with the lurch of the bus, with the whine of the engine, with the tortuous miles unraveling, she thought this decision to go back was wrong, all wrong. Only an insane person would do what she was doing. And by bus.

They should put criminals on buses, she thought, instead of in prisons. But they do, she realized. The bus was full of criminals and half-wits. People who looked as though they'd just ripped apart their parents. People who seemed over- or undermedicated. She felt violated sitting so close to them, forced to participate in their sorry little lives, forced to watch them trade insipid smiles, as if they shared a special bond, like hostages. She couldn't stand it.

"My first wife was beautiful but she was no good. She run off with my uncle." He was young, with stringy blond hair and missing teeth. He was sitting in front of her. He had to twist around to say these things to her, a stranger. What could be going through his head? He

12

said, "We used to go up his house at the lake every chance we got, but not no more."

Slowly she turned her face away from him, to the window. It occurred to her that *she* was the hostage. To the old woman next to her, talking about the bad-seed son she was going to visit in Texas. To the man a few seats behind, reading aloud from his fat Bible. To the screaming kids, smelling of vomit and bubble gum. To the skinheads in the back, drinking beer and rolling the empties up the aisle. To the couple across from her, who waited until dark and everyone was asleep so they could fuck under a raincoat. To the people sitting around them, pretending to sleep. To the driver, hands locked on the wheel, driving for all he was worth, thinking he could get away from these lunatics if he just drove fast enough.

Only two days into the trip, and already her skin had gone gray, her insides turned to rust. Her thin brown hair hung limp as a rag. But then she remembered that she was a criminal before she ever climbed aboard. A woman who had abandoned her child. Unfit. Unsound. Inhuman.

The bus slammed down the dark highway. What she needed was a drink. Across the aisle, the raincoat convulsed. The old woman next to her was whispering. It wasn't clear whether she was whispering to Ellen or to her knitting.

"My red-haired boy's got a Ph.D. and a BMW. He got him a house down to Corpus. Big old house. Nothing but bedrooms and bathrooms. Only, when I get there he's going to put me up in the Remedy Inn. I can't feature it. I don't know what he does for a living. I never asked. I don't want to know."

Something inside Ellen snapped. She reached into the soft cone of light shrouding the old woman. She put her hands on the old woman's hands. She stopped the clicking needles. Into the startled blue eyes, she said, "He *must* understand that I *had* to leave." She knew by this ungovernable urge to explain herself to a stranger that she had become one of them. She was, she thought — the bus rocking through the dark, the night smearing past the windows — right where she belonged.

THE NIGHT REDMOND MET ELLEN, twelve years ago, he was sitting in The Hourglass, going over the good reasons to keep his new job, the good reasons to quit. It was nearly midnight, an hour after his first shift at the weaving mill.

The bar was narrow, dark, dirty, the kind of place where they keep the lights low instead of cleaning. Stapled to the cracked ceiling plaster were three snaky strings of Christmas lights, white and glittering, almost the only light in the place except for the backlit liquor bottles standing against the mirrored wall.

The room was barely wide enough for the bar and a run of café tables no bigger than hubcaps. The stools and bar rail were padded with red vinyl. They'd been done by some customer, done badly, to pay off his tab. Everywhere under the red skin were strange angles and lumps, as if he had sealed up car keys, change, cigarette lighters, and anything else lying on the bartop.

That night there were only a few regulars in the bar. Mostly old men hunched over their drinks in the dim light, nodding to the country music on the jukebox. None of them knew Redmond, and that was the way he liked it. The minute one of them called him by name, the minute the bartender knew his brand of beer, he'd turn around and never look back.

He sat near the corner of the bar, as close to the door as possible. At the far end, three old men and a woman started playing liars' dice, laughing too loud, banging the dice cups hard. One of them was a guy with a face full of burst blood vessels and a laugh like Smiley Burnette's, Roy Rogers's old sidekick. The woman, thin and twisted, with a wig full of meaty blond curls, got up and danced to the bathroom, putting a lot of shoulder and hip action into it. "This rattle your dice, boys?" Smiley Burnette shot off into another fit of high, honking laughter.

On Redmond's right, sitting at the angle of the bar, two old men in limp gray suits picked through some ancient indiscretion.

"You took advantage," one said, nodding, giving his friend a look that said: Let's face it.

The other ran a hand down his wattled neck, then shivered. "My only regret," he said, "is that I behaved so well."

In the last seat, next to the wall, a woman sat by herself, silhouetted by the glow of the cigarette machine behind her. She was about Redmond's age, and she was staring darkly across the room, staring straight through the bartender mixing drinks, wiping up, washing glasses.

Redmond had spent the night learning to run a false-twist machine, a huge contraption built on the order of a walk-through sewing machine. Its purpose was to rewind thread, which ran down one side of the machine from twenty-five fat spools the size of truck tires, dropping through an intricate set of eyelets, crossing under the floor grate, and climbing up the other side, where it wound onto twenty-five cone-shaped spindles. The factory was filled with the machines, and together they sounded like a squadron of fighters ready for takeoff. The company issued earplugs, but they didn't help. The roar was physical, a bone-rattling shudder that traveled up his legs and out his fingertips.

Any other night he'd have offered to buy the woman a drink, but the roar of his machine was still banging around somewhere inside his head. Besides, only a week had passed since he'd been dumped by Cary. Not enough time to figure out or forget what had gone wrong. They'd been together only a couple of months. He told himself he didn't miss her, that what he missed was the feeling of being in love.

He was the kind of man who needed to be up to his eyes in love. When he was alone, he had no personality. He was the invisible man. But when he was in love, he took on the woman's life, hated what she hated, loved what she loved. With a bank teller he talked about the economy over vodka martinis. With an oyster shucker he swore and drank shots of tequila. With a pediatric nurse he talked about auras and past lives and didn't drink at all.

The woman drained her beer and waggled the empty bottle until the bartender brought her another.

The feeling of being in love and the sex, that's all he missed. Cary was a night school psychology student who slept with him because her therapist told her to "expand her person base." She had shiny blond hair and black eyebrows. She had a boxer she took for furious walks. Redmond liked her. But all that ended one night when he knocked on her apartment door. She opened it on the chain. Her mouth had a funny kink in it.

She looked right at him and said, "I can't see you."

"You're busy?" he said. "You have other plans?"

"I mean I can't *see* you. You're not *there*."

"What do you mean?" He laughed nervously, touching his chest with his fingertips. "I'm right here."

She shook her head. "You're just a shadow. You disappeared twenty minutes after we met."

"I love you," he said, but even to him the words sounded irrelevant now.

Other words were passed through that door — about self-destructive patterns and emotional paybacks, about not knowing love if it came up and bit you on the ass.

As far as Redmond was concerned, all relationships were subject to a kind of ten-minute limit. No matter how bad they end up, they all start with ten minutes of grace. Ten minutes in which all your doubts and fears fall away, when your "never again" becomes "maybe this time." For ten solid minutes your life is lit with joy. You stop seeing your friends, and they understand. You spend too much money, eat too much, drink too much. Who cares? All you can think about is her, her, her. You weep over babies, even the ugly ones. Over all dogs, especially golden retrievers. Over the tenderness of new grass. You are so happy you can't stand yourself.

The woman lit a fresh cigarette and blew smoke at the ceiling. She seemed hypnotized. On the jukebox, Patsy Cline was singing "I Fall to Pieces." She listened intensely, keeping time with her finger on the side of her bottle. If the jukebox didn't have the answer, she'd probably throw herself, or someone else, under a bus.

You woo her. You learn her. You tune your instincts to her desires, to the weather of her moods. You're constantly picking up little gifts for her. At a yard sale you find a scratchy forty-five of Desmond Dekker and the Aces doing "Israelites." This, you think, this is just the sort of thing she loves. And you're right. You're always right. But then your ten minutes run out. You realize that intimate knowledge of someone is not love. It's a way of losing yourself. Things have turned out terribly wrong, and you're frightened at what you have become, at the hardening of your heart, at the way your heart has become a weapon. You're not in love. You were never in love. How could you have been such a fool? And who was this woman, anyway? Someone you slept with a few times. Someone you barely knew. Nobody. You tell yourself that this time you're cured, but who are you kidding? You never learn.

The woman got up to go to the bathroom. Light-brown hair just short of her shoulders and swept back. A faded salmon-colored cowboy shirt with white piping. Jeans so worn it was probably a toss-up whether to wear them or throw them away every time she pulled them out of the closet.

He smiled to himself. This was the point in the old movies where the voice-over was supposed to say *She was trouble but I didn't care. I wanted her.* Without knowing it, he had been staring at her.

The woman slowed down as she came closer, stared back at him. Her hard flat gaze felt like a hand against his face. He shifted his gaze, pretended he was reading the sign on the wall behind her — "You were WRONG when you walked in the DOOR." He turned to inspect the softball trophies lined up against the mottled mirror behind the bar, the bowls of boiled eggs and turkey gizzards floating in brine set out along the bar.

He was attracted to troubled women. In a crowded room he'd unconsciously seek out the paranoid schizophrenic, the potential suicide. Ordinary women — happy women, women who gave him room to be himself — scared him. He liked women on the edge. Easier to get lost in their lives.

He went to the bathroom and washed his face, studying the graffiti for a sign. Next to the mirror, someone had scratched "I smell shit — is there a lawyer in here?" On the other side, in a loopy red scrawl, someone had written "Dum-de-dum-de-dum." And under it, in another hand: "And so I got that going for me, which is nice."

When he came back to the bar, she was sitting on his stool, leaning forward a little, having her cigarette lit by the bartender. Every muscle of her face strained toward the freshly lit end. When it caught, she snatched the cigarette away and exhaled sharply toward the ceiling. In the dim light her face had the spooky tint of skim milk.

The two old men on the corner stools had gone, and now a short guy wearing a dark-blue leather jacket sat down at the angle of the bar. "Sake," he pronounced loudly, drumming the edge of the bar with his fingertips and glancing at the woman.

The bartender set a small ceramic bottle and cup in front of him. "Here you go, Dogfood."

The guy stiffened. "I told you not to call me that."

"Why not? It's what you sell, isn't it?"

Patsy Cline was staring at herself in the mirror behind the bar. The steeply arched eyebrows, the critical gaze, the dissatisfied set of her mouth. She knew it was someone she was supposed to know but not if it was someone she was supposed to like. She took a long, thoughtful pull on the cigarette.

The jacket turned his attention to her. "Miss? Oh, miss?" He caught her eye in the mirror and said, "Do you believe in Sandy Claws?"

She tipped her head to the side. One she hadn't heard.

"Because now I do." He raised his thimble of sake to her image and winked. "He just brought me what I always wanted — you."

"Jesus," she said, turning away from him. She took a healthy swallow of Redmond's beer.

"Good beer?" Redmond was standing next to her.

She peered up at him, her face balanced between indignation and amusement. "This place sure got friendly all of a sudden. What do you want?"

"The beer," Redmond said, smiling. "Is it good?"

"It's OK. Why?"

"Because I think it's mine."

She leaned back a little and took another swig, watching him.

"Look," he said, "if you want me to buy you a beer, I'll be happy to."

She set the bottle down and said, "Fuck you, Charlie. I've been sitting here for hours. This is my beer, my stool, and my fingernails that are going to scratch your eyes out if you don't leave me alone."

Redmond turned to the jacket for help, but he was half off the stool, every muscle tensed. This was just the kind of entertainment he'd come for. If he couldn't have her, he could at least beat up somebody on her behalf.

"I suppose I could be mistaken," Redmond said.

The jacket said, "You got that right."

Redmond walked around the bar and sat down in her old seat. In front of him stood a half-empty beer bottle — his brand — and a full ashtray, a lit cigarette perched on the edge.

"What's the use?" he said, pushing the bottle and ashtray toward the bartender. "Let me have what she's having."

The jacket was back at Patsy again. "What's that you're drinking? Beer? No, no, no. That's a white-trash drink." He called the bartender over. "The lady will have" — he studied her — "a Cuba Libre."

She laughed but in an edgy way that said a free drink meant only so much.

The jacket's smile faded when, one by one, Smiley Burnette and his friends bought her a drink, each standing up on his rubbery legs and bowing elaborately. She smiled. She was enjoying this. Soon she couldn't drink them fast enough. Three downturned doubles glasses stood in front of her, marking her free drinks. The bartender started bringing her money for the jukebox, quarters painted red so the service guy would know to return them to the bar. "Please," the bartender said every time he gave her money, "play 'The Rodeo Song.'"

The jacket tried to ignore Smiley. He kept working on her. "One year at Harvard Med and I learned all I needed to know. Why run a good thing into the ground? Now I'm in pet supplies." The guy smiled — a stingy, one-sided smile.

Smiley called down to her. "Here's one for you. Minister's visiting the farmer when the farmer's dim-witted son rides up hell bent for leather. 'Daddy! You know how you told me to watch the bull and brown cow and the white cow? Well, the bull fucked the brown cow!' 'Son,' the farmer said, 'we don't talk like that in front of the minister. We say the bull *surprised* the brown cow.' 'OK.' Boy rides away. Twenty minutes later he's back. 'I know,' the farmer says. 'The bull surprised the white cow.' 'Sure did! Fucked the brown one again!'"

She laughed big and loud. It was her laugh that got to Redmond, kept distracting him.

"Sake is an acquired taste," the jacket said. He held the cup with the tips of his fingers. "I acquired it in Japan."

Smiley Burnette came down the bar. He had slicked-back white hair and sharp sideburns the shape of linoleum knives. He waited patiently while the jacket finished his speech.

"It must be served warm. They say the ancient emperors used to warm it between the breasts of their concubines."

At that, Smiley said, "Come on, little darling," coaxing her off the stool. "Let's you and me do a little stepping."

There, between the bar and the jukebox, he whirled her to a song by Alabama. He played her out, reeled her in. Her hair was flying. She was laughing. She was loving it. The woman in the wig made a mouth at her in the bar mirror. The jacket's eyes went cold and hard. "Hillbilly bullshit," he muttered and took a sip of sake.

The record changed to a stomp-your-heart ballad. Before they started dancing again, the woman in the wig rattled her glass and said, "Say, Georgie? Does this glass seem empty to you? Because it sure seems empty to me. Why don't you park your prostate right here?" She patted the empty stool next to her. Smiley twirled the woman one last time and tipped an imaginary hat to her.

She danced by herself now, head thrown back, arms stiff, eyes closed, barely moving.

The weather makes you wonder if I'm leaving you.

The jacket saw his chance. He slid off the stool and took her hands.

Without opening her eyes, she stepped into him, into the hollow of his body. They turned with the music. She laid her hand on his chest, slid it down a little.

I'm trading dark eyes for dark skies again.

It didn't matter who she was dancing with. She wasn't there. She was in the song. But his eyes were bright. He was looking way beyond that moment, that place.

Suddenly it was last call, with everyone complaining. Come on. Stay open a little longer. Who's to know? But the bartender wasn't drunk enough. "Good night, good night, good night," he said, and then he turned up the lights.

The customers groaned and shaded their eyes, staggering outside like bats. Redmond made a quick trip to the bathroom and then followed the others. Outside, the night was cool and there were stars.

The nose of Smiley Burnette's burgundy LeSabre was three feet from the door of the bar. He stood on the driver's side, fishing for the keys. Even that little movement rocked him. Tufts of his white hair stuck straight out from his head.

The woman in the wig stood next to him, her arms crossed tightly over her chest. "George, I'm driving."

But he had his keys now and climbed into the car, saying, "You are way too drunk to drive this car this night."

Her voice was calm as she looked at Redmond. "If he thinks I'm getting into this car with a drunken madman, he's got another think coming."

"You're drunkerer." George laughed from inside the car. "I'm just trying not to hurt yourself."

At the moment he started the car, the bar's neon hourglass blinked off. He reached over the steering wheel, trying to paw away the sudden darkness. Then, with the engine still running, he crawled between the seats, into the back.

She shook her head. "You men," she said — to George, to Redmond, to the night. "You're none of you any damn good." She climbed in, gunned the engine, and drove away.

Redmond headed for his car. At first he thought someone was trying to break into it, but then he saw that the shadows standing next to his orange Pinto were Patsy Cline and the blue leather jacket. Something was happening. He hurried over.

The guy was leaning up close to her and talking in a thin, brutal voice. "Do you know what you are? Do you? I want to explain it to you. May I have a moment to tell you a few things about yourself?"

She was drunk and hardly knew where she was, but she knew the tone of voice. Her eyes cleared and she gave him the same hard look she had given Redmond when she caught him staring at her. She smiled grimly. She said, "You been telling me something all night long, cowboy, but I ain't going for it."

He cocked his arm and started to swing. She watched through half-closed eyes. She'd seen it coming. Redmond grabbed his arm and yanked him away. The guy swung on him with the other hand, but Redmond let him go and he went sprawling.

Stunned, the guy tried to gather his legs under him, but it was harder than he'd thought. He gave up. Sitting on the asphalt, his legs splayed, he said, his voice shrill and indignant, "Where do you work? Where do you work?" He stood up slowly and took a step toward the woman, but Redmond put himself between them. "Do you want to know what you are?" the guy called out to her. "Do you?"

She was too drunk to listen. She leaned against the Pinto and rested the side of her face on the wet roof.

"A hole," the guy yelled. "That's all you are. A — "

Redmond grabbed him by his leather lapels and shoved. The guy staggered backward, then started to come for Redmond, then thought better of it. He straightened his jacket and pointed at Redmond. His mouth was a knot. "Monday morning, buddy, I'm having a talk with your supervisor!"

But Redmond had already turned his back on him. He touched the woman's shoulder lightly. He was about to ask if she was OK, when she swung her arm back fast, knocking his hand off her shoulder.

"Get off me!" she cried, her voice thick and wet, her fingernails grazing his cheek.

The jacket's Camaro pulled out of the lot with a screech of rubber, horn blaring. The woman winced as if she had been struck, then slowly focused on Redmond.

He said, "Do you want me to take you home?"

In a sleepy voice she said, "You're direct, I'll give you that."

"No, I mean take you home. Do you have a car?"

She looked around the empty lot and shuddered. "I can't remember. Maybe I came with somebody." She looked down at the Pinto. "Maybe this is my car."

"Whoever you came with is long gone. And this is my car."

"Thank God for small favors," she said. "Look, I'm too drunk to resist, so don't try anything, OK?"

"OK." He pulled out his keys and led her around to the passenger door.

"Or do try. As the case may be."

"Right. What's your name, anyway?"

"Don't be fresh."

"I just want to — "

"Carlotta."

"Carlotta? That's your name?"

But by then he had opened the passenger door, and she climbed inside without answering. When he got behind the wheel, she was already slumped against the door, asleep or unconscious. He pried open her leather bag to find a driver's license or anything with her address on it.

"Not worth stealing," she said, suddenly awake. It was true. There was nothing in the purse but a handful of crumpled bills, a lipstick, and a hairbrush.

He said, "I'm trying to find out where you live."

"Sure," she said wearily. "Just drive out the lake highway. I'll tell you where to turn." She leaned her head against the side window.

So he drove. He had the strong feeling that she'd fall asleep and have him driving all night. But a half hour outside town, he was startled to see that she was awake and watching him.

"Turn left at the monstrosity," she said.

"The what?"

"You'll know it when you see it."

And there it was — a barbecue place called Pick o' the Porker, with a huge pink pig next to the highway.

She lived in a trailer park off the access road. "This way," she said, directing him down a narrow rutted lane between bullet-shaped trailers, then: "Maybe we should have gone left back there." When they finally found her place, there were so many cars and trailers wedged in against each other that he had barely enough room to park. He pulled in next to a tow truck. "Cradle Snatcher" was stenciled on the tow arm, and shiny cutouts of reclining nudes were stuck all over it.

Just as he was about to follow her into the trailer, the neighbor's door snapped open. A big guy stood in the dimly lit doorway, a shotgun pointing from the center of his shadow: "What the fuck?"

Redmond said, "I'm just — I — "

The big guy pulled both hammers back. He said, "I got a thirty-ought-six here, mister."

Then the sound of her voice, heavy with boredom, from inside the trailer: "Go to bed, Walter." She took Redmond's hand and pulled him inside. "Don't pay any attention to him. Mix us a couple drinks." She pushed him toward the kitchen and went down the narrow hall to the other end of the trailer, steadying herself with one hand along the wall. The sink was full of dirty dishes. The cupboard doors were sticky. Inside he found two plates, two cups, two bowls. And a bottle of bargain Scotch.

"Just ice," she said from the back room.

He took down two Flintstone jelly glasses, all he could find. He pulled a battered metal ice tray from the freezer and knocked a few cubes out. The ice smelled as if it had been made with dishwater.

The living room was lined with fake oak paneling, a brown water stain cascading down the corner above the TV. One of the panels had come away at the edges. The furniture was old, mismatched — a red vinyl recliner and a scratchy aquamarine sofa whose springs popped and twanged when he sat down. He took a sip of his drink. Bitter, medicinal.

When she came back into the room, he handed her a drink and said, "What's the deal with your neighbor?"

She held out her hand as she sat down. "Name's Ellen Loomis."

"Lloyd Redmond," he said. She pulled her hand away almost as soon as he touched it. "Your neighbor seems — "

"Walter? He's nothing. Don't worry about him. We call him PPK." She made her hand into a pistol, aimed at Redmond, and pulled the trigger. "You know? Like the handgun? Walther PPK? Get it?"

Redmond just sat there feeling stupid.

She shrugged and said, "Anyway, he tries to kill everything I drag home. No offense."

"One of these days somebody's going to get hurt."

"No shit. Him, for instance. Two years ago, his wife shot him in the stomach. He almost died."

"That's terrible."

"You think *that's* terrible? Now his system's so screwed up she has to cook him special meals all the time." She took a swallow of her drink and said, "Come on."

He followed her down the narrow hallway to the end of the trailer, a small square room with nothing in it but a mattress, a desk lamp, a full ashtray, and a tape player with cassettes scattered around it on the floor.

She took his drink and set both glasses on the floor next to the bed. When she straightened up, she said, "Which side of the bed do you like?"

He said, "Look, I only wanted to make sure you got home."

She smiled. "Right." She looked more tired than drunk. Her wariness was gone. Without taking her eyes off him, she unsnapped her cowboy shirt. She was wearing a peach-colored bra, half satin, half lace, a little too big. And it was this, Redmond thought later, more than anything else, that made him want her.

She let the shirt fall to the floor and pulled off her jeans. She uncinched his belt and rocked his jeans off his hips, down his legs. She slid off his underwear. "Nice," she said. She took his hands and pulled him to the mattress.

Everything he knew — his job, his puny life — began to slip away from him. He was moving somewhere fast, and there were hands, her hands on him, his on her. Light sliced through the miniblinds and lay in bars across her breasts, her stomach. With his tongue he stroked a soft brown nipple hard. That he could do that made him think he could do anything.

And then she was on top of him, her breasts brushing against his chest as she moved, as she moved. Then desperate, hard-lipped kisses. The tight muscles gripping him inside. And he was with her, not thinking, not really, about the stale pillow under his head or the smell of cold cigarette ashes. And then, before he knew what was happening, she relaxed completely, collapsed really, her head falling next to his on the pillow, her hair across his face, in his mouth. It smelled of smoke and the singe of a blow-dryer and something like fruit. She lay there, a dead weight, all the energy drained out of her.

He couldn't hold her like that for long. Slowly he slid out from under her, but she didn't wake up. She lay there like a corpse — her mouth open, her hair spread wildly on the pillow, the pale undersides of her arms turned out.

He got up without turning on the gooseneck lamp next to the bed. He stepped carefully through the room, around the doorway, and into the bathroom. Even then, he didn't turn on the light. The room was tiny, windowless. He slid the pleated door shut, and the room went even darker. He felt the slick coolness of magazines underfoot, made out the smell of damp towels. He sat down so he'd make as little noise as possible. In the pitch blackness it made no difference whether he kept his eyes open or closed. The darkness was complete.

But after a minute he was able to make out a few things — the dull silver gleam of the air vent, the quiet glow of the bathtub, and another thing. The tub was filled with something. When he was finished, he reached out and touched dark, scratchy folds of cloth. He ran his hand over it. Laundry, maybe. But there was something more, something firm beneath the cloth, something that moved. He heard a small moan and the wet sound of lips rubbing against each other. He stood up quickly and backed toward the door, sliding it open a few inches.

His eyes were adjusted to the darkness now. The thin light straining through the bedroom window helped. Inside the tub, wrapped in blankets, cushioned with pillows, was a small child, a boy with blond hair that looked gray in the dim light. His eyelids fluttered. He was awake. He raised his head and looked at this man standing naked in the doorway. Then, as if Redmond were someone the boy recognized, he lay back down, burrowing his head into the pillow.

Back in bed, Redmond couldn't sleep. He lay on his side, his arm cocked under his head, watching the woman sleep, this strange woman.

Nick made his way up from the chicken coop. He was scared. The night was cold and wet. Clouds hid the moon. The willows rattled like curtains of bone. Every shadow was alive. Every rustling branch and wing flap was the sound of something being caught and killed.

People said the woods at the foot of the farm were part of a chain of valleys that reached all the way through Maine, into Canada, beyond. They said they'd seen bears and bobcats down there, escaped convicts, leopards. Nick knew better than to believe the stories, but he had only been to the woods once, to leave a salt block for the deer. When he got home, the old man who farmed the next place told him he once found a human foot down there, a foot with bites taken out of it, human bites.

He took the porch steps three at a time, quietly, and opened the back door just enough to ease inside. He stood in the kitchen, feeling like an intruder, waiting for his eyes to adjust to the darkness. The only sound was his deep convulsive breathing. He sounded like some kind of monster. That's right, he said to himself, think monster.

Through the dark kitchen and living room, around the furniture without touching a thing, without making a sound, and up the stairs three at a time, quietly, quietly. And then he was there, outside Redmond's door. He held up his right fist. He had fit a nail between his fingers. He liked the way it took the light, the two inches of chiseled steel. He liked the weapon his hand had become. He closed his eyes for courage.

"I can feel you in there," he whispered. "Are you listening? Do you know what's coming? Do you?" He opened his eyes and stared at the door. "If you want to pretend you're asleep, that's fine. Fine. I'm just going to stand out here. I'm not going to move a muscle. If you want to come and kill me, give it a try. Just try. Or I might come inside that room. I'm not afraid. I'm not afraid of anything."

Before Nick realized what he was doing, he had turned the doorknob and slipped inside. The room shook with nervous gray light from the television. He went to the end of the bed. Redmond lay curled up near one edge, wrapped in the sheet, his face half covered and in shadow. The sheet was so tight it made him look like he'd been sewn into a sack.

Think monster, Nick told himself. His voice was barely a whisper. "I have a surprise for you, you fuck, you thing." He breathed harder, heavier, fighting off the urge to cry. He held out his fist. "One of your nails. I pulled it out with my own bloody fingers. I ought to pound it straight into your fat heart. I really, really ought to."

Lloyd's father, the Commander, has been overseas for six months. It's his first night home. Dinner on the good plates instead of the scratched plastic ones they normally use, and now inspection begins. Lloyd stands at attention beside his bed while his father checks his fingernails and toenails, while he measures the length of Lloyd's hair with a pocket ruler. No strand of hair can be longer than one inch. He checks Lloyd's bedroom to see that the bedsheet is taut enough to bounce a dime, to see that his shirts and underwear are folded carefully and stowed away efficiently, that his shoes are shined to a high gloss. If one pair of socks isn't stuffed into a perfect ball, if even the soles of his dress shoes haven't been polished to a perfect and uniform blackness, if the dime doesn't bounce high enough — he'll have to strip down to his underwear and do push-ups on the cold front lawn. The Commander doesn't know that it's his mother who shines Lloyd's shoes, balls his socks, folds his clothes.

If all goes well, he begins the weighing and measuring, first standing Lloyd against a wall, making sure everything but the small of his back is touching, then laying a pencil across the top of his head and inscribing a line in the wall where it touches. He measures the distance from the floor with a shiny steel tape measure. He weighs him, first standing on the scale himself to check its accuracy. And because he doesn't trust the scale with weights below a hundred pounds, he picks Lloyd up, holding him in his arms but slightly to the side so he can read the number, handling him like so much meat. When he's finished, he enters the new height and weight on a chart he's tacked to the bedroom wall. He stares at the numbers for several minutes. Then, at last, he turns his dead gaze to Lloyd.

"I'm sorry," Lloyd says. Sorry, sorry, sorry.

"Sorry," the Commander says. "Sorry for what?" It's not a real question. It's a test. When Lloyd says nothing, he says, "Do you even know what 'sorry' means?"

His father has been home only a couple of hours, but Lloyd knows he has already failed him somehow. That night he will dream of those eyes staring at him — small, close together, set deep in their bony sockets. Not eyes at all but a microscope like the one the older kids use in science lab. And Lloyd nothing more than a specimen smeared on a glass slide.

WHEN ELLEN WAS A GIRL, her grandfather gave her a diary with pressed flowers on the cover, a metal latch, a key. "This is where you'll find your secret self," he said. Two days later, before she'd even had a chance to write in it, she lost the key. After looking everywhere, she buried the locked book in the backyard, solemnly, with tears in her eyes, sure that her secret self was forever beyond her reach.

The bus pass she'd bought in San Jose was good for two months of travel, so what was the rush? She stopped in Houston, renting herself a room in the best hotel she could find, the Hotel Duquesne. Outside, the long slow southern night was coming on. For the last hour, she'd been sitting at the desk, writing another letter to Nick. The hotel stationery was nice. Creamy white with a dark-blue letterhead and the hotel's motto in sweeping script: "A Century of Graceful Living." Right. She could use a little of that right now. In her letter she was asking herself why she'd rented a room in this expensive hotel when she had barely enough money for the rest of the trip. She almost wrote *for the trip back,* but she was not going back. She merely wanted to clarify a few things, make her motives understood, draw a little — just a little — of Redmond's blood.

She knew part of what she was paying for was the Olympic-size pool in the hotel's basement, a pool she wouldn't use. And the hotel's restaurant, which she couldn't afford. She was paying, she knew, for the complimentary copy of the *Wall Street Journal* she'd find outside her door in the morning, a newspaper she never read. What she was really paying for — and getting — was a night of calm. She was paying for peace the way a man pays for sex. The big room with its thick walls, flocked wallpaper, and linen so clean it hurt to turn her face into the pillow.

But she did read newspapers. Not big-city papers. The world was a neighborhood she knew very little about. Her brown leather shoulder bag was filled with clippings from small-town weeklies. At every rest stop the bus made, she bought a newspaper, spreading it open under her vending machine coffee and sweet roll. She read every word. She was looking for a sign. Of what, she couldn't say. Her secret self. She'd know it when she saw it. When she found the right kind of article, she clipped it out and put it in her bag with the others. Another piece of the puzzle.

In the Calexico *Defender* she read about a Mexico City sweatshop that collapsed during the earthquake. The owner was back as soon as the dust settled. He saved the machines first, then the women workers trapped in the rubble. It took two days to save the machines. They were heavy and delicate — ancient Singers, black with gold filigree. New machines wouldn't be as good, he argued. His machines were one of a kind, collector's items.

In the Show Low, Arizona, *Times-Ledger* she read about a man who stood at the town's main intersection in nothing but a raincoat and flashed the passersby. It was Thanksgiving, he said, and he was giving it. Thanks. "In my own special way." They jailed him for his gratitude. At what intersection had she been standing? And for how long? And with what purpose, what result?

She read the papers carefully, like a deck of tarot cards. She always started with obituaries, moved on to lifestyles, then settled into the police report. She was looking for news of herself, for the story of her life, an indication of its shape, the arc of its fall. She was looking for an account that explained the tangle of bad luck, bad choices, and missed opportunities that passed for her life. She envied every convicted criminal she read about. When they throw you in jail, at least you know where you stand.

She thought of the boy, of the man. For six months they'd been an obstacle in her path, her memory of them. The kind of obstacle you work hard to forget. Later you realize you've been living according to its limits, like a woman adjusting to a dangerous city. The way she decides never to go out after dark, never to go to certain neighborhoods under any circumstances. The way she learns to hang her purse on the opposite shoulder, across her chest, like a bandolier. The way she learns to walk the streets with one hand in her pocket, her keys threaded through the fingers of her fist like a claw. The way a woman learns to live like this, forgetting what she has given up.

She studied the brass lamp on the writing desk, the deep-green leather of its shade, the modest spill of light. Her hands made shadows on the page, the page filled edge to edge with the nervous flow of her thoughts. Not a clear explanation anywhere. Nothing but questions and small talk. She breathed deeply and held her pen over the last band of clean space at the bottom of the paper. She wanted to write down words that would explain what she'd done, that would make her feel she'd done the right thing, that would make Nick feel it, but at every turn of thought and phrase she saw his face.

REDMOND WOKE UP to the picture on the television flipping serenely, a magician looking for the card you chose or think you chose. An endless series of cushy living rooms scrolling upward. An endless series of smiling couples saying smiling things to each other. His mouth tasted like rusty metal. He was exhausted. The day was still only a string of light along the eastern hills.

In the only dream he remembered, he killed someone, though he didn't know who or how — a simple gesture, a handshake, a tap on the arm, nothing at all. But the man went down. Redmond tried to hide the body, kept lugging it from room to room, stuffing it behind the couch, rolling it under the bed. But no place was good enough. The dead man's black shoes kept toeing out from behind the drapes, the kitchen table. An open gray palm kept flopping out from under the bedspread.

Then he remembered Nick, the chicken coop. He got out of bed quickly and pulled on yesterday's jeans and sweatshirt. He looked out the window as he dressed, but from there the willows hid the coop.

What if he was dead? Or worse — alive and laying for him? Let him be alive, he thought. I'll show him my arm. I'll make him understand. But the pain in his arm was long gone, and Redmond himself didn't believe his story, couldn't believe what he'd done. He stamped into his work boots and headed for the stairs. Someone was in the kitchen. He heard cupboards banging, heavy breathing, the sharp thwack of something thrown on the floor hard. He ran, nearly falling the whole flight.

He stepped into the doorway, expecting anything — a cop with cuffs ready or an escaped convict with a knife. But it was only Nick, standing in the center of the room with an empty flour sack in his hand. When

33

he saw Redmond his eyes went dead. He dropped the sack on the floor and turned to the sink. A cloud of flour hung in the air.

The muscles in Nick's back were clenched. He stood there in nothing but his gray Jockey shorts, trying to work a bowl out of the pile of dirty dishes, every muscle an affront, an act of defiance. The pile settled with a sharp crack.

Of course, Redmond thought, I should have guessed. All the cupboard doors were standing open, and dry food was scattered everywhere — loose spaghetti, elbow macaroni, rice. The floor, counters, and table were covered. One burner of the stove was buried under a pile of uncooked popcorn. On the counter, the sugar canister was lying on its side, its contents cascading slowly over the edge. At his feet a cracked bottle of ketchup lay in a slowly spreading puddle of red. A fine coating of flour settled over everything. And in the middle of it all, Nick, getting his ordinary breakfast on an ordinary morning.

Redmond leaned back against the doorframe and waited for him to turn. He ran his fingers through his tangled hair. His head was pounding. He shouldn't have drunk all that bourbon. The kitchen would take hours to clean, but he deserved this and more. Besides, it was a careful mess. No dishes were broken. Except for the oozing bottle of ketchup, none of the mess was wet. The bunched muscles in Nick's back were a snarl. Come on, Redmond thought, let's get this over with.

But Nick ignored him. He pulled down a box of Kix from the cupboard, probably the only food he'd saved. He shook it to hear how much was left. He shook it once more because he liked the sound of it. He honked open the silverware drawer, pawing through the spoons for a long time, rejecting several until he found the one he wanted, even though they were all exactly alike. The clatter of his hand stirring through the silverware was painful to Redmond, piercing, but he didn't say a word.

Still with his back to Redmond, Nick stepped over to the refrigerator for the milk. When he saw the empty gallon jug, he hung in the open door and sighed. He let his gaze fall on the cold shelves, bare except for a nearly empty jar of mayonnaise, a shriveled orange, and a cardboard-colored steak they'd never gotten around to cooking.

He released the door and let it slowly close itself. He took up his cereal and walked around the kitchen table, past Redmond, who stiffened, braced for a blow. But Nick walked right by, pretending not to notice. He sat down and poured himself some cereal, waggling the open box over the bowl so pellets went bouncing across the table, onto the floor — only a few, but enough.

Redmond forced himself not to say, not to do, anything. He tried to think about coffee, tried to quiet the beating in his head. But the pellets careened across the table. And now Nick was spooning dry cereal into his mouth, clacking his spoon against the bottom of the bowl.

Redmond went to the sink, filled the kettle with water, and put it on the stove, pasta crunching under his boots at every step. Out of the corner of his eye, he saw that the refrigerator door hadn't quite closed. A three-inch bar of cold light fell across the food-strewn floor. I'm not going to play this game, he thought. I'm not going to react at all.

More stray cereal pellets were falling off Nick's spoon, bouncing across the linoleum. Redmond knew that no matter how well he cleaned up, some night in his bare feet he'd step on one. That's all it would take to push him over the edge. And he had already been over the edge. But not again, not now, not just yet. He wouldn't give him the satisfaction.

Nick leaned back in the chair, propping his heels on the edge of the table, holding the bowl just below his chin. He ate with his mouth open. He liked the raw crunching sound. He smacked his lips. He tongued the crumbs at the corners of his mouth. More bits of cereal fell off the spoon, spilling onto the floor.

The kid didn't even have the good sense to be nervous. He sat there in his torn gray underwear, tipping the chair on its back legs as far as it would go. The soles of his feet were white with flour. He was filthy and smelled of stale sweat and chicken shit. The heel of his right hand was crusty with dried blood. There was a long scrape inside his left forearm, a bright blue bruise on his left shoulder. And other bruises — on his right bicep, his left thigh.

He's figuring out how to get even, Redmond thought as he waited calmly for his coffee water to boil, listening to Nick eat, to the refrigerator's stumbling whir. He reached into the cupboard for the instant coffee, then saw it spread all over the counter in front of him.

A can of condensed milk stood on the shelf. He took it down. It had a nice heft, like a baseball. He inspected the label. When he turned to Nick, everything stopped. Then, without realizing what he was doing, he said, "Is this any good on cereal?" He held the can out.

Nick gazed at him lazily, like a kid on a street corner waiting for something to happen. Redmond tossed the can to him, and Nick caught it, still balanced on the back legs of his chair. For a second Redmond thought the kid might pitch it through the window. But he only smiled slightly and lobbed it back to Redmond. They were at the edge of something. Forgiveness. Murder. Something.

Jack Teague's pickup pulled into the driveway, brakes squealing, the engine roaring richly as he primed it before shutting it off. They heard him tramp around to the back of the house. He never entered a house by the front door. Front doors were for show. According to him, nothing but bad news and evangelists came to the front door. Real people went in and out the back.

"Holy Jumping Jesus," Teague said when he saw the mess. "What happened here?" When no one answered, he stared at Nick. "Hey, pud, you look like you been dragged around the block too many times."

"Hi, Titty," Nick said, smiling.

Teague raised his chin toward Redmond and said, "How you doing, you old whore?"

Jack Teague — "Titty" to his friends — owned the farm and several other properties in the valley. He was a big man, with a big belly, which he carried proudly, like a prize pig. He had a mottled red face and a habit of making noise. He talked loud, laughed loud, and when he crossed a room, the floor boomed with his footsteps. Teague was a man of conviction: he believed that North Vietnam lost the war and that Elvis is alive.

"So," he said, "how soon do we get to kill us some puppies?"

Redmond gave Teague the last clean mug and took a jelly glass for himself, scraping coffee into them with the edge of his hand and pouring them full of hot water. The hot glass burned the ends of his fingers, nearly bringing tears to his eyes, but he drank from it anyway. He hoped Nick saw how he punished himself. When he couldn't stand it anymore, he set the glass on the edge of the counter. "We've only had those cows a few weeks," he said.

"I know, I know, but I still think we ought to off the little fuckers." Teague pulled a battered metal flask from the pocket of his down vest and poured bourbon into his mug and then into Redmond's glass. He winked. "Let's have us a waker-upper."

The twenty head of Charolais in the field belonged to Teague. His money had bought them, had paid for the feed. All Redmond had to do was see that they were fed and make sure none of them blundered through the fence and got themselves lost. The plan was to split the profits at the end of the season, but it was only May now. The end of the season was a long way off.

"Jack," Redmond said, shaking his head.

"Thing of it is," Teague said, sidling up to him, "I got a little cash flow problem. I mean, we're not married anymore, so why do I have to pay for Dina's therapy? It's like buying her a gun and saying, 'Shoot me!' You see what I'm saying?"

Redmond said, "Pocket change — that's all we'll get for the cattle now. What is it with you?"

"Yeah, yeah, I guess you're right. If we get greedy we might do ourselves out of a lot of money. What the hell. I'll just skip this month's alimony. That ought to fry her fanny."

Nick finished off his cereal. He got slowly to his feet and sighed, stretching his long arms so luxuriously it was like the unfolding of wings. He held the empty bowl in his outstretched hand, twisting his arm — on purpose, Redmond thought, on purpose — until the spoon fell clattering to the floor. He looked at it from a long way off, sighed again, slowly curled his toes around the shaft, and lifted the spoon to his hand. Redmond and Teague watched as he went to the sink and wedged the bowl back into the pile of dirty dishes, but loosely, so he could get at it easily. He headed for his room, dragging his feet through the rubble of cereal, macaroni, and sticks of spaghetti. When Redmond heard his footsteps on the stairs, a wave of relief hit him. The air itself changed, cleared, freshened. He could breathe again.

Teague waited until he heard Nick on the stairs and said slyly, "You believe in dreams?"

Redmond pulled a dirty mug out of the sink and poured his coffee into it.

"I mean, I'll fuck anything that can't outrun me. But I had this dream last night that's got me worried. I dreamed about this chick who kept looking at me, and she says, 'My husband's away.' I'm there unbuttoning her blouse, when I see she's covered with tats — eagles, flags, skulls, all that shit. And on her chest there's this big blue cobra, ready to strike. I fucked her anyway, but I don't feel right about it. Even in the dream I didn't feel right about it."

Redmond sipped his coffee.

"Thing of it is, Dina says one of the reasons she left me was because the sex wasn't right. What the hell's that supposed to mean? Sex is sex, isn't it? She's so beautiful she made me nervous, that's all. She's the most eye-popping, tie-your-dick-in-a-knot, flat-out beauty I ever saw. If you ask me, we were fine until she started taking courses at the community college. Then she goes and gets herself into city politics. The bitch has had me singing soprano ever since."

Ellen had slept with Teague. She threw the fact in Redmond's face the night she left. It didn't mean anything, she told him, except to show what a dumb, desperate animal Redmond had turned her into.

Since then, all Teague's talk about sex seemed like an elaborate apology. He thought it was still a secret, and Redmond let him believe it. They sipped their coffee and stared at the empty doorway to the living room, as if Nick were still standing there.

"What happened here?" Teague asked finally.

"Nothing," Redmond said. "What do you mean?"

Teague pulled out his flask and poured more bourbon into their mugs. "You whipped him pretty good. What'd he do?"

"Nothing. I mean, *I* didn't do nothing. He did that to himself."

"Sure. Look, I understand these things. I know what kids are like. I took my nephew fishing last summer. Soon as we get in the boat, I give him a little whack to the back of the head. He's there, 'What'd I do? What's that for?' I acted like I didn't even hear him. I wasn't looking to hurt him. I love the little fucker. I just wanted to put in his mind the idea that if he did anything stupid, he *could* get hurt. You see what I'm saying? Since then, that kid don't give me a bit of trouble."

Redmond, righteous, sputtering: "It wasn't like that. I didn't touch him. I wouldn't."

"Right. You stick to your story. Hell, I'll take a good lie over the truth any goddamn day of the week. Besides, what's it matter whether it's the truth or a lie? Only thing that matters is how many chumps you get to believe you."

"I didn't hit him."

"I believe you." Teague smiled and held up a finger. "That's one chump."

"But I didn't."

"Right. So you said. No problem. I'll stand up in court for you, if it comes to that." He took a quick look in the living room in case Nick was hiding there. "Thing of it is," he said, "between you, me, and the cow shit, I think you went a tad too far."

Redmond would never hurt Nick, not ever. How could he convince Teague of that? How could he convince the kid? How could he convince himself? Nick was like his own blood. He'd lived with Nick and his mother on and off for twelve years. And now he was raising him, wasn't he? He was the closest thing Nick had to a father. He wanted to rush upstairs now and tell him how sorry he was, how it was somebody else out there in the field yesterday, some wounded thing lashing out. But how could Nick believe him after what he'd done? But what had he done? He hadn't even laid a hand on him. I know that, Nick would say, smiling, sitting there in his cuts and bruises.

Redmond felt the anger rising again. This kid. This kid. What does he know about anything? His muscles are strung too tight. His hormones are climbing the walls. He's all appetite and sweat. You think you've been mistreated? What do you know about anything, about anything at all?

Teague set down his empty mug. "If you're not going to let me kill the puppies, I guess I better get my ass in gear."

"Wait a minute," Redmond said. "As long as you're here, why don't you haul away some of that lumber out by the barn?"

Teague let his head droop. "It's Sunday, the day of rest. Besides, this is a farm. It's supposed to have shit like that lying around."

"That stuff is piled so high it's caving in the wall of the barn. It's full of rats and snakes and I don't know what all. I want it out of there."

"All right. All right. Don't get your blood in a flood." He drained his coffee like it was cool water. "Let's do her."

Teague headed for the door and Redmond followed, walking straight to the barn while Teague fired up his truck, an old Ford he'd rebuilt and painted candy-apple red. Its fenders reminded Redmond of muscles. For somebody with perpetual cash flow problems, Teague owned a lot of trucks and showed up regularly in new ones. Redmond had always suspected that his idea of being broke and Teague's were very different. For him it meant a month of macaroni and cheese. For Teague it meant having to dip into his principal.

Up on the main road, a two-lane blacktop that led through the hills to the county prison five miles away, a white clump of something lay in the roadway. A balled-up sheet of newspaper, maybe. Redmond went up there to see what it was, while Teague backed the truck toward the barn and started hoisting long pieces of lumber into the bed.

It was one of his hens, its head and neck crushed by a passing car, one wing broken, the other sticking straight out. Sometimes it happened. A hen found enough strength to flap up and over the four-foot fence around the pen, or it scratched at the ground near the fence until there was enough room to duck under. He thought he had it all figured out, simple, and now he'd bury the carcass in the mulch pile.

But then he heard, from the bushes along the edge of the road, Fatima's raspy warble. She stood among the uncurling spring leaves, rocking from foot to foot, her beak flicking nervously, fifty pounds of lice-infested feathers.

All the hens were loose. Down in the paddock garden, they trampled some of the new tomato plants. They wandered among the apple trees. They staggered through the melon vines. He couldn't believe it. He couldn't fucking believe it.

When he got back to the barn, Teague was holding up one end of a four-by-four. The wood was pale green and covered with razor-thin hash marks, all running in the same direction.

"You see this baby?" he said. "There's a whole shitload of them here. They're treated with some kind of chemical to keep them from rotting. I figure I cut them up, throw them in my wood burner, and they keep me warm all winter." He hoisted the four-by-four into the truck alongside several others and tapped his temple. "That's the old brain, always ticking away. Tickety, tickety, tick."

But Redmond wasn't listening. He was looking past Teague to the chicken coop. It looked like someone had thrown a stick of dynamite in there. Three one-by-twelve planks had been knocked out of the uphill wall, knocked out from inside, and lay on the ground like enormous teeth. There were chickens all over the place. A hen was perched on the raw, ripped edge of the hole, sleeping, its head sucked into its chest.

When Teague saw what Redmond was looking at, he whistled. "Son-of-a-bitch. The kid do that? No wonder you beat the shit out of him."

Redmond walked toward the coop, snatching up two hens by the legs as he passed them. Teague followed. When he got close enough, Redmond flung one of the squalling birds through the hole.

"Yeah!" Teague said. "Let me do one." He grabbed the other hen by the feet and went into a windmill windup, whipping the heavy bird around and around. He yelled, "Tenderize, you motherfucker!" and pitched the bird through the hole. He chased down another one, grabbing it by the feet, and pitched it through the hole. The air was filled with crows of outrage. But soon the hens got smart and ran farther than Teague was willing to chase them. He fell to his knees. "God," he panted, "I love country living."

They saw birds as far as two acres away, stepping serenely among the grazing cattle, heading into the woods below the pasture.

"What about them?" Teague said.

"Let them starve."

Together they nailed a sheet of chicken wire over the hole, making sure there were no gaps wide enough for the birds to squeeze through.

When they were finished, Teague said, "I'm out of here. I don't want to be around when the fur starts to fly." Redmond looked at him, confused. Teague made his hand into a karate blade. "You know — chop, chop, slap, slap. That kid is dead meat now. Am I right?"

NICK WATCHED from his bedroom window while Redmond and Teague chased chickens. It made him feel a little better about things. He was doing his tai chi moves, or what he imagined were tai chi moves — his arms stretched out, floating, his hands in slow orbit around each other, one leg raised, bent at the knee. He stepped forward, raising the other leg, moving silently, slowly, a man under water. He turned in a tight pivot, sweeping his arms out, then pulling them back to his sides.

He wanted to shake Redmond, the animal. He wanted to say, "I was that close to killing you." But he was too scared. Scared of Redmond, yes, but more scared of himself, of what he'd almost done, of what he still wanted to do.

The old floor creaked with every lunge. When he did his spinning kick, the lamp on his night table rocked and the edge of his Doors poster drifted lightly away from the wall. He stepped carefully, with grace and cunning, over the piles of dirty laundry scattered across the floor. He imagined they were the lifeless bodies of his enemies. As he moved he counted in a quiet whisper: "One hundred forty-one thousand three hundred sixty-nine. One hundred forty-one thousand three hundred seventy. . . ."

His secret project was to count aloud to one million. It was something he thought he had to do. He didn't know why, he just had to. Every day he found a little time to count. Usually it was at night, before he fell asleep. Counting helped him keep his hands off himself. But he also counted in the shower, in study hall, and sometimes at the dinner table, quietly, while Redmond was busy watching the news, stuffing his face. The pig.

Last night when it got dark and cold in the chicken coop, he curled

41

up on the floor next to the space heater and counted. Counting got him through. It helped him focus his energy to kick out the boards. Counting saved his life.

When he finished each day, he wrote down the numbers in a worn blue notebook. The pages were crammed to the edges, front and back, with numbers. The paper had gone crinkly as old parchment with the weight of all those numbers, with the heavy pressure of his pen. This was something he wanted to last, something that would still be legible fifty years from now, a permanent record of the life of Nick Loomis. For future civilizations, like the *Voyager* spacecraft.

Back in the beginning, he'd made a false start. It was right there in the notebook. He'd counted nearly to seven hundred before realizing that if he wanted to do it right, he should really start at zero. He began again, but he kept those pages in the notebook. They reminded him to be careful.

He believed that when he finally got to a million, something would happen, that his life would somehow change. Maybe that was the day his mother would come back for him. Or maybe that's when he'd finally put an end to Redmond. He crossed his forearms in front of his face. He pulled one knee up close to his chest, exhaled through clenched teeth, then kicked out, knocking his pillow off the bed. He had to be ready, even if the day brought dark forces and disaster, or death.

"Let it come," he said.

AFTER A RESTLESS NIGHT at the Hotel Duquesne, Ellen found a bus heading northeast, and now it was blundering down some dusty two-lane. She wanted a drink, she wanted to stop her head, but there was nothing she could do. The landscape kept reeling away from her window.

She'd grown up in a small factory town in the Midwest. After high school she kicked around for a while — clerking, waitressing, answering telephones. She married Bob Whitney two weeks after meeting him, because he was a guy who liked a good laugh and a good drink. In those days that was enough. A while later Nick was born.

Bob was a big man with a beard, who wore his army jacket wherever he went. When he drank too much, he'd tell stories about what happened in 'Nam, the friends he'd lost and how he'd lost them. Once, when they were out walking with Nick, a car backfired and Bob dove behind a hedge. Sometimes at night he'd wake up screaming. By the time she'd get him calmed down, Nick would be crying.

Three years into the marriage, things were bad. Bob couldn't work. He was having flashbacks pretty much every day. Their rent was a couple months late. The little money she was bringing in went to booze and medication.

Then one night the phone rang. Bob was out drinking with some vets he knew. She and Nick had just come back from the laundromat. An old friend of Bob's was calling. She recognized the name at once, a friend from 'Nam, a friend who'd been torn in half by a booby trap.

She held the receiver in both hands, pressing it tightly to her ear. She said, "I don't understand. You're supposed to be dead."

"What?" The word fell like a hatchet stroke. The guy laughed nervously. "Is this a joke?"

"But Bob said — "

More nervous laughter. "Look, I don't know what Bob told you, but I had a desk job in Saigon. Not exactly the front line. Not then, anyway."

"But Bob *saw* you die."

"Now I *know* you're joking. Bob was never in country. He never even served. I was there when he flunked the physical. Where is that joker? Put him on."

From the kitchen, where she'd left Nick, she heard a bump and the sound of something rolling. "I have to go," she said, and hung up. Nick was sitting on the floor, dipping his hand into a jar of peanut butter.

"Peanie-buddy," he said, looking up with wide eyes, ready to be yelled at. But Ellen just turned around and walked into the bedroom.

The bed was piled high with fresh laundry. She began to separate Bob's clothes from hers. The khaki socks and T-shirts, the fatigue pants. She carried them into the bathroom, dropped them into the tub, and emptied a gallon of bleach over them.

She put the rest of the clothes back into the basket and brought it to the kitchen. She set it on the floor and threw her purse on top. She wet a paper towel and wiped Nick's hands and face.

"Come on, peanie-buddy," she said as she picked up the laundry basket.

Nick clapped his wet hands. "A ride! A ride! A ride!" And then they were gone.

It seemed so long ago, like an episode from someone else's life. But her whole past was beginning to feel like that.

After leaving Bob, she saw other men but never let them get too close. Then she met Redmond. "I'm not ready for this," she said to herself, to him, the second night he stayed with her at the trailer. But it was already too late. She was like the passenger in a car who sees the accident coming but can't do a thing about it, her fingernails digging into the dashboard as she rides it out to the last sickening thud.

Twelve years she and Redmond were together. Twelve years. It didn't seem possible. How could she have stayed with someone so screwed up? Someone who crippled her with passion one minute and threw his face into his hands the next, crying, "I can't do this anymore." How?

Twelve years. But how long really? Six, if she didn't count the time he spent away from her. Washing dishes in a diner in Little Rock. Running a grease gun for a road crew in Flagstaff. Jobs too stupid to be lies. But how much time really? How long was he really there with her, *really* with her, not watching himself be with her, not shooting nervous glances over his shoulder at whatever was chasing him? Two hours, maybe?

More, if she counted the sex. He was himself during sex. He was all there. It was one reason she let him come back and come back and come back. A man who knew her body better than she knew it herself. She fell to pieces at his touch. He made her laugh and cry at the same time. When his mouth worked at the wet fold between her legs, the world fell away. And when she came, her muscles jumping like wires, he was so caught up in her, sometimes he came too. So when she found him at the trailer door, an old record in his hand, a fistful of flowers, a face twisted with repentance, she let him in.

There were other men while he was gone. Some of them good men who made her happy. Some who hurt her, men she stayed with to spite him, even though she knew she'd never tell him about them, what they did to her. Every one of them was a better drinking partner than he ever was. But the day after he'd show up, she'd quietly call the latest one, tell him not to come around anymore.

Maybe she should have told him about the men. The one who cut hearts from sheets of newspaper and hung them around the trailer. The one who liked to fuck on the floor until her knees were raw, until her shoulders were blue and sore. Would it have made a difference if she'd told him about them? Would it have made him jealous enough to stay? But she didn't tell him. She didn't want to know that he didn't love her enough to care.

But what about Nick? She never meant to leave him. To her the last six months had been a kind of vacation, a chance to get her head straight, to get Redmond out of her system. Nick was a smart kid, he understood these things, he wasn't the kind of kid who needed to be told every little thing. Besides, she wrote to him from California. She just never mailed the letters, afraid Redmond would read them. She carried them in her purse, her don't-hate-me letters. She'd give them to Nick when she saw him, and then he'd understand everything and they'd go off together like the old days, when he was little.

She thought of that night years ago when she left Bob, of their long drive through the dark. How Nick never once asked what they were doing, where they were going. How he just sat there staring at the glove compartment, pressing his blue plastic harmonica to his lips, breathing through it slowly, in and out.

N ICK WOULD MISS TEAGUE if he didn't hurry. He dressed quickly, made sure Redmond was still out by the coop, then went down to the kitchen and eased out the screen door. He headed into the orchard, away from the house, from Redmond, ripping through the blackberry bushes, already showing the tiny red knuckles of new fruit, then over the fence and onto John Sterling's property. Out on the road and a good quarter mile from the house, from Redmond, he stopped on the shoulder, panting, leaning on his knees, waiting for Teague's truck.

Across the road was the hippie house, a run-down place where there was always a party — old, old music and old guys with long hair sitting out on the porch smoking grass. The place was trashed. Sheets of siding had come off the house. The wall around the front door was spray-painted with daisies. There were dogs and cats everywhere and an old VW bus that had been caught in a paint storm. The two or three acres that went with the house were all overgrown with weeds and brush. Hasn't anybody told these people the sixties are over? But it was quiet now. Nobody was outside, and that made Nick even more nervous. It made him feel as though they were all inside watching him.

He heard Teague before he saw him, heard the throaty guzzle of his pickup's engine, the loose lumber bucking around in the bed. He stepped out into the road and flagged him down.

When Nick climbed in, Teague said, "Hey, kid, what's the haps?"

"Nothing," Nick said. "I'm just going to the mall. I thought you could give me a ride."

"Sure, why not." Teague sniffed wetly, like a dog. "No offense, kid, but you smell."

Nick was wearing his clothes from yesterday, his gray T-shirt with the neck and sleeves carefully torn out, his new black sweatpants. They were stiff with sweat and dirt. He lifted a pinch of the shirtsleeve to his nose. It smelled of chicken shit.

"I hope you're not trying to bag a babe, smelling like that," Teague said.

Slowly Nick straightened. "I'm *not* going to 'bag' a 'babe.'"

"Hell," Teague said, "so what if you are? You smell like a farmer. What's wrong with that? There are worse ways to smell. Some women don't know how a man's supposed to smell."

"Anyway, I'm not going there to look at girls."

"What are you — sick?" Teague laughed. "Either that or you're getting some. Which is it?"

"Some what?"

"Some what," Teague said, looking into Nick's face for a second. "You're a riot."

Nick was starting to think this ride was not such a good idea. He liked Teague so much he forgot how uncomfortable he felt around him. Teague got him alone sometimes and made sidelong references to "nooky" and "hair pie." Once Teague asked him if he'd ever dated Mrs. Thumb and her four ugly daughters. Nick told him kids his age didn't really date anymore, tried to make dating sound as old-fashioned as knickers. Teague laughed and laughed.

Buda Road was a narrow two-lane connecting the farm to the highway. It followed Buda Creek and was full of dangerous switchbacks, but Teague had a rule never to let the needle fall below fifty. When he took the turns, rubber whined against blacktop.

Looking straight ahead, Nick said, "I'm going to the mall to get my ear pierced."

"Ear pierced?" Teague said. He swung wide into the next switchback, then seemed disappointed when there were no oncoming cars he could bully onto the shoulder. He turned his big loose face to Nick for a long moment. "You're putting me on." When Nick didn't say anything, didn't even look at him, he said, "Kid, I'm worried about you. I really am. One of these days you're going to push your old man too damn far."

"Lots of guys have done it. Besides, he's not my father."

"I know that. You know what I mean."

And because Nick did know what he meant, he said nothing for the rest of the drive, not even when Teague decided to drop him across the highway from the mall instead of taking him all the way in. Nick got out of the truck without saying a word and slammed the door.

"Don't fuck anything I wouldn't fuck!" Teague called out as he sailed off down the highway. But Nick wasn't listening. The pierced ear had become a holy quest.

He crossed the busy highway, horns blaring, shouts. A small kid looked out at him with dead eyes from the back window of a station wagon. When he got to the other side, he started down the long, curving ramp that led to the mall but decided instead to climb down the embankment, across the gully, and up into the parking lot.

The climb wore him out. He'd slept an hour or so on the cold floor of the coop, maybe two hours more when he got back to his bed. Usually, unless he got at least ten, he was wasted the whole next day. His bruises ached, and he was starting to hate the way he smelled. He hoped he didn't see anyone from school.

Even though he was tired, he didn't walk straight through the lot. He invented a game, a kind of gauntlet he made for himself. The first one was easy — a new green Porsche parked diagonally across two spaces. He went up to it, put his foot on the front bumper, and rocked the car hard. He was right. The car alarm began to whoop. He looked around for his next victim, past all the station wagons, pickups, and econoboxes, past an MG with a ripped-up roof, an old Pacer. There it was — a silver Lexus. He went up to it carefully, treating it like a loaded gun, and pumped the bumper. This one was wired to the horn, loud, regular as a heartbeat.

More than halfway across the lot he saw a red Corvette, the finish dull as an old apple. He wasn't really sure about this one, but he'd barely set his foot on the car's fiberglass lip when the alarm sounded. A siren, an inconsolable wail. He looked around carefully for his next car. The siren rattled him, but he had to take his time. If he rushed he might make a wrong choice. And then what? What would it mean? He couldn't get his ear pierced? He'd have to go home and be the good little man? Yes. That would be his sign.

Aᴏᴏᴛᴇʀ Tᴇᴀɢᴜᴇ ʟᴇꜰᴛ, Redmond went to the barn and found a large
burlap sack. He filled a pail with chicken feed and went into the field,
dragging the empty sack over the new grass. Down below, near the
stone wall at the bottom of the field, three hens were strutting back
and forth, patrolling the perimeter. And there were others all over the
field, lurching along for a few feet, then stopping to peck at something.
Redmond made for the nearest cluster of them.

The cattle had been grazing along the fence, but when they heard
the clatter of the pail, they came lumbering toward him. To them it
meant corn and oats rolled in molasses. Twenty head came charging
at Redmond from all sides of the field.

"No," Redmond yelled firmly, then louder, "*No.*" But they kept
coming. When the hens heard the noise, they scattered.

And now the cattle were there, all around him, butting their heads
at Redmond, rolling their runny eyes, nosing the bucket, moaning,
tails whipping.

"Back off!" he yelled, swinging the bucket at them, spilling some of
the feed. But the cattle crowded in and began tonguing up what he'd
spilled. He slapped at them and they moved aside, but sluggishly. They
turned and followed him as he worked his way down the field toward
another cluster of hens.

"Here chick, here chick," he called when he got near them, scat-
tering a handful of feed. But before they came close enough, the cattle
charged in and dragged their slimy muzzles over the grass, each tongue
scraping wetly at the feed, until they realized it wasn't what they wanted.
By then the hens had wandered away.

"All right, you stupid sons-of-bitches!" Redmond yelled, throwing the pail into the middle of the cattle and taking off after the nearest hen.

Up on the road a blue pickup drifted to a stop, drifted so slowly it seemed the engine must have lost power. Built onto the back was a handcrafted wooden camper. When the truck drifted a little too far, the driver backed it up so he could see better, so he could see that crazy boy of his down in the field chasing chickens, catching some, stuffing them into a sack, waving his arms, shouting.

The Commander sets up the tiered shelf on the living room rug. He arranges the candy carefully so it covers each tier edge to edge — Snickers, Bit-O-Honey, Red Hots, M&M's, Three Musketeers, Sugar Daddy, Good & Plenty, Licorice Whips, Hershey bars. He calls Lloyd in from his bedroom, to face the wall of candy standing as if by itself. Lloyd kneels on the rug in front of it, more candy than he has ever seen in one place, candy his father sells to him at discount, so his allowance will last longer.

"Store's open," the Commander says, smiling, opening his record book and the tin box of house money, but never taking his eyes off Lloyd, who waits for the calculations, knowing what's coming.

"Let's see. . . . " His father's pencil point scratches at a page of the notebook. He's pretending to figure up what he already knows. He stops scribbling and rests the eraser end of the pencil in the dent above his lip. He holds the notebook close and then far away. He lays it down solemnly and looks at Lloyd, who's glad the ritual's almost over.

"Seems to me as though you spent this week's allowance three weeks ago. Remember when I gave you that advance? Well, you still haven't caught up, sport. Would you like me to give you another advance?" The pen is poised over the open book of Lloyd's appetite, his debt, his failings.

"No."

The Commander squints and cocks his hand behind his ear. "I'm sorry?"

"No, sir."

He bends his ear forward. "How's that again?"

"No, sir. Thank you, sir."

"All right, then. Now give me a hand putting these goodies away."

Carefully, they remove each bar and bag of candy from the display and lay it in its box. His father stacks the boxes in Lloyd's arms, stacks them right up to his chin. Lloyd carries the boxes to the hall closet and holds them while his father makes a show of putting them one by one on the top shelf. The weight of all that candy. The sickly scent of cheap chocolate. Its piercing sweetness, like a needle between his eyes.

Late morning in Louisiana. Ellen and the other bus people were sitting beside the blacktop, crouching on or next to their luggage, empty acres on both sides of the road. They were waiting for a replacement bus. Theirs sat beside the road, canted dangerously over the irrigation ditch. The driver paced, frowning at his watch as if it were a malignant growth. In the distance a farmer was plowing the gray stubble of his land into strips of rich black earth. From so far away the tractor's roar was nothing but a soft stumbling drone. An hour ago, the same farmer waved to them. The driver, thinking he needed help, yanked the bus off the road, churning up a cloud of dust and thick diesel fumes, cracking the back axle. Not only, she realized, had she spent too much money in Houston, but now she found herself on the bus of doom.

"It's what you do when you're out in the country," the driver pleaded to a young guy sitting on a suitcase. "You see somebody in trouble, you stop. It's the southern way."

The guy looked up, shading his eyes against the new sun, and said, "Jesus — "

"Yeah, well, fuck you," the driver said, turning away before he saw the open Bible in the guy's lap.

Ellen dragged her suitcase to the other side of the road, away from everybody, and sat down on it.

She didn't remember much about that time, six months ago, when she left Redmond. And Nick, she had to admit, she left Nick too. She remembered the events, the details, what was said and what was left unsaid. What she couldn't call up was the wave of feeling that had swept her away.

The day had started badly. She and Redmond had gone out the night before. Lots of drinking. He was still sleeping it off. She made coffee and looked out the window. The sun was shining, but the world looked gray. Nick stood in the yard, a shovel in one hand. He was staring at the ground by his feet. Then with a sudden movement he took up the shovel in both hands and jabbed it at the ground.

Her love for Nick was the one thing in her life that constantly surprised her. It was so surprising that she never got used to it, never fully enjoyed it. And now he was growing up so fast, especially since he'd started karate. She was toasting an English muffin for herself, but she loaded it with grape jelly and brought it down to Nick instead. The world was gray, but she would try. She would make the effort.

"What's up, kiddo?" she said as she got near. Then she saw the snake writhing in the grass at his feet, a garter snake, its bloody halves twisting and turning.

The muffin slid off the plate, flipping onto the ground. "What have you done?" she said.

He poked at the snake with his boot. "It's interesting. You can't kill it." He raised the shovel and chopped at it again.

"Stop it," Ellen yelled, flinging the plate away.

But Nick just watched the snake. Its freshly cut quarters curled up against the blade of the shovel and then coiled away. The pieces were moving more slowly now.

When he did finally look up at her, she was staring at him coldly. "You're just like all the others," she said. She turned and went slowly back to the house.

"What?" he yelled after her. "It's just a snake."

That night, after the fifth or sixth drink, Redmond made things worse. It wasn't what he said or didn't say. It was the look in his eye. He was turning her into some kind of specimen. She knew then what it was like to be that snake lying under the shadow of the shovel's blade. The look meant he was about to leave. For once, she decided, she'd beat him to it. See how he liked it. And there it was — the memory brought it back — the rage that rose inside her and swept her away.

They were alike, Nick and Redmond, not happy unless they were killing, breaking, wrecking. And that wasn't enough. Later they expected you to feel sorry for them over the pain they'd caused. Well, no more.

So she left. She threw everything she owned into her old LeSabre and headed west on Highway 80, opening it up until the engine was nothing but a steel scream. The only destination she had in mind was away. That's when she turned on the radio. There was Dionne Warwick, asking her did she know the way to San Jose and telling her she was going there herself. Ellen took it as a sign. But when the engine seized in the desert, and she had to hitch the rest of the way, she wondered if maybe Dionne was singing about the San José in Costa Rica.

If she was only planning to make a little surgical strike on Redmond, why had she closed her checking account and turned in her apartment key? Because, she knew, there was a door somewhere that she had to either open again or close and lock forever. And you couldn't know for sure what to do if you gave yourself a way out, a life to return to.

In San Jose she lived next to a psychotherapist, a wispy-haired blond who wore colors so bright they hurt your head. Ellen figured she was asserting her place in the world. The therapist had a remarkable son, Milton, a seven-year-old who was building a fort with bamboo and blankets. He'd go out there every day after school and work on it. Ellen was bereft and unemployed, which is to say, weepy, drinking a lot, inclined to chuck it all. It helped to watch Milton build his fort.

She was also broke, but temp work always brought in enough money to keep her going. Sitting at the window, drinking vodka tonics, she wondered what she'd do if she ran out of drinking money. Was it the world in general that had wronged her or just a few particular inhabitants? Some days she wanted to know. Other days she wanted to climb into Milton's little fort and never come out.

Instead, she mostly sat in a crippled recliner, drinking, watching the therapist's clients come and go. Most of them were women in career suits, who walked nervously to the house, heads lowered. Like they were sneaking into a porn palace.

Some of them had obvious problems. Once a week a couple came by — he in a black Testarossa, she in a van that looked like a lunar rover. Who needed a therapist to figure them out?

After a while, and after a certain amount of drinking, it always seemed to Ellen that the therapist and her clients were watching her, that they'd given up counseling and being counseled, that they spent each session staring at her from behind pinched curtains, shaking their heads, saying, "We think *we've* got problems."

Ellen started saying things as the clients walked back to their cars. Things like "A good stiff drink will do more for you than a year of therapy" and "I'd be in therapy, too, if I had your hair." To Mr. Testarossa she said, "Why don't you trade cars, you little prick?" In short, she became the neighborhood crazy. Everybody on the block began to watch her. The old man who walked past the house every morning in his frayed pants and greasy tweed jacket. The burly guy jogging to the grocery store, his big dog running on ahead and his little dog trotting in crazy yelping circles behind.

One day she found a neighborhood committee at her door.

"There are places," they said, "for people with problems like yours."

"What problems?" She took a defiant sip of her drink.

"You're an alcoholic."

"Nope. You're only an alcoholic if you go to meetings. I'm a drunk."

"Think of the children," they cried as she flipped the door shut in their faces.

Sanctimonious pissants. The nerve of them. Besides, she had no desire to stay in a place where her special insights weren't appreciated.

Drinking as much as she did taught her many things. She learned that bottling companies are not very careful. She could get an extra ounce or so of tonic if she compared bottles. She learned that cheap vodka is easier to drink than cheap bourbon, Scotch, gin, and what-have-you, because of the tastelessness, though the fumes might curl your eyebrows. And she learned that she was not an alcoholic unless, having purchased equal volumes of tonic and vodka, the vodka was the first to run out. So there.

She liked to think of herself as a steady drinker, liked to pretend there was some virtue in sticking to it, as if drinking were a kind of diet or a form of exercise. In life, she told herself, it is important to do a few things well.

WHEN REDMOND WOKE UP after their first night together, Ellen was sitting on the other side of the small bedroom, staring at him. She'd dragged a chair in from the kitchen. She wore a brown terry-cloth robe and held a mug of coffee in one hand and a cigarette in the other, a hard, tense woman chewing the inside of her mouth.

When she saw that he was awake, she took a sip of coffee and said, "I don't want to hurt your feelings or anything, but who invited you?" Her soft brown hair hung limp with sleep. There was a pale-red crease down her cheek where she'd slept on her face. She looked like a woman who was always nervous unless she had a drink in her hand.

Redmond sat up, stuffing the pillow behind the small of his back, and leaned against the wall. He felt the flimsy paneling give. The details of the night before were pretty hazy, but they were there. He remembered the empty parking lot, a woman weeping, this woman. "You invited me," he said.

Her face became even more tense. She nodded slowly. "The hell I did," she said. She took a hit off her cigarette and exhaled sharply. Her voice trembled. She said, "I want you out of here."

He sat up more, pulling the covers tighter around his waist. "You needed a ride home, so I gave it to you."

"You lie."

"You saved my life," he said.

She was raising the coffee mug to her mouth but stopped.

"You saved me from Walter PPK, the guy with the shotgun."

Either she remembered now or she liked the picture it brought to her mind, because she smiled. More like a kink, really, a smile so spare it could be used only for contemplating the ridiculous but true.

"I think," she said, but more gently now, "that you ought to get out of here anyway." She stood up. "The bathroom's around the corner." She went out and down the hall, dragging the kitchen chair behind her.

It was hard to get out of bed when the bed was just a mattress on the floor. He felt like he was climbing up out of a deep hole. As he pulled on his pants he toed through her cassettes: Billie Holiday, Edith Piaf, Etta James, Aretha Franklin — songs about the hard bargains men and women make with each other and the wreckage that results. He shook out his shirt to freshen it, but it still smelled of beer, cigarettes, and sweat.

Hanging on her wall was a framed diploma. An A.A. in liberal arts conferred upon Ellen Loomis. Taped to the wall around it were a hundred photographs of parents and children, grandparents, pets. Families sat around picnic tables, stood beside new cars, sprawled on beaches. A fat boy wearing black glasses pushed a pretty girl into a swimming pool. Ten or twelve kittens and puppies hung from the hands of grinning kids. Dozens of couples stood smiling in front of dozens of waterfalls, fountains, redwoods. A laughing man forked a charred and flaming steak off a grill and dangled it in front of the camera. Each figure in the photographs appeared only once. It had to be the largest family on record, and all of them smiling. Later, after they'd been together for a while, she told him she'd bought them from a camera store. They were pictures no one had ever picked up. A bargain. All those unclaimed families for a dollar.

The bathtub was full of blankets and sheets, a pillow that still held the impression of a small head. So I didn't dream it, he thought. He scrubbed his face hard, hoping it would help him make sense of things. He studied the crosshatched lines under his eyes. He was only twenty-five, but he felt old, too old.

He looked himself hard in the eyes and said, "What we need here is a graceful exit."

The kitchen was at the other end of the trailer. On the four-foot square of linoleum stood a round wooden table and two chairs. She sat on one and a small boy knelt on the other, the boy from the bathtub. He was eating a piece of toast with nearly an inch of grape jelly on it. He had a shock of dirty-blond hair and skin so white it seemed poached.

Redmond headed for the door, nodding to the woman, who looked at her son and said, "Say goodbye to Mr. Fields, Nicky."

The boy twisted around on his knees and stuck his hand out to shake. He threw his head back, waiting, smiling. Redmond shook the hand gently. It was sticky with something Redmond hoped was only jelly. When the boy spoke, he made his voice sound like a small robot's, cranking Redmond's arm once for each syllable: "Good-bye-Mis-ter-Feels." He held on to Redmond's hand, staring up at him. Redmond looked at Ellen, who stared back at him woodenly.

What did these people mean to him? Nothing. Even less. But Redmond couldn't help himself. He said, "You know, I don't think I can leave without straightening things out."

"Oh, they're straight," she said. "You can just hit the road, you and your clean little conscience." Her smile was like a wince.

"My name is Lloyd Redmond. I don't know what you think you have against me," he said. "All I did was give you a ride home. I almost got my head shot off for it. And anyway, nothing happened between us. So don't give me shit like I did something wrong."

The boy's head spun around to his mother. In his robot monotone he said, "I-heard-the-*s*-word."

Her chin bunched and the corners of her mouth turned down. "Shut up, Nicky." Then to Redmond, in a small frightened voice: "You got what you wanted. Why won't you just go?"

He took a deep breath. She stubbed out her cigarette. She was like a child playing at toughness, barely pulling it off. That's what he wanted to tell her. Come off it, he wanted to say.

The boy took a noisy drink of milk, slurping and humming as he swallowed. Then he leaned his head back over the top of the chair, looking at Redmond upside down. When he smiled, a thin trickle of milk ran out the corners of his mouth, ran into his ears.

"You said 'shit.' "

Redmond left, snapping the door shut quietly behind him. It was early and cold. The grass was stiff with frost, what little grass there was in the narrow passage between the trailers. Her trailer listed slightly toward the downhill side. There were dings and dents everywhere. One corner of the thing — the bedroom corner, Redmond realized — was crumpled. Walter, the neighbor, had probably backed his tow truck into it. The rusted skirting had fallen off the trailer long ago, showing the eight pairs of ancient, decayed tires the whole thing sat on. From the darkness far under the trailer, eyes stared out at Redmond, yellow cat eyes.

He hated this Ellen Loomis, hated her for what she made him want to do. He wanted to put his shoulder to the uphill side of the trailer and push the whole mess over. He was so mad he thought he could do it. But he also wanted to scare up some cinder blocks and mortar and build a more solid foundation under the trailer, tack up some new skirting, rebuild the sagging wooden steps, maybe lay some flagstone so she'd have a place to sit on hot days and cool evenings. This desire to please her was the stronger impulse in him and the one, he knew, that would do more damage in the long run.

NICK WATCHED ALL THE happy, smiling Sunday families walking through the mall, walking so slowly, with all the time in the world. Every last one of them was going to end up a cold gray thing in the ground. Didn't they know that? He hated them. This one wearing his work clothes even on the weekend, his hair slicked back and snaking down his neck. His wife all dressed up so nobody could tell she was married to the weasel beside her. Their two kids slurping strawberry ice cream cones. He felt like rubbing it in their faces.

Don't look at anyone. Keep your eyes on the floor passing under your feet, at the store windows sliding by. He knew where he was going. He'd passed it many times. The Earring Pagoda sat in the middle of the mall, a square of display cases topped by a red roof with curled-up corners. He could find his way with his eyes closed. Only, today was different. He wasn't just passing by. He was going to do it.

But when he got to the Pagoda, he lost his nerve. Two girls were inside, getting their ears done. One was already finished, looking into a hand mirror, teasing her bright black hair out to set off her new gold posts. The other sat in the chair, her eyes flipping back and forth in nervous delight as each ear was done. They were the kind of girls who made him nervous — sure of themselves, pretty. He ran his hand along the display cases and kept walking.

One reason he wanted the earring was to get girls at school to notice him, girls like them. The coolest guys in school had at least one pierced ear. But he didn't want witnesses. If he was nervous, they'd laugh, they'd embarrass him. Why should he care? They weren't from his school, they weren't from anywhere. Still, he decided to hide out in the Orange Julius until they went away.

He finished his Julius and walked back to the Pagoda, trying not to

61

look too eager, but it cost him. By the time he got there, another customer had stopped, a small, pretty woman with long dark hair that hid part of her square face. She was pushing a stroller that seemed too big for her.

This time, he knew, if he didn't wait he'd never go through with it. Then Redmond and all the dark forces would win. He stood there studying the earrings, the simple gold and silver hoops, the tiny inscribed shields that made him think of knights in armor, the wavy scraps that looked like an alien's teardrops, the turquoise pendants. Some were even wilder — fish earrings, cow earrings, hot dog earrings, and, the best of all, two tiny waitresses wearing pointed glasses and holding platters of burgers, fries, and Cokes.

The woman was counting eight dollars into the clerk's hand. The clerk was old, bored. Her mouth was such a thin, tight line that her lips looked sewn together. She held one hand out for the money. In the other, she held the gray metal earring gun loosely and down by her side like a six-shooter. Something seemed wrong to Nick. The customer spoke with a heavy accent he didn't recognize, but that wasn't it. It was her ears — they were already pierced. Before he figured out what was happening, she bent to the stroller and lifted a little kid out of it, a baby, and sat down in the earring chair, holding her on her lap, because the kid wasn't old enough to sit up by herself.

The clerk was pissed because she had to bend down low to get at the baby's ear. And then the ear was too small to get at very easily. The baby had this wide, peaceful face, not pretty but peaceful, like a frog's face. When the clerk swabbed her ear with alcohol, the baby batted her hand and smiled, but her mother pulled the arm down and held it. The clerk brought the barrel of the earring gun alongside the baby's face and fit the lobe into the little notch at the end. It took a couple of tries, because the lobe was small and the baby kept turning her head to see what was going on. The clerk finally got it right, though, and triggered the gun with a loud snap.

The baby began to scream, her face all red and running with tears. The mother held her, very calm, while the clerk reset the gun and swabbed the other ear. The baby tried to squirm away, but her mother pulled her up, held her tighter.

"Don't do this," Nick said, his voice a raw whisper. And then, louder: "Don't do this."

"Hold on," the clerk said to him. "I'll be finished here in a second."

"Don't do this," Nick said, stepping between the display cases, stepping in next to the mother, who was pinning the baby's arms to her sides.

The baby screamed so loud she stopped making any kind of sound, her head shaking, her mouth open, her face a blister. The clerk tried to line up the gun over the other lobe.

Nick dug out all his money, eight dollars and change, money he'd stolen from Redmond's wallet last night, stealing from him instead of killing him. "Here," he said. "Take it all. Just stop." He held the money near the mother's face, but she only looked up for a second, confused. "Here," he said to the clerk. "I'll give it to you. Just stop."

But she didn't even look up from the baby, from the baby's ear in the gun. "I'll be right with you," she said sharply. "Will you give me a break here?" And then it was done, another loud snap and the baby screaming, her eyes all water, her mouth a wet hole.

Nick backed away from them, sick to his stomach. The mother turned the baby, inspecting the bright gold bead in each ear. She dug a pacifier out of the blankets in the stroller and stroked the baby's lips with it. The baby quieted down some and took it, sucking furiously, her face blotchy and red.

"You're next, cowboy," the clerk said, her elbow on her hip, the gun pointed up and away, like some kind of Dirty Harry. Nick, his money still in his hand, moved toward the chair in a daze, sat down, waited.

"Just one," he said hoarsely.

She swabbed the ear roughly, the way you'd clean a dirty ashtray.

The small woman held her baby with one arm and pushed the stroller with the other. The posts in the baby's ears made him think of the tags they used to keep track of animals in Africa. He felt sicker. Why was he going through with this? Because if he didn't, he'd regret it later. He'd wake up tomorrow no more special than today. He had to give the world a sign, had to give himself a sign, a sign that things were going to be different from now on.

It took him a moment to realize that someone was watching. The man he'd seen when he first came into the mall, the man wearing his work clothes — dark-green pants and shirt, with a white oval above the pocket and "Bud" in red stitching. He was alone now and smoking a twisted little cigar. He stared directly at Nick, wouldn't take his eyes off him. When it was clear that Nick saw him, he took the cigar out of his mouth, puckered his lips, and made a loud kiss. Then he smiled, put the dark wet cigar back into his mouth, and walked on.

Nick felt like running away, but it was almost over now. Dirty Harry stepped toward him, swabbed his ear, laid the barrel of her gun along his cheek, fired. It was over. She was talking now, telling him how to prevent infection, telling him to turn the post once every four hours or six hours or twenty-four hours. Nick couldn't listen. He wanted out of there. He paid her and left, his ear throbbing, feeling that everyone in the mall was staring at him, throwing obscene kisses. The nearest exit was a football field away, a distant rectangle of sunlight. He made for it. He ran.

Redmond liked to drink in places with women bartenders who called him "honey" and "doll" — places like the Sip 'n Sup, the C'mon Inn, and the Club Moderne. Ellen liked them too. She said she felt safer being served by a woman. Sometimes he thought the only thing that kept them together was the fact that they got drunk at the same rate. They didn't go out every night, but when they did, they started at four and drank hard until last call, when they ordered two drinks to carry them to closing. They drank until they became suspicious, resentful, and frightened of the people around them. Eventually, they turned on each other. Back at the trailer, they passed out in separate rooms, smoldering with distrust over something said or unsaid, something damning, unforgivable, forgotten by morning.

One night at the Club Moderne, they decided to leave the bar early. They were already half drunk, but they wanted to surprise Nick at his new job, his first. He'd wanted extra money, so Redmond told him about the sign at the supermarket — "Stock Boy Wanted." Nick hated the job. He spent his hours "fronting" — moving cans, packages, and boxes forward to make the shelves look full. He had to wear black polyester pants and an ugly blue tunic supplied by the store. As a protest, he never washed the pants, wearing them day after day until they were shiny and sour-smelling.

Whenever Ellen threatened to come by, he said, "You'd only feel bad when you see the way the manager pushes me around." So they felt like spies when they snuck into the store, laughing, getting stares from the checkout clerks. They were nervous and forgot to pick up a cart, and now their arms were full of bread, milk, cheese, cereal. When they found everything they wanted, they went looking for Nick, prowling the aisles, arms overloaded with groceries.

He was leaning against a shelf near the rice and pasta, talking to a kid who looked about the same age but harder, rougher, a kid with a silver ring in his nose and a torn black leather jacket. Redmond had seen his type before — full of hatred for any pure emotion, always peering around the corner of a person, looking for this one's weakness, that one's foolishness. A kid with no talent for anything but irony, his face balanced between scorn and rage. The kind of kid Redmond had been.

Ellen tried to wave, but her arms were so loaded she only managed to flutter a few fingers at Nick. She began to laugh, and then Redmond laughed, both of them falling against each other, laughing drunkenly. Nick was no more than ten feet away. They watched as he began to turn to them, then saw his glance stop short. The kid next to him, though, stared right at them with eyes that said everything, everything in the world, was beneath him.

"Maybe he just can't see us," Redmond said.

"Yup," Ellen said.

When Nick turned back to his friend, they snuck up behind him, then lunged into his line of sight. This time when she waved, Ellen dropped a can of soup and kicked it straight at Nick. She fell against Redmond, laughing. That's when she saw the trail of spaghetti following them, spilling from the box Redmond had crushed under his arm. They laughed louder. It was all so funny. Couldn't the kid see how funny it was?

Nick looked at them then. He couldn't help but look at them. The whole store was watching. But he looked through them, canceled them out. Redmond suddenly realized what the kid felt about him, about his mother, about the whole world.

"Nicky?" Ellen said, dropping her groceries loudly and wringing her hands. But Nick said nothing. His hard eyes pushed at them. His hard eyes said, *I don't know you people.*

Later she lay in bed staring at the ceiling. "I hate him," she said, her eyes brimming, tears running into her ears.

Redmond turned to her, stroked her shoulder tenderly, and said, "He's an ungrateful little shit."

She flung herself out of bed so suddenly it was like she'd been yanked. She grabbed the pillow and the top cover and dragged them to the bedroom door, then turned back. "You're talking about my *kid*," she said, pounding her bare chest. "*Nobody* talks like that about my kid. *Nobody*." Stunned, Redmond listened as she went to the living room and arranged herself on the couch, where she lay whimpering for most of the night, wounded in too many ways to name.

B EING A HUSBAND, TEAGUE THOUGHT, was like being one of those lawyers who handle the same case all their lives. You have to come to hate it. If you don't, you're nuts. Usually it's got nothing to do with the actual woman, but for him it did. His old lady was a case, all right. Dina. Dinette, he called her when she started porking up. They used to have fun, but those times were getting harder and harder to remember. The happiest day of his life was the day she walked out on him.

Getting mad is the only way to get a job done, he thought, and Dina gave him plenty of reasons. Teague was out beside his house, working with the wood he'd collected at Redmond's. He backed his truck up the driveway and pulled the ends of the four-by-fours a little off the bed. He wiped away the cobwebs and rat droppings, then powered up his saber saw and started cutting the wood into one-foot chunks, just right for his wood burner. Redmond. That spooky fuck. Someday they'd find out he had a few relatives buried in the basement. And Ellen. Who could figure her out? They played a little grab-ass once that turned into something more. Just the one time. Redmond had walked out. Again. And Dina had split. He was feeling drunk, wasted, full of self-pity. So was Ellen. It was a mistake. And now she was gone. Finally came to her senses, probably. Finally figured Redmond out. Him with those eyes that flip from don't-hit-me to come-here-while-I-kill-you. And the kid, all scratched up and smelling like that. Some really weird shit was going on out there.

Dina hated everything about him. The way he ran his real estate. The survivalist literature he used to get. The empty beer cans he left lying around. She said he didn't eat like a normal person. So what if he just sucked the food right off the plate? And then there was the sex. The not-right sex. The incorrect sex. Every day of his married life, the first thing he did when he woke up was toss his cookies. The morning after she left, he woke up in perfect health. What more proof did he need? So now she's a high mucky-muck in city government. What's that to him? And so what if she looks even better now than she looked in high school? Her with her Teflon suits and titanium tits. Now who's going to save you when the Arabs come over the dune, you dumb bitch?

It was tough work. The four-by-fours cut like rock. He was pushing the saw too hard. He knew that. He smelled the wood burning against the screaming blade. Even the handle was getting hot. He went into the house for some help, into the dining room, his bedroom since Dina moved out. He never liked the blue flowered wallpaper she had him put up in the bedroom, the oak woodwork, the dried weeds in old medicine bottles. And now it all reminded him too much of her. The day she left, he dragged their queen-size mattress downstairs and into the dining room. The walls were cracked and greasy, salmon-colored. That was more like it.

The mattress filled a corner of the room, the blankets and gray sheets trailing off the end. A drill press stood in the middle of the room, left over from some project he couldn't remember. There was a row of empty army surplus filing cabinets against another wall. Someday he'd put his life in order, get it all in there according to the alphabet.

But right now he needed a little help. His stereo system was piled on top of itself in another corner of the room. He hoisted the speakers into the window facing the driveway, wedged them in, and cranked up some Little Feat. He fished through the pockets in a pile of dirty jeans until he found the stingy little joint someone had given him at a party last week. He didn't feel like rolling his own. "Any joint in a jam," he said. He stroked it straight. He lit up and took a hit. It was like sucking on a Q-Tip.

When he went back out to the truck, his next-door neighbor made a show of slamming her kitchen window shut. The old guy in the house behind his came out on his deck and stared at him angrily. The music was so loud you could feel it, you could wrap your arms around it, straddle it. Teague dropped into a bass player's crouch and hit a few hot chords on his air guitar, dancing around, pumping hard. The air boomed and buzzed. The old guy shook his head slowly, a prune in a Porsche cap.

Waverley Place wasn't the neighborhood where you lived the sort of life Teague lived, especially on Sunday. The street was full of retirees and young families. He'd had trouble with them before. Trouble over the old cars in the front yard, cars he worked on or meant to work on — three Monte Carlos (one to drive and two for parts), a little Ghia, and the pickup he'd restored, the red so syrupy you could eat it with a spoon. They're just jealous, he figured, with nothing to drive but those little ricegrinders.

They hassled him over other things too. Over the ladders, lumber, engine parts, old washer, and dead doorless refrigerator lying in the yard. Over the loud fights he and Dina used to have. Over the midnight home improvement projects he'd get into after a little Mexican bug water. What did he care? Like the song said, he was fightin' the good fight, hangin' on to the good times.

Jack Teague was the grandson of Congressman Luther Teague, who represented the district for over forty years, a dapper old man who always wore a white suit and a panama hat, his mustache elegantly waxed. In his youth, in the twenties, he could be found every summer afternoon leaning languidly in front of the Rialto Theater with an unlit cigarette in his mouth. Women loved him, his look, anyway. He was a man known for his artful ways, especially with the taxpayer's dollar. When he died they found a solid-gold telephone in his study.

Teague modeled his life on the old man's, his version of it. As a boy he ran wild, wrecking every car his father gave him, chasing women, ducking the law. His father, who ran a small law firm, gave up trying to control him. He decided to let the bad blood run its course, until the wildness worked out of his system or landed him in jail. But then Teague's grandfather, the Right Honorable Luther Teague, died.

This was the moment Teague had been preparing for. With a fat inheritance, he'd be equipped for some serious depravity. But the old boys were too crafty for him. They booby-trapped the inheritance, setting up a foundation that released money to Teague in the form of low-interest loans. And even then, the largest percentage of every loan had to be spent on real estate. Over the years, kicking and screaming all the way, Teague had come to own a couple dozen houses and farms up and down the valley.

But he found a way around the inheritance. "Creating wealth," he called it. He bought two-story houses or ones that could easily be broken down into separate living units. He threw up some drywall, rerouted the plumbing, rewired a little, and soon he had an extra little moneymaker nobody knew about, at least until Dina came along.

He turned porches into kitchens, pantries into bathrooms, and walk-in closets into "junior bedrooms." He turned a rat-infested cellar into what he called a "maisonette." "Year-round comfort," he said to the new tenant, slapping the cast-iron furnace that stood in the middle of the kitchen.

In the beginning, the tenants used to complain, but then he learned to rent to people no one else would rent to, bad risks, people who knew better than to complain, people who were happy to have a roof over their heads. And anyway, what did they really have to complain about? Hell, he hadn't seen his own upstairs since Dina left. Who needed all that space? He didn't mind eating his meals over the sink, so why should his tenants? You want a sit-down dinner, you go to McDonald's.

But the more he owned and the more he finessed, the more pain it caused him. Where he used to spend his days drinking, shooting pool, and hanging out with his friends — "low-life cronies," according to his father — now he spent them knocking together kitchen units, buying used furniture, tacking down carpeting, and snaking out septic systems. Whether his father knew it or not, his vengeance was complete.

He had about half the wood cut, a dozen foot-long chunks. That was plenty. It had to be. Piece-of-shit saw. The blade was so hot the cut end of every piece of wood was a burned swirl. He tossed it on the ground and walked into the waves of music pounding out of the window. He unclamped the speakers from the sash and lowered them into the room. The volume dropped so suddenly that every other sound seemed muted. A thin, faraway whistle sang in his head.

He went back to the truck and hiked his new chunks of firewood one at a time through the window. Some of them landed on the bed. Some of them fell with a thunk on the floor or bashed against the empty filing cabinets. He thought of the chickens, the way he and Redmond pitched them through the hole in the coop. He thought about Redmond and the kid in that kitchen, their faces like fists.

He hauled what was left of the four-by-fours off the end of the truck and let them fall in the driveway. They were heavy and hard to get hold of. Later on sometime he'd stack them against the house with the rest of his lumber. He tapped one of them with the steel toe of his work boot. The pale-green wood looked like it was fresh from the lumberyard, even though it had been lying against the barn since before he owned the property. And all those hash marks running in the same direction, laid out so carefully, like a secret code. It wasn't just Redmond and that scratched-up kid and Dina and Ellen and all his nice nervous neighbors. Weird shit was happening everywhere.

THE KID WAS GONE. Redmond had stayed away from the house all day, recapturing the chickens, working in the barn. They both needed time alone. But now it was late afternoon, and he was feeling hungry and tired and sorry. He looked all over for him — in his room, in the barn, in the orchard — but he was gone.

He went back to the room to see if he was just gone or gone gone. The air held his scent, sour and waxy. The only clothes in his closet were the chinos and polo shirts he'd stopped wearing when he started his karate lessons. Now all he wore were T-shirts and black sweatpants, and they were strewn all over the floor. It was hard to tell if anything was missing. He couldn't be gone for good — he'd left his mother's tape player and a pile of cassettes. He wouldn't go anywhere without those. Seeing the player there next to the mattress made Redmond think of her, of that first night. In the end she left without the tape player, so maybe he was gone too, gone like his mother. Good. Give me a shot at a normal life. Get off this fucking farm. Get an apartment like a normal person, a regular job. No more deals with Teague. No more unloading trucks for Kinsey's. Maybe they'd hire him back at the weaving mill, but that didn't matter. Any factory job would do. He was sick of having to make so many decisions for himself, of having to live with the consequences.

But when he really thought about it, about Ellen's leaving and now maybe Nick gone too, an emptiness opened up in front of him. He felt paralyzed. He hoped the kid wasn't really gone. Even if he couldn't tell the kid how sorry he was, he might be able to show him. He grabbed a light jacket, his car keys, and drove to the grocery store.

Mealtime used to be when Redmond and Nick got along best, when they had their most important talks, at least when Nick was little.

71

Nick, looking up from his bowl of cereal: Oak meal is hot and Krispies is cold, right?

Right.

And we like cold better than hot, right?

Well, I don't really like cereal.

And Nick, with a big spoonful of dripping cereal in his mouth: Me either.

At the grocery store, Redmond moved quickly up and down the aisles. He knew what he wanted: a gallon of milk, a twenty-four pack of frozen burritos, a box of Kix, a quart of peanut butter, a quart of grape jelly, a loaf of white bread, a box of Quik, cold cuts, corn chips. When he got to the checkout, he realized he might not be able to afford all that food. He had something like thirteen dollars in his wallet. As he waited he calculated what he could afford, what he might have to give back. He unloaded his groceries onto the conveyor, the milk and burritos first, then the rest, ranked according to what the boy needed, wanted.

The man in front of Redmond was taking his time. Old wool overcoat with a T-shirt under it, pin-stripe slacks, brown corduroy bedroom slippers. He'd bought a lottery ticket and was scraping it right there, holding up the line. One end of his mouth was a hitch higher than the other. He had a mustache like an old scab, dark, pushed-in eyes, and a few black wires of hair. When he finished scraping the ticket, he said, "I changed my mind," and flipped it at the clerk. "I don't want this. I never wanted this. I want my dollar back."

The clerk ignored him and started dragging Redmond's groceries one by one across the scanner. She was about Nick's age, but she'd given herself a hard-edged, older look. She wore heavy blue makeup on her eyelids, and her black hair was cut raggedly, the ends of it dyed white.

"Did you hear me, you piece of shit?" The man raised his arms like a boxer. In another second he'd vault over the conveyor.

But then the clerk, in a small, shattered voice, the voice behind the blue makeup and dyed hair, said, "Go home, Dad, OK? Just go home. I'll give you your dollar when I get off work. Only just go home. OK?"

The scabby mustache squirmed. He pointed at her as he backed away from the checkout. His head shook. "You want to know something? I am sick. To the death. Of you."

Redmond wanted to do something, but she shifted her gaze to him and said evenly, "Twenty-four seventy-eight."

"Oh no," he said. There was nothing in his wallet but three dollars and a receipt from Kinsey's for chicken feed. "I thought — God, I'm sorry. I — I guess — "

She closed her eyes and breathed once, deeply. When she opened them, they were wet.

He gripped the side of the conveyor with one hand, squeezing the three dollars in the other. "I'm really — I don't — Look, I'll put everything back."

But the clerk had already begun moving the groceries from the conveyor to a cart behind her. Redmond grabbed the sweating gallon of milk before she reached for it, held it against his chest. "I'll just have the one thing," he said.

Bᵧ ᴛʜᴇ ᴛɪᴍᴇ Nɪᴄᴋ ɢᴏᴛ ʜᴏᴍᴇ, hitching rides with half a dozen drivers, it was already dark. His last ride was in a rusted-out Impala owned by a guard heading out to the county prison down Buda Road. He was a gray-faced man who chewed tobacco and spit into a Coke bottle he kept between his legs.

"We got a guy out there at the prison who cut up his neighbor's dog and fed it to him. Roasted it like a pig, with an apple in its mouth and all. A poodle, I do believe. You got an earache?"

"No," Nick said, but he was holding his right ear, the one with the new earring in it. He didn't want to have to explain anything to this man. Maybe the earring had been a terrible mistake.

He hadn't thought anyone could drive Buda Road faster than Teague. He had to brace himself against the dash to keep from being thrown all over. The guy took every turn too sharp or too wide, tires flumping off the asphalt and kicking up dust and gravel, low branches whipping the sides of the car.

"Reason I ask about the ear is because ears remind me of this old boy we got who used to cut the ears off of children. He only took one from each, just for his collection. He was crazy about ears, especially young, tender ones. He even snuck one inside with him. It looks a lot like a dried apricot."

"Let me out," Nick said.

"I thought you said you lived — "

"Here," he said, slapping the dashboard. "Right here is just fine."

"Suit yourself," the guard said and hit the brakes.

The car pulled away, leaving Nick beside the road, waiting for his heart to stop beating him to death. He was still a mile or more from the house, but that was all right. This way Redmond wouldn't hear him coming. He walked, willing his heart to slow down, stepping back into the bushes when he heard a car coming, in case it was Redmond.

The evening sky was dark blue, nearly black, except for a sulfur-yellow streak of light along the western hills. Most of the houses he passed were lit up. He saw families moving around inside, working in kitchens, setting and unsetting Sunday dinner, changing channels on TVs. In one living room he saw an old couple dancing. The man stood with his left palm pressed to her right. They held each other lightly, barely moving, and looked straight into each other's eyes.

The front window of the hippie house was open, the living room lit up. He saw a kid his age shooting a basketball up at the ceiling, catching it, then shooting it back up. Nick heard each throw hit the ceiling. Upstairs the bedroom light came on. The boy stared up and smiled.

And then he was home. Down through John Sterling's property, over his split-rail fence, under the apple trees, to the house, to the maniac. When he came clear of the orchard he was ten feet from the side of the house. The lights were on here too, but because the rear of the house was one story off the ground, he couldn't see inside.

He leaned back against the nearest tree and thought about climbing up into it so he could see what Redmond was doing, whether he was sprawled on the couch in front of another Perry Mason rerun or waiting beside the door with a loaded shotgun. A small breeze came up the hillside, and the tree shifted slightly against his back. He felt the flutter of wings in its hollow trunk. Birds must be nesting inside. Or bats. He moved away quickly, silently, downhill, away from the orchard, the house.

When he got to the coop, he carefully undid a corner of the chicken wire and stepped in through the hole he'd kicked, then pulled the wire shut again. Redmond would never think to look for him here.

Most of the hens were asleep already, stuffed into their nesting boxes or huddled together on the perches. A few flapped and moaned a little when Nick came inside, but when he spread a little scratch in their feed trough, they forgot all about him and went for it, beaks stabbing at the grain.

He snapped on the space heater and sat down near the hole in the wall so he could keep watch. His ear felt sore, but he carefully turned the silver bead, the way he thought he was supposed to. An hour after the lights went out, maybe two, he'd sneak into the house, get some sleep. He'd drink a lot of water before going to bed. That way he'd be sure to wake up before Redmond and slip back outside. That's the way a warrior would do it.

ALABAMA. LATE. It was so dark, or she'd been on the bus for so long, that colors stopped registering on her retinas. Everything was a shade of blue or gray.

The bus made a rest stop at a diner called The Majestic, only twelve miles from the next station. When she asked the driver why they couldn't go right on into Birmingham, he mumbled something about company policy, hiked up his pants, and led the passengers inside. Everyone shambled after him and obediently ordered a dry little sandwich from piles stacked on the cutting board. Sitting there for hours, she figured, waiting for them.

The driver and the owner stood at the end of the counter, talking out of the sides of their mouths as they watched the passengers eat. She was sure of one thing. Before they left, money would pass between them. She asked the waitress for a glass of water. On principle she would not eat. Let them try to throw her out. Let them just try.

Nick couldn't sleep. He lay on the hard floor of the chicken coop, his eyes tightly closed, but nothing would shut out the noise. One of the chickens was about to lay. For an hour it had been cooing quietly, like someone talking in her sleep, but then it began to moan, and now it was making a noise like a rusty gate in a windstorm.

He tried to distract himself by picturing his mother's face. He didn't want to lose her, didn't want to forget what she looked like. He wanted to fix her in his memory for all time. But instead of her face, he saw the face of his English teacher and then the face of a woman he'd seen from the window of the school bus. His mother was transforming herself from a particular woman into all women. The chicken curdled the air with one sharp cry and then fell silent.

The night before Redmond nailed him into the coop, Nick had decided to ask him questions about his mother. Redmond was cooking their dinner, stirring up a pot of canned ravioli with one hand and drinking from a tall bourbon and Coke with the other. It was a subject Redmond had declared forbidden, and it was obvious he was in no mood. Still, Nick couldn't resist.

He said, "I just want to know a few things. Like did she have a job when she was my age? What kind of friends did she have? Did she even have friends? What did she like to do? Things like that." Things he never wondered about until she was gone.

Redmond stood at the stove with his back to Nick, slowly stirring the pot.

Nick cleared dirty dishes and yesterday's newspaper from the table, but kept at him, kept asking questions. "What was she like when you first met her? I don't remember much from back then. I must have been about three or four. I remember she liked to dance. What kind of clothes did she wear? What did she do on the weekends?"

Redmond just stood there and stirred.

"What were the things she couldn't live without?" And why, Nick wondered, wasn't I one of them?

"It's hot," Redmond said, bending over the pot. "Let's go."

But Nick wouldn't quit. "That night she left, what did she say? What did *you* say? Did she give you a message for me?"

He knew some of it, how she stormed through the house, collecting her things, saying, "I can't do this anymore. You hear me? *I* can't do this anymore." He stayed in his room, afraid to find out that "this" meant being his mother. And then she left, without explaining anything to him, without saying goodbye, without waving to him where he stood at the window, watching.

He got spoons and tore off paper towels for napkins, while Redmond stood at the counter scraping the ravioli into bowls. "Where do you think she went? Didn't you even bother to try to find out where she went?"

Redmond put the bowls on the table, then dropped heavily into one of the chairs and began to eat.

Nick sat down across from him, but he didn't eat, couldn't let it go. "Tell me," he said. He wanted Redmond to talk. He wanted to see his mouth make the shape of her name. But Redmond kept his eyes fixed on his bowl.

"You don't understand." Nick's voice shook. "It's like she's not real anymore. It's like she never existed." Redmond kept eating. "Say her name," Nick said. "At least that." He was holding the edge of the table now. He felt strong enough to snap it off. Say it, he thought. Say it.

"Mary," Redmond said, without looking up. "All women are named Mary. Or Carlotta."

Nick felt the muscles in his neck go thick and hard. He could barely speak. "What do you get out of this?" he said. "I mean, what's the point?"

"The point?" Redmond said, his voice mocking. He threw his spoon on the table and shoved his bowl away. "Grace, Jane, Janet, Larry, Lucy, Joe. What's the point of that, of her name? You think you'll be any more real if you hear her name? Don't kid yourself, bucko. It's still you. That's all you've got — always only you. And when you forget that, you're really alone." He stood up now and started moving toward the back door. "I don't want to hear any more of this. As far as I'm concerned, your mother is dead. OK? That's all there is to know." He went out on the porch, slamming the screen door behind him, his eyes filling.

Nick cleared his throat. "Ellen," he said. Then, louder, loud enough for him to hear out on the porch, "Ellen Loomis."

But Redmond said nothing. He was standing at the banister, staring into the woods at the bottom of the farm, at the dark branches spattered with pale flakes of new green.

Nick remembered some things about his mother from back when he was a kid. The way she left him by himself when she went out on a date, telling him not to answer the door, not to answer the phone, and to call Walter next door if anything bad happened. "But nothing bad's going to happen," she'd say and kiss him on the forehead. Still, after she left, Nick stayed awake until she came home, worrying, waiting for the glare of headlights to sweep through the room, waiting for her to come back to him, smelling of cigarettes and liquor. It was a small trailer and they had to share the same bed. If she was happy she'd want to talk. She'd kneel beside him and whisper, "Wake up, Sneaky Neeky. I'm home."

"Did you have a good time?" he'd ask, trying to make his voice sound full of sleep. "Did you get to dance?"

"We danced all night," she'd say. "And then we danced some more."

"That's good." He'd pretend to yawn so he could stare at her face through his nearly closed eyes. He memorized those moments in the dark, knowing somehow that he needed to. He listened to her, to the soft sounds her mouth made when she was happy. He watched the way the moonlight lit up her hair.

Sometimes, when he heard her key in the lock, he kicked off the covers and pretended to be asleep so she'd pull them back up to his chin. And sometimes he moaned and whimpered, to make her think he was having a bad dream. She'd stroke his hair and whisper-sing to him.

"Did you get to dance?"

"This one" — she laughed — "this one danced like he was gut shot."

Sometimes they gave her things, these men. A gold necklace once, silver earrings, an old record. And sometimes they made promises. He knew this by the change in the way she talked. She'd say, "Look around you, kid. Someday soon we're going to kiss this crap goodbye."

"Did you dance?"

"It would have taken a block and tackle to get this one on the dance floor."

Once in a while a man spent the night. Nick heard two sets of footsteps, a low voice. She'd come into the bedroom, still in her coat, gather him up, and lay him in the bathtub. It wasn't so bad. There were plenty of blankets. It was like being held in someone's arms, in someone's cold arms.

Usually the men were long gone by the time Nick woke up. Sometimes they stayed for coffee, laughing nervously, calling him "little man" and "bub" and "half-pint." He made faces at his mother, but she'd ball up her fist, mouthing "Be nice" at him. He remembered one who sat with his legs crossed, knocking his cigarette ashes into the cuff of his pants, making sure he left no evidence behind.

But sometimes no headlights came washing through the room, and there was no sound of a car pulling in. He heard only her key scratching at the lock. On those nights she didn't come right to bed. She stayed in the bathroom for a long time. He heard her soft whimper through the wall, behind the sound of running water. When she finally came in, he'd be lying there with the blankets down around his knees, his skin all goose bumps, but she wouldn't notice. She crawled quietly into bed, turning to the wall, holding herself still, her pillow rolled up hard under her head. Nick stayed awake for the rest of the night, wanting to say something, to touch her the way she touched him. But she wouldn't allow that. If she knew he was awake, she'd only laugh and lie about the great time she'd had. So he kept still too, staring all night at the back of her head, helpless.

And now she was gone. Too hard to believe. Like a theorem in algebra that you just can't get your mind around. He never got to feel sad or angry, because he never really believed that she left him. He knew she was gone, but every knock at the door, every footstep in the hall, was hers.

If he had known she was going away, he thought, he would have paid more attention. He would have written down all her words so he could keep her somehow. He would have written down the names of the kids she grew up with, the records they liked. He would have written down how the neighbor girl came in one day and poked the eyes out of her goldfish. He would have written about her drunken uncle who pushed her into the closet one New Year's Eve and held her tight in there among all the coats. And how her mother slapped her when she told about it, like she was the one who did wrong. Like what was wrong was telling about it and not what her uncle did to her in the dark. If he had the chance, Nick would even write down the little things she said, like "Pick up your toys, kiddo" and "Come and eat or I'll throw it out" and "You do that again and you're one dead kid." If he had known she was going away, he would have written out every word she ever said, right down to the last yes, no, and maybe.

He'd have written that one morning it was Redmond shambling out of the bedroom, guilty eyes flashing toward the door. Redmond shifting nervously from foot to foot, not sure whether he should sit down or run away. Nick couldn't remember what they talked about, but he remembered that they were mad at each other, that Redmond said mean things, there in the kitchen and from outside the trailer. And he remembered the way his mother answered the door a half hour later, stepping back stunned as Redmond came inside with a bag of groceries and the morning paper.

"Sit," he said before she could react. And she sat, watching while he poured them glasses of juice. "Take these," he said, shaking vitamins into her hand. "A multivitamin, a C, and a B-complex. And eat this banana. Drinking makes you lose a lot of potassium." And then he turned to Nick, pulling another bottle of vitamins out of the bag. He dug one out and said, "You look like a Dino kind of guy to me."

Then he went to the stove and put together some breakfast. They both just sat there watching as he moved from cupboard to stove to sink, cracking eggs, whisking them frothy, laying strips of bacon in a pan, toasting bread.

Later that night, in bed, she joked with Nick about it. "I thought maybe I should call the cops, but what would I tell them? 'Officer, Officer, he forced us to eat breakfast! He made us take vitamins!'"

She got him laughing. She always could. But Nick knew his mother was scared. This was not the kind of thing she was used to. This strange man moving into their lives, waving a greasy spatula, with eggs and bacon crackling in the pan and the toast just beginning to burn.

T HE LITTLE KID across the aisle was driving Ellen crazy. For hours, it seemed, he fussed and cried and wriggled away when his mother tried to comfort him. Finally the woman shook him and said, "What is it? *What* is the *mat*ter?" Grinding his fists into his eyes, he said, "Everything's bugging me."

Ellen pictured Redmond's face. The nervous eyes always looking for the exit, the weak smile that appeared as soon as he saw her looking at him. The dead eyes he sometimes turned on her. She began to talk to the image in her mind.

For a while, she said, it was a good life. But then little things began to matter. It began to matter that you always let the car's engine lug down when you drove, the way you changed lanes without looking, the way you waited until the last possible second before braking at a red light. It began to matter that every plant I ever gave you died. It began to matter that you couldn't fall asleep unless all the dishes had been washed. It began to matter that you slept with one leg out from under the covers, like a fireman ready to go.

It began to matter that you hated country music, that you made me feel guilty for listening to it. It began to matter that we went to parties where you talked and laughed all night with strangers and then drove home with me in silence. It began to matter that you always rubbed your hands together when you were nervous. It began to matter that you were always nervous. It began to matter that you whistled when you were bored and that you whistled a lot. That missing tooth, the one that only showed when you smiled, began to matter. And when I stopped seeing that missing tooth, it began to matter. It began to matter when your first words in any conversation with me were "Well, no. . . ." It began to matter that you started looking past my face when

82

you talked to me. It began to matter that you checked out the other tables at a restaurant before sitting down, hoping for better company than mine. It began to matter that you never said my name when we made love.

It began to matter that you can't dance worth shit. The hair on your back began to matter. It began to matter that you once offered to mail a letter for me and then I found it weeks later under the seat of the car. It began to matter that you never insisted but somehow always got your way. It began to matter, that day in the park when you fell, when you twisted your ankle, the way you brushed my hand away like I'd made you fall, like help from me would be the greater injury.

It began to matter that you made me need you and then started leaving me. The way you held my face that first time, tenderly, and said, "I can't do this anymore." The way you slunk back a few weeks later and made it all seem like a bad dream. And two years after that, the way you turned on your way out the door, dropped your duffel bag, and divided the air with your slow, cold hands. You said, "You're killing me." You made the word a knife. "Killing." And the way you turned up a few months later, full of drunken repentance. The way you made me afraid to open my mouth, afraid of what I'd say that might tip the scales toward your leaving. The way you left and left and left, no matter what I said. The way you made things worse by coming back. The way I made things worse by taking you back.

If you'd just left, it wouldn't have been so bad. But you had to keep leaving, keep coming back. I'd get used to your being gone, and then one day you'd turn up with a bottle of rum, a rose, a bag of Chinese food. "We have to talk," you'd say. That was the line that always got you in the door. But we never talked. We got drunk, we fucked, but we *never* talked. We woke up the next day like nothing had changed, and we never, never talked. I was so goddamn stupid. I *knew* you'd only leave again. I *knew* you'd wake up one day and say, "I have to go." And always when things were good. That's what killed me. I actually thought each time you came back was the time you'd stay. Is that the only kind of relationship you can have? One that's always falling apart? Stupid, stupid.

Little things began to matter. It began to matter that you never gave me a back rub, that you never covered me with a blanket when I fell asleep on the floor in front of an old movie, that you never opened the car door for me before you got in. It began to matter that you never bought me *Linda Ronstadt's Greatest Hits*. It began to matter that these things began to matter.

When the Commander is overseas, he keeps in touch with Lloyd through the coins. He sends a set from every port. He's given Lloyd a collector's album and a jar of metal polish. Lloyd is supposed to shine up the coins and slip them into the paper pockets under the country of origin, but he quickly loses interest. Half the time he can't tell where the coins come from, and he hates the greasy gray scum that gets all over his fingers when he cleans them. His fingers smell for days.

Now, as soon as they come, he throws the coins into a Seagram's bag he found in the junk drawer. His mother has begun to drink alone at night. There are enough bags for several coin collections. He likes the blue cotton with its gold piping and drawstring, the "Seagram's" scripted on the side. That's how he thinks of the coins — as sea-grams from his father. But the messages they bear, the strange symbols and letters, make no sense to him — this one with its cluster of grain, that one with its woman in a sheet looking like she's about to throw a fastball. There are lots with flowers, mean-looking faces, and eagles biting small animals. The only one he likes is the ten-pence piece from England, because the words are pretty much in English and because the queen is smiling and because on the back there's a lion wearing a crown, its paw raised defiantly.

The last time he was home, the Commander said, "I don't want you fighting with other boys, but if you can't help it, make sure you win. Anything less is unacceptable. Win and you'll get one of these." And he held a silver dollar up to his bright eye.

Now, after a long description of every fight to prove he's won, the Commander turns his son's face in his hands and says, "A few scars will make a man out of you." He lays a silver dollar in Lloyd's hand, the coin almost as big as the palm. He says, "Remember, if you ever lose, you're not to come home. Not ever. You hear? You understand? You will not be welcome in my house."

MONDAY AND STILL NO SIGN OF NICK. Redmond stayed around the house, half hoping Nick was gone for good, half hoping he'd come back. He fought off the sense of loss that rose in him. He told himself it wasn't loss, that it was just the need to explain, to straighten the kid out on a few fine points.

There were certain things about the kid he hated, things the kid needed to know. He hated the way Nick dragged his feet on the rug when he walked through a room. The dry scratchy sound of it wore away at him. He hated the long-suffering sighs. The kid hadn't been alive long enough to feel that much grief. He hated his withering gray gaze, his mother's gaze. He hated the food crumbs trailing to the stack of dirty dishes next to his bed, dishes so dirty the dried food had to be chiseled off. "Would it kill you to put your dirty dishes in the sink and run some hot water over them?" And he hated the kid's reaction when you gave him a little advice he didn't care to hear. He looked up slowly, coldly, from whatever he was doing and pinned you to the wall with his hate. Where did that hate come from? Even when he was a little kid, and Redmond asked him to do something, Nick sometimes shook his head and said, "You're not the boss of me."

That's what he was saying now. Nick wouldn't give him a chance to explain. Redmond checked all over the house. Nick wasn't in his room, wasn't anywhere, but the new jug of milk had been opened, and there was a new layer of breakfast rubble on the kitchen floor.

He spent the morning cleaning the kitchen, vacuuming up all the cereal and pasta from the floor, wiping down the counters and the table, even running the dust mop over the walls to clean off the fine layer of flour. He washed every dirty dish in the house. He liked the work. Besides, he wanted to stay near the phone in case Nick called.

But that was such a joke. Ever since his mother left, Nick had stayed as far away from Redmond as he could get — eating at different times, going out without telling him, coming home at all hours. So how was this any different? He was only making his move complete.

Then the phone did ring. He jumped for it, nearly breaking his leg on the vacuum cleaner, but it was only Mrs. Kinsey, asking him to come down and unload a truck.

"I've got another union driver here." She was talking loud, so the driver would hear. "He says his contract won't allow him to unload, only to drive. Right now, his contract's making him sit on the loading dock and eat an egg sandwich. How's your contract look this afternoon, Lloyd?"

Wherever Nick was, there was no point in hanging around the house, waiting for him. What was he trying to prove? "I'll be right over."

He spent the afternoon hauling hundred-pound sacks of feed off a flatbed and stacking them in the warehouse at the back of the store. It was hard work. At first he carried them two at a time, one on each shoulder, but by the end of the afternoon, he was so tired he had to drag the sacks off one by one.

Mrs. Kinsey took over Kinsey's Feed and Supply after a stroke killed her husband. She expanded the stock to include equipment for camping, hunting, and horseback riding. She was a large woman who wore flower-print dresses, shiny black high heels, and a choker of pearls. Redmond liked her. Even the real farmers liked her. She had a settled, no-nonsense attitude about things. Even so, after Ellen left, she gave Redmond a copy of an astrology book she'd had privately printed. She said, "It's so foolish." Redmond nodded but didn't know whether she meant astrology, Ellen's leaving, or life itself.

By the time he finished unloading the truck, he didn't care about anything anymore — about Ellen, about the kid, about anything. He felt like he'd been hit by a car. When he turned his head, the muscles in his neck cracked sharply. He decided to go home and sleep.

That night, very late, he woke up feeling exhausted, shattered. It wasn't fair that he couldn't sleep when he was so tired. Then he heard the thin whistle of water running in the bathroom sink, the creaking of a floorboard.

He told himself he should be happy to have the kid staying out of his way. But it shook him to hear Nick ghosting around like that. All right, maybe he had lost control — not without cause — but this, this was more than Redmond deserved. The kid was making him feel like a criminal. Which was just what he wanted, Redmond figured. The kid was so messed up, the sneaking around probably had nothing to do with him at all. He'd probably gone off and gotten himself into some kind of trouble, just for spite.

He heard Nick creep from the bathroom to his room, next to Redmond's. He heard the ache of his mattress springs. The tape player came on quietly, the Doors. It galled Redmond that the kid talked about the band like he owned them, like they belonged to his generation instead of Redmond's own, like no one else knew how to listen to them until he came along. Never mind that at Nick's age Redmond liked only folk music, that he'd never really listened to the Doors until Nick brought home the tape and played it every night for a month.

Redmond got out of bed, hunted for his robe, and went to Nick's room. He was going to settle this. He was going to settle it right now. But by the time he pushed Nick's door open, the music had stopped. Nick lay under a mound of blankets, under the twisting shadows of tree branches, pretending to sleep.

Redmond lightly kicked the end of his mattress. "I just have two questions for you," he said, not even waiting for the kid to pretend to wake up. "One: Did you kill anybody? Two: Did you get anybody pregnant?"

No answer. Nick just lay there with his eyes closed, his face slack, his mouth slightly open.

Redmond sighed. "I'm going to take that as a no." He started toward the door, then stopped. He stood there for a long moment among the dirty clothes scattered all around, breathing in the heavy scent of the kid, feeling the weight of all that darkness.

"I remember once," Redmond began slowly, "she told me about a job she had when she was in high school."

There was no sound from the bed behind him, but he felt a pressure. Something with claws and fangs was watching him from the underbrush. He went on anyway.

"Selling lingerie in a department store. Three clerks, all teenagers. They could never seem to make their register balance out at the end of the night. The owner decided someone was stealing from him. He was a nice old guy from Bavaria. And he liked them all too much to fire anyone. But he couldn't ignore the missing money. He decided to hold back ten dollars a week from each paycheck. And because he was a sweet old guy, a guy who sang them German love songs in the lunchroom, nobody quit or complained. They each took ten dollars a week from the cash drawer, just to even things out."

Nothing behind him but that terrible pressure. Redmond felt like a fool. What did he think he was doing? He headed for the door. He got halfway out of the room.

In a voice that reminded Redmond of the little robot voice from long ago, but colder, quieter, Nick said, "Don't ever come into my room again without knocking."

Redmond looked up at the ceiling. "Fine," he said flatly. "Fine." Nick's word. The one he used when something wasn't fine at all but he didn't have the power to change it. As soon as Redmond pulled the door shut behind him, the music came on again, but louder. Back in his room, he snapped on his television and threw himself into bed. A man with flashing eyes and teeth stood in front of a small group of people, his hands beckoning, cajoling, his mouth moving nonstop, the look of madness. The words "Act now and take advantage of this once-in-a-lifetime opportunity!" crawled across the foot of the screen.

Redmond felt angrier than ever. He'd handled it all wrong, it's true, but couldn't the little son-of-a-bitch see that he was trying? Nick seemed to read his mind and turned up the music, turned it so loud Redmond's bedroom window buzzed.

S OUTH CAROLINA. Another unscheduled stop. The passengers didn't mind being forced more or less at gunpoint to pay good money for sandwiches made from roofing material, but when she told the driver she wasn't going on, that she wanted him to open the baggage compartment and pull out her suitcase right here, right now, they stared at her hatefully. She'd committed a desecration.

At a grocery store, she bought some waxy-looking sliced ham, a loaf of dried-out bread, a jar of mustard, some iceberg lettuce, and two apples from a bin marked "Unknown Variety."

It was only later, in her room at the Rebel Yell Motel, that she noticed what was printed on the side of the bag in bold red letters: "For a free informative booklet about the facts and warning signs of mental illness call . . ."

She sat on the floor, her back against the end of the swayback bed, three feet from the TV, half watching the news as she ate two sandwiches. On the screen, sirens, smoke, flames flashing against the night sky. Then the camera jumped to the morning after. The couple looked so vulnerable standing there with firemen's blankets wrapped around them. Their house was a smoldering ruin, only one wall left standing. "What will you do?" the newsman said, waving the wand of his microphone between their faces. The man held his wife closer to him. Their cheeks were sunburned from watching the flames all night. "We'll go on," he said. "After all" — he pointed at the one remaining wall and smiled — "it's not a total loss." Just then the wall collapsed, caving in the side of his neighbor's house.

Ellen shivered. She got up, shut off the TV, closed the blinds, turned off all the lights, and lay down on top of the bedspread.

She loved cheap motel rooms. The brown and orange bedspread, the faded landscape painting, the cigarette burns on the nightstand, the plastic glasses wrapped in cellophane in the cinder-block bathroom. The stink of disinfectant, old cigarettes, the barely held back smell of decay. It was a place where you could make anything happen. Leave the lights on all day, steal the towels, break up the furniture, screw a stranger. Anything. It's what she wanted and what she feared. The anything of it.

She loved the instructions on the back of the door. All her life she'd wanted a set of bolted-down instructions, a cheat sheet for living. She loved the simple clarity of the rules — follow a few guidelines and they promise not to shoot you. Most of all, she loved the concept of checkout time, the belief that a voice from the darkness will tell you when it's time to cut your losses and hit the road.

But the room wasn't working. She needed a drink. Memories of Redmond kept surprising her, moments from their past kept flying out at her.

Once, on the way home from the movies, the Pinto broke down. Nick was sleeping over at a friend's house. It was the coldest night of the year. Too cold to wait for help. They decided they'd walk the three miles to the farm. After the first few minutes, they were so cold their hands ached and their faces felt stripped of skin. When they finally got home, they piled every blanket and piece of clothing they owned on the bed and burrowed under them, but the warmth was as painful as the cold, needles of fire. Still, they couldn't stop laughing — dark, desperate laughter. They'd gone to a revival house to see *Dr. Zhivago.*

She remembered other times too, but for some reason, she couldn't really remember the night of their last argument, the night she left. Was that a good sign or a bad one?

And where was Nick that night? She couldn't remember. There were a lot of things she couldn't remember. Every day for the past six months, she'd been telling herself he was a big kid, that he could take care of himself. But there was a hole in her where he'd once been. She stared at the ceiling and tried not to think.

In the next room, a kid was crying faintly. She waited for someone to do something about it, but the kid kept crying. She sat up. Sleep was impossible. She'd seen a bar down the street called The Philosophers' Club. Just what I need, she thought, a little eighty-proof philosophy.

The bar was dark and seedy, a place to lose yourself. The front wall was a plate-glass window that had been painted black. Light filtered through the brush strokes where the paint was laid on too thinly. The front room held the bar and a row of stools. The back room was filled with pool tables and loud men. What other kind was there? The Redmond kind, of course. The long-suffering, spiteful kind who made you pay for every misery anyone had ever done to them.

She ordered a light beer, letting herself believe she wasn't really drinking. You're not an alcoholic if you can drink dishwater like this, she said to herself. After three quick beers, she was still too sober to look at herself in the bar mirror. The brush strokes of light coming through the painted window felt like an accusation. She wanted complete darkness, circles within circles of darkness. She wanted it to be as dark outside as it was in the bloody chambers of her heart. A few of the boys in the back room came out with their empty pitchers, whooping it up. She realized from the sudden cut of their eyes that she was the only woman in the place. The happy boys took their fresh pitchers into the back room, leaving her out front with the solitary drinkers, the losers. She didn't care. At least they weren't trying to hit on her.

After the first hour, she started drinking highballs, her mother's drink. That's how the old lady died. Highballed herself straight to hell. Ellen laughed, then quickly covered her mouth, but no one seemed to notice. This was the part of drinking she liked, when she felt high and loose. The trick was to keep it going. But that was getting harder and harder. The liquor kept turning on her, made strange thoughts fly into her head, made her say things, do things. She'd seen it in her mother, and more and more she was seeing it in herself.

She remembered a time when she was four, her first fever. She remembered how everything looked ten times bigger than it was, how the words in her Dr. Seuss book wormed off the page. Her mother was never one for kids, especially sick kids. She drove her to a friend's house far away. She made Ellen hold her highball while she drove, and left her with the friend for a couple of weeks, until she was sure Ellen was well.

"How about a little whiskey in this one?" she said to the old man behind the bar. He gave her a look.

When she tasted her fresh drink, she slapped the bar and said, "God*damn*. Now *that's* a highball." She got the same pinched look, as if she'd spoken in tongues.

He zeroed in on her as soon as he walked in, this man with the red face, with the vein throbbing in his forehead, with his thinning white-blond hair brushed back bravely off his forehead. He smiled at her, already half in the bag. He took a step backward, made a cross out of his index fingers, and said, "Just don't tell me you're an architect!" He

to him. For all his talk, for all the ways he looked at her, he hadn't done this very often or very well. He stroked the hair back from her face, a strand catching on the corner of his fingernail. His right knee knocked hers as he climbed suddenly on top of her. He was breathing heavily, and not with desire. It was the beer and the cigarettes and the heavy burden of himself. He began to rock against her, but it was no good and he stopped moving after a few minutes, just hovered over her with his eyes closed.

She thought about the days when she and Redmond lived together. Toward the end, the sex turned so solemn, so much like work. How had that happened? In the beginning it was a friendly wrestling match, a tussle. His mouth on her, her mouth on him. His hands, her hands.

Once, when she and Redmond were lying there sweaty, exhausted, the sheets twisted around them, she said, Gee, this is better than aerobics.

Yeah, he said, and you don't need special shoes.

She said, I don't think I'll ever walk again.

No problem, he said. He scooped her up into his arms and carried her slowly through the trailer, carried her naked like that, just carried her. Everything looked different from his arms, better — even the dirty sink, even the coffee table slathered with magazines. There were times when he made her so happy she thought her eyes would pop out like a cartoon cat's. She smiled at the memory.

The man's eyes were open now. He smiled down at her. "You know what?" he said, frowning comically. "I think I'm cooked."

She pressed her hands against his temples and kissed his forehead. In an odd way she was grateful, for the truth the body tells. She kissed him again, thinking of Redmond.

"Baby," she said, "it's not supposed to be work." She rolled him off gently — he seemed so much lighter now — and pulled the edge of the covers to his chin. "You sleep now," she said, kissing the rim of his ear. And as quickly as that, he was asleep.

She lay there for a few more minutes. Then she got up and slowly dressed. She looked once more at the man, with his mouth open, his face half buried in the pillow, then slipped out and went back to her room, three doors down.

She locked herself in, checked the lock, washed her face, checked the lock again, and fell into bed. Before sleep came, she reminded herself to be careful in the morning. It would be embarrassing to run into him. It would hurt his feelings.

Next door, the kid was still crying. She got up and turned on the shower, turned it on full blast, then climbed back into bed.

How DARE YOU come into my room like that, Nick thought. He dragged his sleeping bag down from his closet and gathered up his cassette player and a few tapes. His mother could never have been in love with Redmond, not ever. The Doors were still playing, but the machine was on batteries, now that he'd unplugged it, so Morrison's voice sounded even slower and muggier than usual, a funeral march. *Try — to — set — the — night — on — fi — yer.* He turned the volume as high as it would go, but it wasn't enough. It would be enough if Redmond ran screaming from the house, from his life, forever.

Nick's lamb lamp began to blink. There was a short in the cord. The lamp stood on his night table, something he'd made in shop from a thick birch board he jigsawed and painted to look like two frolicking lambs. Lambs. That was the pattern the teacher dealt him on the day projects were assigned. He tried to trade plans with someone else, but no one wanted the lambs, so he decided he'd make the lamp and give it to his mother as a joke.

The more he worked on it, though, the more he came to care about it. Instead of letting the cord hang loose from the socket — the way the plans directed — he drilled a hole through the length of the board and inserted a pipe for the cord. He took his time cutting and sanding, joining the board to the base. He mixed his paints until he got the right white for lambs' wool. He painted a red and blue neckerchief on one and a small blue bell on the other. He painted leaves on the bubblelike trees in the background and violets around the lambs' feet. He haunted thrift stores until he found the right lampshade for it — white cotton with a border of fuzzy dingleberries.

He'd given his mother many presents over the years, all of them homemade — a crooked paper heart with fringe, rock candy earrings, a macaroni-covered cigar box spray-painted gold. But he was always too excited to wait for her birthday or Christmas. He'd go around the house singing, "I know something you don't know." And she'd chase him — "What? What?" — until she caught him and tickled him, both of them laughing until they couldn't breathe.

He was just as excited making the lamb lamp. And once he even said it: "I know something you don't know." But things were already bad between her and Redmond. She looked at him dismally and said, "Join the club." In the end, he took so long with the lamp his teacher gave him a C. In the end, he took so long his mother left before he could give it to her.

He never thought she'd leave. It was something he didn't know about her, that she'd do that. And now he wondered if anything else he thought he knew about her was true. Maybe the lamp would have made a difference. If only he'd finished it soon enough, if only he'd given it to her. She would have seen what a good lamp it was. She would have said, "This lamp is *amazing*," and she would have stayed.

His idea for the cord had been a mistake. Because it ran right out the bottom of the base, the lamp never stood straight. And the edge of the pipe had pinched a bare spot in the cord.

The bulb was flickering steadily now. He turned it off and then on. With a quick searing flare of blue-white light, it died. A sign, Nick thought. He looked at the wall between his room and Redmond's and said, "I'm not spending another night under the same roof with you." He wanted to hear what the words sounded like, more words he heard his mother say that night. It felt good to say them. From now on he'd live in the chicken coop, if that's what it took. Until he was twenty-one, if he had to.

There wasn't much moon, but somehow the way down to the coop was not as dark as that first night. What had he been afraid of? Everything was so clear. Each thick black branch of the apple trees stood out sharply in the night air. A few of last year's apples clung there like tiny scorched fists. The whitewashed fence of the paddock was so bright it seemed electrified. Gray clouds streamed across the blue-black sky, and their shadows followed across the field like ghosts. Everything felt unreal, the way it is in dreams. He could make it all disappear with one good blink. When he listened he heard nothing but the wind in the trees. There was nothing to be afraid of, nothing at all. But at the foot of the farm, beyond the fieldstone wall, the woods were as dark as ever. Maybe there was a mountain lion, and maybe it was waiting for him, two yellow eyes floating in the darkness. Maybe it was crawling through the underbrush right now, claws flexing, digging in for a good pounce.

He undid the chicken wire covering the hole and crawled into the coop, then wired it up again. Most of the hens were stuffed into the nesting boxes that lined the divider wall, heads sucked between their shoulders, ass feathers and old straw sticking back through the wire mesh at Nick. Lovely. A few stood on the perches, half asleep, groaning mournfully: *I knew it. I told you so. We're all going to die.* One was awake, pecking at the empty feed hopper, too stupid to quit, beak ticking against bare metal.

He hung the space heater from a nail overhead so he'd have more floor space. He set his tape player on a piece of the coop's framing and unrolled his sleeping bag. It was so long it bunched against the other wall. He climbed into it anyway and curled up. On his right side he had to stare under the cage at the foul-smelling scum of chicken shit and loose feathers fluttering in the breeze that came through the cracks. He rolled over. Three inches from his face was a fifty-pound sack of feed. Still, he thought he'd have a better chance at sleeping this way. The heat billowing from the space heater made the dusty orange air swim and shudder.

It was never, never love. That much he knew. Redmond crept into his mother's life like a thief. It was burglary, not love. By the time his mother realized this, the damage had been done. All her valuables missing and no evidence at the crime scene, only conflicting reports from the witnesses. Still, first his father's out of the picture and now his mother. It was hard for Nick not to blame himself, not to think that he had something to do with it.

When he and his mother lived in the trailer, he used to play down along the muddy bank of the river. One day he found a half-drowned puppy in a burlap bag. He brought it home and begged his mother to let him keep it. After three days in a box, barely conscious, it died. He went back to the river every day, looking for another dog. Eventually he found one, an old dachshund whose back legs were paralyzed. But soon it died too. He found another, then another. When he saw each one struggling up the muddy bank, he called out, "I'm coming, doggie. I'm coming, boy." He was going to keep trying until one of the dogs survived, but none did. One by one, he took them back to the river and buried them, believing it was all his fault that they died.

Outside the coop, there was a scratching sound. Fatima. Big, stupid Fatima, who'd gone up the wrong ramp again, the exercise ramp propped against the blank wall of the coop. Unless he got her, she'd stand out there all night waiting for the solid wall to open up for her. She was a bird who believed in magic.

Fatima was the last of their turkeys. The other four all died one day during a rainstorm, running around the yard with their mouths open to the sky, drinking until they drowned. Stupid birds.

He got up, crawled out the hole, and climbed over the fence into the pen. She was there, waiting patiently at the top of the ramp, cocking her head at the mystery of the solid wall. She didn't fuss when he took her into his arms. She was huge and heavy and old, like a stuffed chair that had been left out in the rain.

"You stupid bird," he said, smiling, petting her a little. He set her at the top of the right ramp and pushed her gently toward the opening. By the time he crawled back into his hole in the coop, she was already settled.

He tried to sleep, listening to the brittle, rattling sigh of the space heater. Not love, he thought. Never love.

The rest of that first day, back when Redmond brought breakfast to their trailer, Nick's mother sat at the kitchen table smoking cigarettes and drinking coffee, or letting cup after cup sit in front of her until it turned cold and slicked over with an oily rainbow. She didn't seem to notice Nick. She just sat there staring out the window. He played with his trucks on the living room rug, making loud engine sounds, the way she hated. He slammed the door to the medicine chest so she'd think he was getting into the pills. She paid no attention. Maybe she was hypnotized? He realized now that she must have been thinking, making plans, unlocking doors that had been closed for a long time.

Did you dance?

This one . . . this one . . .

He almost never thought of his father. All he remembered was a hairy face and a voice that boomed off the walls. He remembered big hands. He remembered grabbing hold of a wiry beard and being lifted off the floor like that, being swung back and forth, his father's face bright red and laughing, both of them laughing. No one, least of all Redmond, could ever measure up to that man and that laughter.

Around suppertime his mother started getting spooky. She walked around the trailer straightening things up, smoking nervously. She did the thing she knew he hated. She sat down where he was playing on the rug, licked her thumb, and cleaned his face with it. She sat there with his chin pinched in her hand, wiping off the crust of milk still on his upper lip from lunch, wiping his cheeks. That was not his mother, and it was never love.

Before long, Redmond showed up with dinner, like some kind of food delivery service. Meals on heels. He brought homemade clam chowder and salad. Nick hated salad. His mother never made him eat it. And this one was filled with paper-thin parings of apple. He liked apples but not in salad, not drenched in vinegar and oil. And hidden among the lettuce leaves were raisins, dark squashed pellets he never ate because they looked too much like dead bugs. Tasted like them too, probably. But he ate the dinner, some of it. He ate because he was afraid not to.

Supper was usually Nick's favorite part of the day. That's when he and his mother talked. They did more talking than eating. That's when he caught up with her, when he had a real mother instead of someone who went zooming from room to room, to work, to the bar, who always had something more important to do, something more important than him.

Every meal started the same way. They tore into the pork chops or meat loaf, then moaned in mock ecstasy and called each other "greedy guts." It never took them more than five minutes to eat.

When they were finished, they relaxed. His mother made herself a highball, opened the newspaper, and said, "Did you get enough?" He nodded while he drank some milk. He saved his milk for last. His glass of milk was his highball. He took a long, noisy swallow, set it down, and licked his lips. There was only one thing more that made the meal complete. He wanted her to say the words. He said, "I saw a cat with three legs." His mother nodded. He said, "I saw Walter shoot a bottle." She made a sound in her throat. He said whatever it took. "I saw the mailman drop a letter in the mud and step on it." And if he was lucky enough and clever enough, she shook her head and said the words: "Such is life in Scaryville." He loved it.

But this time they didn't talk, they ate. Redmond sat bent over his food, Nick's mother stealing glances at him.

"Chowder's good," she said.

"Little touch of brandy," Redmond said. "Gives it bite."

To Nick the chowder tasted like booger soup. He ate in horror.

The night was cold, even with the space heater. Nick rolled onto his back and watched the sky through the wired-over hole of the chicken coop. It was no use. He couldn't sleep. He tried counting.

"One hundred forty-three thousand two hundred fifty-one. One hundred forty-three thousand two hundred fifty-two. . . ."

Thinks he can interrogate me. Did I kill anybody, did I get anybody pregnant. I have a couple questions of my own. One: Just what the hell *are* you? Two: Why are you alive?

"One hundred forty-three thousand two hundred fifty-three...."
From where he lay, he could see the new moon like a bright sickle
and the old moon in its arc — faded, gray, like a face hidden in the
shadows. Three stars hovered close to the moon. The pale-red one,
he knew, was Mars. And the small one was Venus. But what was the
third, the big bright one?

I T WAS THE SECOND MONDAY of the month, when Teague liked to settle down with a six-pack and watch Dina on what he called "public asses" television. Used to be it was enough for her to boss Teague around. Now she had half the valley on their knees. She was the head of the city zoning board, telling people who could build and where they could build and how high they could build. *Dina, can I add a bedroom onto my house? Dina, is this setback OK? Dina, please, may I please be granted a variance?*

He was a little early. He watched the last few minutes of "Look Good — Feel Good" and promos for "Hamilton Avenue Forum" and "Heavy Metal Meltdown." Then the picture fuzzed out for a second, and there she was, leading a bunch of rumpled suits and skinny neckties into the city council chambers. Teague cracked a beer and saluted her. "Heeeeere's Dina!" She was wearing a shiny green suit with shoulder pads. Her blond hair was poofed out. She looked like a mobster from Mars.

When they'd all sat down, she said, "I call this meeting to order." She whacked the gavel against the tabletop. And then she whacked it again, just for good measure.

May's episode of The Dina Show was a real hoot. The Montgomery Street Citizens Coalition presented a petition asking the board to make one of their neighbors repaint his front door.

The ringleader came to the microphone and ticked off their reasoning: "Our property values will plummet. Not to mention aesthetics. Not to mention neighborhood spirit."

Teague yelled, "Give the guy a fucking break, man!" and bounced a peanut off the screen.

When it was his turn, the neighbor said, "I like red. I thought everybody liked red."

"Pinko!" Teague yelled. "Sic 'em, Dina! Fry his fat ass!"

When everyone had spoken, Dina covered her microphone and whispered to the white-headed board member next to her. He made a mouth and nodded. Then they all began to whisper. Teague heard only the muffled scratching of Dina's hand against the microphone. The sight of it cupped lightly over the head of the thing gave Teague a deep twinge.

She turned back to the petitioners. "It is unfair to expect someone to repaint a door he painted in good faith. Yet" — here she turned to the neighbor — "to expect members of the community to live with something they consider an eyesore is also unfair. It is our determination that the Citizens Coalition pay for and repaint the door themselves. I'm thinking burnt sienna, boys."

Teague laughed. "Oh, you're good." He crushed his empty beer can. "You're Judge Wapner with tits!"

He tried to get interested in the next case, a guy who wanted the city to save the heritage tree on the parkway in front of his house. The guy read the woodsman-spare-that-tree poem, his voice shaking. You'd think they wanted to chop down his grandmother. After another off-mike confab, Dina said, "The tree must go. It's full of Dutch elm disease. But we'll put you on the list for replanting next year." That seemed to satisfy the guy. No drama. Teague was getting bored.

"Now on to new business," Dina said, turning to the camera. To Teague, it seemed. "For too long, this board has cast a blind eye on those who violate zoning ordinances, who treat them like suggestions instead of laws. For too long we have allowed these people to put a strain on public services, parking, and overall quality of life for the law-abiding home owners of our city. It's time this was put to an end."

At these words, Dina ceremoniously set aside the gavel she'd been using and pulled out a Sears Craftsman clawhammer. Teague's hammer. One she borrowed months ago and never returned. Teague cracked a new beer and leaned forward. His face was a foot from the screen.

"Tonight we are inaugurating our new get-tough policy." She whacked the table with the hammer. "Tonight is the beginning of the end for cynical self-interest." She whacked the table again. "Tonight we're serving notice on the housing scofflaws and schemers who've had their way for so long. To them we say, 'No more.'" She whacked the table three times in slow motion, stage lights glinting off the drop-forged steel. Teague was getting a bad feeling in the pit of his stomach.

Dina laid down the hammer and picked up a sheet of paper. "I have here a list of illegal living units within the city limits. Units that have been built in violation of the zoning ordinances. Units that represent many thousands of dollars in lost revenues." Teague set his can of beer on the floor.

"We're not just talking taxes and technicalities here. These rental units were constructed without building permits, without inspections of any kind. We're talking about a house where the back door opens twenty feet off the ground."

"It's a French window, you dumb bitch!" Teague slid off his chair and put a hand on each side of the TV.

"We're talking about an attic 'apartment' where the fire escape is a rope dangling out the bathroom window."

"Dina, don't." He was so close to the screen he felt the soft electrical haze against his forehead.

"We're talking about slumlords with absolutely no concern for the health and safety of human beings." She began to read a list of addresses from the paper, all of them Teague's moneymakers.

"Dina, Dina, Dina." He stood up, turned, and kicked his beer across the room. "Jesus Creeping Christ." He grabbed his keys and ran.

He backed the pickup into the street. He was ready to do whatever it took to stop Dina. He'd burn down City Hall if he had to. That's when the idea hit him. He sat there in the truck, blocking both lanes, thinking. A Volvo wagon slowed down and stopped behind him. The driver gave the horn a discreet tap. Teague jumped out, leaving the door open, the engine running. A quick flutter of horn taps followed him to the house.

Back in the kitchen, he slopped through the phone book until he found what he was looking for.

When the night man at City Hall answered, Teague said, "This is Dennis. Across the street at Copy-rama? I think I see flames shooting out of your second-floor windows."

The phone was dropped so hard it felt like someone had punched him in the ear. Back on the TV, Dina was still sticking it to him when a guy in a brown uniform came charging into the council chambers yelling, "Fire!"

The visitors jumped up, knocking over chairs, toppling the microphone stand with a loud boom and a shriek of feedback. In a few seconds the room was empty, except for Dina, who kept reading from her list: "352 Maxson Road, 834 Juniper Lane, 205 Emerson Street . . ." When she finished, she looked up. She and Teague were the only two people alive in the universe. Outside, the Volvo driver leaned on his horn.

"Jack," she said, aiming her beady blue eyes right at Teague, "nothing in that twisted little brain will save you now."

TUESDAY MORNING. There was no sign of Nick in his room. In the kitchen more milk was missing and more cereal was strewn on the floor. A dirty bowl and spoon sat in the empty sink. The kid was trying to drive him crazy.

He went out behind the barn to rebuild the upper gate near the stable door. It had been rotting off its hinges for years. It was a tough job. He took it slow. He didn't want to finish too soon. He was only trying to keep busy.

When the phone rang that afternoon, he took his time getting there. It was probably Mrs. Kinsey. If she hung up, he'd call her back. But it was one of Nick's teachers, calling from school, wanting to talk to Nick.

"What do you mean?" Redmond said. "He's there at school. Isn't he?"

"Oh," she said. "Oh, God. Nobody called you? Nick didn't call you?"

"What's going on here?"

There was a pause. He heard her hand covering the receiver, heard the muffled sound of typing in the background. Then her voice again, apologetic. "I'm sorry. I shouldn't have called. I should have waited."

"For what? Waited for what?"

"Look," she said, and now Redmond could tell she was holding the receiver close to her mouth. Her voice dropped to a whisper. "There's been some trouble. Nick's been hurt. He's been suspended. I can't talk about it."

Redmond felt his stomach begin to clench. "What has he done now?"

"Nothing," she said. "He hasn't done anything. He's been hurt. It was all over that silly earring."

"What earring?"

"*His* earring."

106

"He doesn't have an earring."

Look, Mr. Loomis — "

"Redmond. The name is Redmond."

Her voice caught. "Do I even have the right number here? I mean, you *are* Nick Loomis's father?"

"I'm coming right over."

"Maybe you should wait to hear from — "

"I'm coming. I'm coming there right now." He hung up, grabbed his car keys and jacket, and headed for the door.

He wanted to rescue Nick. He wanted to beat the shit out of him. This was just like Nick. When he didn't get his way, he manufactured a crisis. Illness, accident, or some other emergency rose up, requiring your sympathy, your efforts. Ellen was the same way. She kept getting into car accidents. Nothing major — a crumpled fender, a dented bumper. Nothing you could say was her fault. She was just in the wrong place at the wrong time. Still, there was something so deliberate about it all.

Redmond was driving Buda Road too fast, evening out the turns, passing cars blind. He had to get to the school. He had to prove something.

And the way she crossed streets. Redmond knew the world wanted him dead, so he nearly ran across, reaching the other curb long before Ellen even got halfway. In fact, she seemed to walk slower in traffic, giving every maniac a fair shot at her. It wasn't that she had more faith in the world. It was a need to know the worst the world had to offer, to confirm a vision even darker than Redmond's. If a car ran her down in the street, Redmond knew her last words would be "See? What did I tell you?" And Redmond would be screaming in her face: "Are you happy now? Are you?"

And then there was Nick, whose accidents were too well planned to be believed. When he cleared leaves from the rain gutters, the ladder collapsed under him. When he washed the car, a wheel rolled over his foot. When he took out the garbage, a twist tie punctured his finger. Redmond swore the kid could vomit at will. And now this. He swung off Buda and onto the highway to town, cutting in front of a white station wagon that braked so hard its antenna whipped angrily.

He remembered an evening from their first year together, when they were still living in the trailer. He and Ellen were listening to her tape player in the living room, slow-dancing to Aretha Franklin, with Nick elbowing between them, singing, "And when my shawl was in the lost-and-found, you came along and claimed it!" And how much fun it was when he didn't know why they were laughing, and how all the fun went out of it when he caught on, when he sang it wrong on purpose, with sly looks as he waited for them to laugh. And when they got tired of laughing, how he stomped out of the room and, within ten minutes, pinched his finger in a door — "Mom! *Mom!*" The rest of the night was full of hot cocoa and extra stories at bedtime and breathless whimpering. No more Aretha, no more dancing, no more fun.

And another time, when Nick was about eight, just after they moved to the farm, the place where he thought he might finally feel settled. No more running away. That's what he told them. That's what he hoped was true.

Ellen and he were going out to dinner. They were running late. She called down from upstairs, "Be right there." Redmond stood in the living room with his coat on, believing her.

Nick was lying on his stomach, aimed at the TV, his hands propped under his chin, watching a herd of antelope swerve suddenly across the tundra, fluid as a flock of birds. Behind them, alongside them, a gray streak, the shadow of a wolf.

"You're going to be OK, right?" Redmond asked.

Nick said nothing, switching the channel to pavement-level shots of police cars stopping inches from the camera lens, doors flying open, men in uniforms running with guns drawn.

"Hey," Redmond said, "I'm asking you a question."

A man in a suit leaned over a SWAT sharpshooter aiming his rifle across the hood of a squad car, his eyes fixed on a distant doorway. The man in the suit said, "You're not going to have much of a target." "No problem, Captain," the sharpshooter said, laying his cheek against the gunstock.

Redmond was about to grab the kid by the collar of his ninja pajamas and drag him to his feet, when Nick rolled onto his side, looked at Redmond, and said, "No problem, Captain."

"Great," Redmond said, thinking, I could string you up by your little balls — no problem. But he smiled. "I think you'll be just fine."

"Where you going, anyway?"

"I told you — dinner."

"Yeah, but where?"

"Why do you want to know? You planning some hot date?"

Nick pointed at Redmond's suit, at his shined shoes. "Is that what *this* is?" he said slowly and deliberately. "A hot date?" But before Redmond could speak, Ellen came down the stairs, leaning her head to the side to hook an earring. She knelt beside Nick.

"Hey, kookaburra," she said, one hand on his shoulder. "I put the phone number of the restaurant on the kitchen table. OK? If anything happens, you call us. At The Lamplighter. OK? If you see anyone strange outside, if someone starts calling and hanging up, if you just want to know where I put the peanut butter — I don't care what the reason. Nothing's going to happen, but if it does, just call. OK?"

"OK." And then Nick did something Redmond couldn't quite believe. He reached up to her face. He pulled her closer to him, pulled her by the arm, then kissed her lightly, awkwardly, on the side of the neck. Redmond heard the small snap of his lips against her skin, saw Ellen kiss the boy's matted yellow hair. Redmond looked away before they saw him watching, pretended to be pulling on his coat.

When she stood up she said, "What do you want us to bring you from the restaurant?"

Again Nick rolled to his side, looking up at her, his eyes bright with unforeseen pleasure. He shot a quick look at Redmond, who pretended to be searching for his keys. "Clam strips?" Nick said. The wildest desire he could imagine.

"Clam strips," Ellen said, smiling. "You got it."

Then Redmond, who couldn't help himself, said, "We'd better go before they give our table away." And at the door, with Ellen halfway to the car, he looked back in at Nick and said, "No funny business while we're gone." He knew that he was trying to undo the small pleasure Ellen had given the boy, and knew that he had not succeeded. He wanted to see the kid turn his startled face to him, but Nick just lay there on his stomach, watching his program, one small vinyl moccasin crossed over the other, rubbing together lightly at the pure promise of fried clams.

"You realize," Redmond said as they climbed into the car, "that The Lamplighter doesn't serve clam strips."

"Of course I do," Ellen said. She said the words wearily. The pleasant part of the evening was over. The rest was work. "But Zeno's does."

"I don't want to eat at Zeno's," Redmond said quickly. "They fry everything. The place is full of pushy waitresses and fat families."

"We're not eating there," Ellen said. She was ignoring his tone, treating him like a child. "We're eating at The Lamplighter. We'll stop at Zeno's on the way home."

"He's just a kid, Ellen. He'll be in bed asleep by the time we get home. He'll forget all about it."

Slowly, she said, "That's not the point," her voice hard and sharp. Redmond hit the gas, taking the next turn wide, the dark trees flipping by. He didn't know, didn't care, whether another car was coming, or if the headlights might pick up the green glow of a deer's eyes floating out there in the dark road. Ellen gasped, her hand flying out to the dashboard. Redmond felt better about the evening ahead. Now Ellen was as upset as he was.

They pulled into the lot of The Lamplighter and parked beneath the glow of a gas lamp. Neither of them had said a word since Redmond had tried to kill them. He was overwhelmed with happiness. It was all he could do to keep from backing out of the space and heading off down the highway to Zeno's. Suddenly all he wanted in the world was to be sitting in that grimy cellar, with the heat and smoke of frying fish pouring from the kitchen, with gum-snapping waitresses in hair nets, with all the fat fish-eaters crowded around platters of Fishermen's Delight. More tartar sauce! Suddenly all he wanted in the world was a plate of clam strips.

He turned off the ignition, set the brake, turned off the lights, and waited for a moment while Ellen redid her lips in the twisted rearview mirror. Was that so very much to ask out of life? A plate of stinking clam strips? Why was this woman, this woman who *claimed* to love him, denying him the one thing that would make him happy?

"S'nice to see you again," the host said, quickly stubbing out his cigarette. It was something he said every time Redmond ate there, even the first time.

The restaurant itself was a cavernous room with blood-red carpeting that had suspicious dark stains in several places. Hung all over the walnut paneling were lumpy oil paintings of Venice and Rome. Over the doorways and at random around the walls were great draperies the same red as the carpet and belted with elaborate gold ropes. Across the room from the booth where Ellen and Redmond were seated was a grand piano, with padded edges and stools around the sides. On the wall behind it was a mural of happy people listening to "Margi Atwater, Mistress of Melody!" The mural was supposed to show a mix of celebrities and the restaurant's regular customers, but all the faces had the same stunned, half-human features.

At the table nearest them, a heavy man with wiry gray hair was lecturing a woman who looked like a secretary. He leaned across the table, pointing his fork for emphasis, pointing, as it happened, at the woman's veal piccata.

"One of my best features," he was saying, "is that I'm very, very bright. I've been blessed with a great deal of insight. Do you see how I listen to you, how I bring you out?"

The woman took a weak sip of her water, her eyes sliding back and forth. No escape. "You're good at your job," she said.

"You'd better believe it!" he said, fork flashing with the certainty of the stupid.

A waiter pushed the roast beef cart past them, an elaborate silver dome with lots of scrollwork. "I hate this place," Ellen said. "Why do we come here?"

Redmond pretended to read the menu and said, "You think you might want to share a seizure salad?"

Ellen laughed weakly and tossed her napkin on the table. "Order me a drink and anything that won't bite back. I'm going to play the cigarette machine." Redmond smiled as he watched her walk away. One night, after hours of drinking, she pumped three dollars' worth of quarters into a cigarette machine and kicked it when it wouldn't play any music. They'd traded their standing jokes. They were keeping things alive for another day.

Halfway through dinner, a cop came into the restaurant and spoke briefly with the host, who led him around the room, table by table. Redmond had the terrible feeling he was about to be arrested.

"Yeah," Ellen said, half rising from her seat. "Nick is my son."

"There's been some trouble," the cop said delicately, his leather creaking as he leaned over Ellen, as he helped her up. "He's fine now, but he's had a nasty shock. He's a little banged up too. But really, he's fine. He's outside."

Nick looked small and helpless in the back of the squad car, black ninja pajamas against black vinyl. He seemed dazed, a little cranky, the way he sounded when his mother woke him up for school. Someone broke into the house, he said. He heard the doorknob jiggle. Before he turned around, something hit him on the head. When he came to, the front door was wide open and the stereo was gone.

Ellen crawled into the backseat as he told his story, and pulled him into her arms. Redmond stood next to the cop, watching the wounded child stare darkly back at him.

And now, here was Nick's school, on a hillside overlooking the highway. Redmond took a deep breath, bracing himself for a fresh trauma. His Pinto had trouble making it up the long drive. He'd never been here before, hadn't been inside any school for years.

He parked in the crowded lot, where kids sat in their cars with the doors wide open, smoking, playing their radios too loud. He thought he smelled marijuana. He thought he felt Nick watching him.

The morning after Nick was attacked and the stereo was stolen, he stayed home from school. He had a small knot on the back of his head, and Ellen thought it would be better to keep him in bed for a day. She'd gone off to town to get him some comic books and Kool-Aid. Redmond headed out to the paddock garden to do a little weeding.

It was still early. Cobwebs damp with dew stretched between the blades of long grass. He carried his coffee mug, sipping as he walked. Weeding was his least favorite chore, but if he didn't do it, they wouldn't have as many vegetables to get them through the winter, and he'd probably have to get a real job.

A few steps into the garden, his foot came down on something that cracked. He knelt, set his coffee cup next to the row of cauliflower. He'd have to tie the leaves over the heads soon. They were already turning yellow in the sun. He scraped the dirt away from whatever he'd stepped on. The dirt was loose. He pawed at it until he could clearly see the cracked dust cover of his stereo and through that the turntable itself, his Simon and Garfunkel record still on it. He looked up at the house. Nick stood watching him from his bedroom window.

It's late, but Lloyd isn't asleep. He's found a way to make himself go blind. He lies on his back with his arms crossed over his chest and stares at the ceiling, focusing his will until he can see nothing but grainy blackness. It's his way of sneaking up on sleep when he's too frightened to close his eyes. It's his way of imagining what death will be like. Not too bad. A long mysterious illness will make him paler, thinner, will carry him quietly, bravely into darkness. But not before everyone comes weeping to his bedside.

"We're sorry. We didn't know. Please forgive us."

"It's too late," Lloyd will whisper, his voice like a sigh. "I must go."

Almost before he hears the turn of the doorknob, the creak of the floorboard, the Commander's face presses through the murk of his blindness. His big hand grabs him by the hair, twists his head back against the pillow. " 'If his sons forsake My Law and don't live by My rules, if they violate My Laws and don't do what I order, I will punish their wrongs with a rod and their sins with blows. But I will not stop loving him or prove Myself unfaithful.' "

And then, very close, sharp as a blade: "You think I don't know you, boy? I know every move you make. I know every filthy thought you think." And then the true dying begins.

W ASHINGTON. Brakes crying, the bus rocked slowly into the terminal, floundering into its stall at last with a jerk and a hiss. The driver peeled the door back and climbed down to help passengers off and new ones on. Everyone seemed to move in slow motion. There were several empty seats, so Ellen put her leather bag on the one beside her. It was a Coach bag she'd awarded herself for leaving Redmond, the only good thing she owned.

Outside, beyond the finger-smeared window, the air was pale blue. Haloes of hard yellow light hung over the numbered doors of the terminal. Two middle-aged black women climbed on, holding Styrofoam cups of coffee. They moved slowly down the dark aisle. The larger woman, who wore a nurse's uniform, said, "Your Frederick used to kick at you in the old days, right?"

"Yeah," the smaller woman said, stepping carefully past a knee jutting into the aisle. "When I was bad."

"He don't kick at you no more?"

"I ain't bad no more. Not *that* way."

What drove her away from Redmond was not exactly something he did. It was more what he didn't do. Some lack, some failure, some missed connection. She couldn't name it, but she could sense its absence. An emptiness inside him that seemed to deepen the longer they stayed together.

She remembered why she let him move into the trailer with them. Because he made her laugh. But things changed after he moved in. The meals he used to cook for fun turned into duties he carried out with cool efficiency. He became a demon for neatness. He seemed to be waiting for Ellen or Nick to make a mess so he'd have a reason for being there. He built things — a bed frame, a flagstone patio. At first

114

she joked about her live-in maid, her handyman, but after a while it was eerie. He'd become their keeper.

And what about her? Was there something she did to ruin things or could have done to save them? There was her drinking. But hell, it was never really alcohol she was after. It was the dim light and honest talk of a good bar. Besides, she liked to dance, he didn't. If they'd spent time on the dance floor, she wouldn't have gotten drunk so many times. No question about it. Was it her fault he couldn't dance?

Toward the end, good bar or not, they just sat there and drank. She watched as, night after night, he silently counted her crimes, working up the courage to leave again.

She never could figure out what it was he needed and wanted, and whether she could give it. She always pushed things too far, trying to find out. Meanness, he called it. But with a man who won't talk, who doesn't even know his own mind, what else could she do? So she started dancing with whoever asked. What was so wrong about that?

Now she remembered. That's how their last night together went wrong. A guy who called himself Dag stepped up to the table. Nodding toward the jukebox, he said, "I got myself a slow song, and now I'm looking for a fast woman." On the dance floor, he told her he'd just been released from the county jail. When she asked him what he was in for, he said, "Being smarter than the next fellow." She liked that. She liked the way he danced, too. Close. And she was just drunk enough not to mind when his hand slid down low on her back, lower. He held her tight, humming softly in her ear.

When the song was over, he nodded toward the door and the night beyond. "You want to?"

Redmond sat behind his drink, his empty gaze trained on her, but he said nothing. She was an experiment he should have known would never work out.

Dag threw a quick glance at Redmond and then lightly grabbed Ellen's wrist. "What do you think?"

In one swift movement, Redmond drained his glass, stood up, and headed for the door.

She pulled free of Dag's grip and followed Redmond out of the bar. "Don't you care?" she said. "Don't you even care?"

They drove home in silence — angry, injured, filled with self-pity. This time, Ellen decided, she wouldn't wait for him to leave. By the time they got back to the farm, she'd made a mental list of everything she owned and how much of it would fit in the car.

Everyone on the bus seemed to be asleep. She picked up her purse from the seat beside her, wishing she'd let someone sit there, to keep her from thinking so much. She dug around inside — pulling out her makeup case, the packet of letters to Nick — until she found what she was after. A clipping from an Arizona paper about a couple visiting the Grand Canyon. Their marriage was going bad. Seeing something so much larger than themselves, they thought, would make them realize how puny their problems were. They took pictures of each other against the vastness. The husband squinted through the viewfinder, said, "Back up," said, "Back up," said, "Just a step more." In the end the camera caught only the pale flash of her open hand as she went over the side.

The bus whined across a metal bridge. Far below, the crazy face of the moon shimmered on the dark water.

I T HAPPENED TOO QUICKLY for Nick's karate instincts to take over. In the locker room after Tuesday's gym class, Stoesser said, "I'm talking to you, faggot." He was standing two feet away from Nick, wearing nothing but a worn-out jockstrap. Nick had already taken his shower and was trying to fiddle his locker open. Two turns to the right? The left? It always took him a couple of tries to unlock it.

He turned to Stoesser and made his eyes go cold and hard, but Stoesser was too dumb to be scared. He was a wrestler, a guy whose skin always looked and smelled like rancid butter. He liked strutting around the locker room in his jockstrap, snapping a wet towel at guys, knocking them into their lockers, throwing wrestling holds on them.

Nick hated gym — the slap and squeak of rubber soles against the hardwood floor, the way Coach made them yell like animals when they played his idiotic games. He hated the stinging showers, the smell of sweat, the slamming of lockers. All of it. He'd flunked gym twice so far. "How?" Redmond wailed the last time he brought home a report card. "How can anyone flunk gym?"

Nick could have told him. It's easy. You don't show up. You hide out in the bathroom. You find a dark corner backstage in the assembly hall. You slip outside into the parking lot.

Anything was better than gym. But this time there was talk about holding him back a grade, and about how it would look on his permanent record. So he made sure he didn't miss any more classes. Every Tuesday and Thursday he tried to get excited about dodgeball and calisthenics and shinnying up the rope with a marker in his teeth to write his name on the ceiling of the gym.

But there was Stoesser, edging closer to him, leading with his chest, flexing his biceps, his face hardening into a sneer but the mouth

117

trembling a little, like he was having trouble holding it. This guy wants blood, Nick thought. Anyone's — even his own — would do.

"That earring mean what I think it means?" Stoesser said.

Nick said nothing. Didn't all the cool guys wear an earring?

"Because I think it means you're a queer." His puzzled voice, someone trying hard to understand. "That right? You queer?"

Nick didn't know what to say, to think. The earring weighed ten or twelve pounds.

Three weeks ago he danced with Clarice Vellequette, right there in the gym. The big dance at the end of Spirit Week. She walked right up and asked him.

"Clarice Vellequette," he said. "It's a nice name."

"Are you kidding? It makes me sound like a bottle of wine. Call me Chase."

"Chase. That's nice too."

She pressed herself against him. The band was playing "Whiter Shade of Pale." She said, "Most of the guys at this school are dorks."

"Yeah?" Nick said. "Am I a dork?"

"Well, yeah," she said, smiling, closing her eyes to the music. "You are." Then she opened her eyes, slowly, brilliantly. "But you're the kind of dork I like."

She held him tight, so close he felt her warm breath in his ear. At the end of the dance she whispered, "Call me," and drifted back among the girls she came with. Nick could barely stand up. But he never called her. He was too scared. Now he'd call her. He'd definitely call her. Soon.

Stoesser was standing so close that Nick felt the waves of heat coming off his body, close enough for him to see a flaming pimple hidden in the crease next to his left nostril. He couldn't help staring at it. Somehow, staring at it made him calm, even as Stoesser moved closer, close enough now for Nick to smell the tuna fish he'd eaten for lunch.

"Come on," Stoesser whispered, his mouth an angry twist, "you can tell me. Is it true? Are you a shit-dick?"

Nick laughed. He couldn't help himself. It started as a dry tick deep in his throat. The laugh had something to do with Stoesser's pimple, with Nick's memory of Chase, with how scared he felt. He didn't exactly know why, but the laugh grew louder, turned into a whooping cackle. Something to do with Redmond nailing him up inside the chicken coop and with his lost mother. He put his hand over his heart and doubled over a little, helpless with laughter and tears. Now others were laughing. Wet from the shower or still in their sweaty gym clothes, they gathered around, laughing.

The first punch landed in Nick's face. Pain shot up his nose into his skull. He tasted blood. But still he couldn't stop laughing, laughing at that furious red face. And before Nick knew what was happening, Stoesser had him down on the concrete floor, straddling him, slamming him, doing the work he was made for.

Nick tried to defend himself, but he was partway under the bench and couldn't raise his arms. He tensed his body and swung his legs up hard, knocking Stoesser over the bench and into a locker. He slipped out from under. By the time Stoesser was up on his feet, Nick was ready for him, arm cocked, ready.

But as Stoesser turned to him, someone grabbed Nick from behind, pinning his arms back. He twisted his head, hardly believing what he saw. It was the gym teacher, Coach Carlino. When Nick tried to shake free, Carlino held him tighter. He was leering, watching Stoesser, waiting. His mouth was a fat pink scar. And then Nick saw what he was waiting for. Stoesser stood there, breathing hard, lining up his last punch, taking his time. Nick never actually felt the blow. A sweep of darkness dropped over him, and when it lifted, he was sitting against his locker, looking down at his gold gym shirt streaked with blood. His earring burned like a pinpoint of fire.

WITH ITS MODULAR CLASSROOMS laid out like wheel spokes, Emerson High looked more like a self-storage facility than a school. The glassed-in principal's office was in the hub of the building. Redmond found it right away but hung around the display cases of debate and football trophies before going in. He had to figure out how to handle himself, but it was hard when he had no idea what had happened. The best thing is to go in peacefully, he thought. Get the facts. Still, even without the facts, he couldn't help feeling that Nick was in the wrong. He had to fight the urge to go in apologizing, promising to set the kid straight if they'd let him come back to school. Ever since Nick dropped out of sight, Redmond had the feeling that he was being watched. Like living with a ghost. He couldn't bear the thought of the kid being free for three solid days of spying.

A teenage boy and girl with cruel haircuts and baggy black clothes sat in molded plastic chairs next to the door. From their sullen looks, Redmond figured they were waiting to be punished for something. They were talking in low, angry voices, but when he came near, they stopped talking, pretending not to notice him or each other.

He stood there with his hand on the doorknob, feeling like he was the one about to be punished.

The secretary held a computer manual in one hand and poked at her keyboard with the other. When Redmond asked to see the principal, she made a face and ticked her head toward the assistant principal's open door, on the other side of the room.

"School policy," Mr. Leidner said when Redmond explained who he was and asked why Nick had been suspended. The spring in Leidner's chair popped when he leaned back. He sighed, his voice full of weariness. "Fourteen years I've had this job," he said, "and I still don't know the first thing about kids. They're not like real people." These things, he was saying, are out of our hands — like the weather, like death — but particularly out of my hands.

Redmond leaned forward. "Mr. Leidner, I'm still not straight on exactly what happened. I mean, who started it?"

"It's not our place to lay blame." He drummed his pen against a manila folder lying on his desk. "But as I understand it, your boy jumped the other boy. Nobody's sure just why." Leidner spread his hands magnanimously. "But does it really matter exactly what happened? In my experience, a three-day suspension gives both boys a chance to cool off and forget their differences. And between you and me, it makes things a lot easier on the rest of us."

It was just as he thought — Nick had gone crazy, attacked someone. Now what was he supposed to do? Apologize? Promise to punish the kid? "What's in the coach's report?" he said, pointing his chin at the folder.

"Report?" Leidner said, chuckling softly. "This is a school, not a police station." He picked up the folder in front of him and tossed it lightly aside, something that had interrupted his real work, nothing. When he looked at Redmond again, the same thought showed behind his polite gaze. You're nothing. An interruption. Go away and let me do my real work. "I wish I could help you, Mr. . . ." He tried to remember the name, failed. "But there's really nothing I can do."

Redmond was suddenly very tired. What was he doing there? What did he want from Leidner? All he could think about was what it was like when he was a kid, before his own school days, when he was small enough to fit under the kitchen table and listen to his father and his father's friends play poker, small enough to hide behind the sofa, small enough to crawl under the sink and behind the drainpipe, holding himself so still that no one, no one, no one could find him. He wanted to be there now, away from this place, away from everything, sitting somewhere quietly in the dark.

Redmond heard footsteps outside the door behind him, a sharp rap on the glass. The door opened immediately, and a voice said, "You wanted to see me?"

Leidner stood up, relieved. "Coach," he said, "come in. Victor Carlino, this is Mr. . . . He's here about the incident in the locker room."

Redmond stood up and turned to see a man barely in his twenties, short but powerfully built. In his left hand he held a folded handkerchief. He kept pressing it to the edges of his nostrils, which were red and sore looking.

"Incident," the man said after blowing his nose delicately. "That's good. More like a slaughter."

Then it was true — Nick had sent some kid to the hospital and now there would be lawyers and bills and vengeance.

For a second there was no sound in the room but the wet ripple of the coach's breathing. Then he said, "So what can I do you for?"

"I just wanted to know who started it," Redmond said.

Leidner came around the desk until he was standing next to the coach. "That is not the issue," he said, "as I've tried to explain."

"Dick's right, but for the record," the coach said, pointing the handkerchief at Redmond, "it was your kid started it. He really beat the crap out of the Loomis boy."

Leidner winced.

It took Redmond a moment to realize what the coach had said. "Nick Loomis is my kid," Redmond said. And then to Leidner: "You told me it was the other way around."

Leidner smiled tightly and glanced at the coach. "What I told you was that it doesn't matter," he said.

So it was Nick in the hospital, Nick cut, bruised, and broken, Nick lying in the street. Nick. "You're telling me you gave my kid a three-day suspension for getting beat up?"

"They were both suspended," Leidner said. "I told you."

"Is that your idea of fair?"

"We've gone through all this. It's not a question of fairness. It's a question of school policy."

"In my experience," Redmond said, standing straighter, his face flushed, his heart banging, "the best policy is to punish the guilty, not the innocent."

"Now look — "

"It's called justice. Ever hear of it?"

Carlino stepped forward, pointing his damp handkerchief at Redmond. "Your kid is really the one to blame," he said, "wearing that earring. This ain't California, you know. That's why he got jumped. You want to be talking to him, not us. What kind of father lets his kid do that, anyway? That's what I have to ask myself. The way I see it, you're just as much to blame for that fight as anybody else."

Redmond was ready to grab both of them by the throat and shake them. But no words came to him. The thought almost knocked the wind out of him: it was true, what the coach said. Not true the way he meant it, but true all the same. Everything — Leidner's heavy oak desk, the shiny brown linoleum, even the secretary in the outer office, quietly cursing at her computer — everything seemed to prove it.

"This isn't over," Redmond said weakly.

Leidner looked from the coach to Redmond and said, "Of course it is."

The couple waiting in the hall were still there. As Redmond pulled open the door, he saw the boy shoot the girl a quick, menacing look, his face bunched and red, and heard him say, "I ought to kick you right in the cunt."

Redmond's heart stopped. He'd never heard, could not imagine, anything more foul.

The boy turned slowly to Redmond. His hair was cut to the scalp in places. He said, "Bite me bloody."

When Redmond took a step toward him, the girl stood up. Her lips were bright red, her face white, brittle. She said, "What? What? Can I help you with something?"

NICK KNEW HIS NOSE WAS BROKEN. No way it wasn't. His whole face was swollen and tender. There was a bar of pain across the back of his eyes. He felt like he was wearing a mask. Or like he had an extra layer of face. It hurt to breathe, to move his mouth.

After the fight, Coach Carlino dragged Nick to his feet, Nick still only barely conscious, and checked out his face. "You done it good." He held a folded handkerchief against Nick's nose to catch the blood, but pressed until Nick screamed and his eyes filled with tears. Carlino shook his head at Nick and said, "I'm only trying to help you out a little, boy." Stoesser laughed. "Good one, Coach!" Then Carlino hauled them both off to Leidner's office.

Leidner — the "Assistant Dick" everybody called him, or "Ass Dick" — suspended them both without hearing either of their stories. Stoesser stood there with a pursed-lip smile, and Nick stood there his face all blood, but Ass Dick just looked up for a second and said, "Don't drip on my desk, kid."

The secretary gave Nick a pass to see the nurse. Outside in the hall he watched the coach and Stoesser go off together, Carlino's meaty arm draped over Stoesser's shoulder. Nick wadded up the pass and threw it after them.

He headed for his locker, trying to figure out which books he'd need to keep up with his homework while he was suspended. The earring was supposed to be a sign. It was supposed to change his life. It sure did that. When he laughed, his nose felt like it was splitting open. He wanted to hold his face, to dig the heels of his hands into his eyes and make the pain stop. But even the thought made his face pound. His tears fell in searing streaks. His nose ran blood. All he needed was to lie down for three or four months. That would do it. He laughed again.

He'd read ahead in history, so he wouldn't need that. He dropped the book in the bottom of his locker. He never read his health book until the day before tests, so he dropped that one too. He was behind two chapters in civics, though, and he still hadn't memorized the President's cabinet. He slipped the civics book into his backpack with his English book. Math. He'd have to keep up with math. Harwich kept you after school if you didn't hand in your homework.

"Well, if it isn't the Nickster."

He closed his locker and saw Clarice Vellequette, Chase, leaning against the locker next to his, watching. She had dark, loopy hair that looked hard to comb, and a wide mouth, cynical but soft-looking.

"You scared me," he said. It hurt his nose to speak.

She smiled. Not really a smile. She never really smiled. It was more a way she had of stretching her mouth, like she didn't want to waste a smile on you if you weren't going to appreciate it. "What happened? Change a tire with your face?"

Nick started to laugh, then caught himself. "Don't. It hurts."

She stopped smiling when she got a good look at his nose. "It looks bad. Are you OK?"

Someone had hammered a nail into his face. "Sure," he said.

She pointed at his backpack. "So what's with the books?"

He said, "I don't want to fall behind."

She shook her head. "I believe you've suffered some brain damage." She gently took the backpack from him and set it inside his locker. "When they give you a three-day suspension, consider it a vacation."

"How did you know I got suspended?"

Chase tapped her head. "Knows all, sees all." She closed his locker and clamped his padlock shut.

Nick stood looking at the locker as if it had closed by itself. "What about homework? Finals are in four weeks."

"Four weeks? Four weeks is eternity. Some life forms live and die inside of four *min*utes." She took him by the arm. "Come on," she said. "I've got a car." She led him out of the school and across the parking lot to a faded olive-green Mustang convertible.

"Nice car," Nick said, climbing in. "You shouldn't leave it with the top down."

"If I didn't, one of the numb-nuts around here would slice it open for me."

She headed out the lake highway, talking all the time, telling him things. How she hated green and thought of the car as taupe. How the car was her father's idea of an investment and how she was more like its caretaker than its owner. "One of these days he'll sell it out from under me, so I try not to get attached. Her name's Angelique."

He told her how Stoesser jumped him and Carlino helped. "Sean Stoesser," she said, "is dumb as a bag of hammers. He doesn't know any other way to be. But Carlino . . ." She shook her head.

Nick felt a rush of relief. He leaned back in the bucket seat. The sun was warm. The sky was clear. For a little while, at least, Chase had brought the world back into line. He watched her drive, her tangled hair whipped by the wind. She was wearing baggy black pants and a blue cowboy shirt with gold threads that shimmered when she turned to him. He imagined they were together and that they were going someplace special, someplace that was theirs, someplace far away.

At first the wind burned against Nick's face, but after a while it didn't hurt so much. His face stiffened. Was he in shock? He touched it with the tips of his fingers, but he couldn't feel anything. It was like touching someone else's face.

When they got to the lake, they stopped to eat at The Grotto, a place Nick had heard other kids talk about. The ceiling was hung with fishnets. Anchors and harpoons were bolted to the walls. There were fake portholes. The owners were trying to pretend Lake Chabot was the North Atlantic instead of an open sewer for the vacation cottages strung along its shores.

Chase brought their orders to the table and sat down. She pointed at the paper plate piled high with french fries, the two hamburgers propped against them. She said, "You're about to sink your teeth into the finest cuisine Lake Shabby has to offer." She picked up a french fry and the plastic squeeze bottle of ketchup and ran a bead along it. She made her mouth into an O and stared at him.

"What?"

"O-o-o-o," she droned, pointing at his mouth.

He made an O with his mouth, and she slid the french fry into it. She said, "We don't want to give that face any more action than it can handle." She dressed another french fry and slid it into his mouth. "This is the way mama birds feed their young."

"No," Nick said, chewing. "They regurgitate into their babies' open mouths."

"You'd be happier if you didn't expect so much," Chase said, smiling.

She fed him like that until his half of the french fries was gone. Then she cut up his burger with a plastic knife and fed him a pinch at a time. She couldn't believe that he'd never been to The Grotto. "You live closer than I do, and I'm out here all the time." He didn't tell her that the only thing he had to drive was a '49 Ford tractor. And she laughed when he told her the dance where they met was the first and last one he'd ever gone to. She teased him about being from another country, from another planet. But it was fun. She made him feel like an old friend. More than a friend.

"Time for the mama bird to eat now," she said, pulling the plate toward her.

Nick looked out the window at the lake lying just beyond the highway. He saw a slice of it between a body shop and a boatyard. No one came out to the lake much anymore, not since the amusement park closed down. It sat there on the other side of the lake, faded yellow, the arc of the roller coaster like a giant Tinkertoy construction. "My mom used to bring me out here sometimes when I was a kid. The first time, I was about six. She made me go into the water."

Chase looked up from her hamburger. She swallowed and said, "Toxic," then took another bite.

"The water was like up to my thigh. I remember it was all brown and murky. I was looking back at my mom, when something floated up against my leg. It was a dead fish."

Chase dropped her burger on the paper plate.

"I got out fast. I think I was screaming. I held my leg like a shark had bitten me. She took me there lots more times, but I'd just sit on the beach and read. Really I was watching the water. I think I thought like Godzilla was going to rise up out of there and come after us." Chase laughed when he held his hands like claws and made his eyes bug out. For a second he thought of Redmond and how, in a way, a monster had come into their lives. "You're not eating."

Chase scowled and stuck her tongue out, making the choking sign with her hands. "All this talk about Lake Shabby is turning my stomach. Besides, we've got one more stop on our itinerary." She grabbed his hand and pulled him up out of his chair. "Come on," she said. "We're going to climb a mountain."

They drove around the lake, to the north shore, where there were no houses and no mountains, only the stunted pines that grew everywhere in the valley, and the abandoned amusement park, McNeal's Playland.

A tall fence of wide planks ran along the road, keeping them from seeing anything but the great faded hump of the roller coaster. The fence was stenciled all over with the words "No Trespassing" and covered with mostly unreadable graffiti. In balloon letters someone had spray-painted "Class of '79." And above it, in neat block print, someone else had come along later and added "Bobo sucks . . ."

Chase drove to the end of the property and pulled over. There was barely enough room for the car between the road and the fence. Nick had to climb over the door to get out. Across the road there was a short drop-off and then the lake, right there, pawing at the shore. Chase climbed out of the car, wordlessly leading Nick to the end of the fence and around the corner. They walked under the dark canopy of pine trees. The ground was thick with rust-colored needles.

On their right was a chain-link fence as high as the plank fence out front, with a wing of barbed wire angling off the top. He saw the park now, but there wasn't much to it. A gauntlet of yellow game booths made of plywood warped from years of bad weather. A cinder-block band shell at the back of the park, also covered with graffiti. The rides were gone. Sold, he figured. All that remained were oil stains where the engines had stood and short stumps of piping fingering up through the asphalt, for running power lines to the rides. Nick and Redmond had run a line like that down to the chicken coop last summer.

What had survived, though barely, was the roller coaster, sitting starkly in the center of the park, huge and rickety, a set of reconstructed dinosaur bones. Its high hills and sweeping curves were all a little twisted, a little out of line. The steepest hill leaned dangerously out of plumb.

Chase led him along the fence until they reached a place where it bellied out. She pulled on it, and the bottom of the fence lifted off the ground like a mouth opening. She made an after-you gesture with her hand. "Be careful how you crawl under. This thing can snag you good."

He could tell how often she'd been there by how quickly she followed him, slipping under the fence and back to her feet so fast that a flash of jealousy shot through him. He wondered how many other guys she'd brought there.

On the other side of the fence was a small octagonal food stand made of cinder block. A sign around the top advertised foot-longs, pizza, burgers, cotton candy, and caramel apples. There was nothing inside but a jumble of rusty napkin dispensers.

"You come here often?" he said, brushing off his pants. It hurt his face to lean over.

"Often," Chase said. "Yeah, I guess. Sometimes it feels like I live here." She grabbed his hand and led him deeper into the park, past the empty bumper car pavilion, toward the roller coaster at the center.

When he was a kid, Nick liked amusement parks, liked climbing into machines that flung him out to the wild edge of himself. But this place wasn't like that. They wandered past a dismembered tilt-a-whirl. "It feels like a cemetery," he said.

"You get used to it," she said, "and then you get to like it. It's cool."

They were standing in front of the roller coaster now. Beams and crosspieces were missing in many places, and rotted yellow lumber lay everywhere on the ground. One good wind could have blown the whole thing away. But the sign still hung over the staging area. In letters painted to look like logs, faded now from rain, from sun: The Mountain.

Chase said, "Once I brought a sleeping bag and stayed all night." She shaded her eyes and pointed to the top of the highest hill.

"Up there?" Nick followed her gaze. "Are you crazy? You could have been killed."

"Worth it," she said. "I'll show you." She ran to the foot of the scaffolding and started to climb it hand over hand, pulling herself up onto sagging beams, steadying her feet against flimsy one-by-four crosspieces that shivered with her weight. When she was fifteen feet off the ground, she stopped and looked back down at Nick.

"Come on," she said. "You won't believe the view."

"I'll take your word for it." He reached out and touched one of the stout posts, trying to look casual. Weather had worn down the wood, more gray than yellow. The grain stood out like the whorl of a fingerprint. As he ran his hand over it, he swore he felt the whole roller coaster shift slightly in the breeze. In another minute, he was sure, it would all come crashing down. "This is insane," he said.

"Trust me," she said. "You'll love it." She swung through a crosspiece and started climbing up inside the scaffolding of struts and beams. She scrambled nimbly, not even pausing to test the places where she set her feet. Risking her life on a derelict thrill ride was the most reasonable thing in the world.

He didn't want to be left behind. Besides, if he stayed on the ground, he'd be crushed when the thing collapsed. So he started to climb. If he was going to die anyway, he might as well enjoy the view.

Ten feet up, one of the crosspieces that looked solid tore free when he kicked it lightly. And every time he rested his weight somewhere, he heard the wood ache and felt it start to give way. It seemed safer to keep moving. He climbed higher. "This is *so* insane," he said, but Chase was much too far away to hear him. The roller coaster trembled and creaked with every move he made. In his imagination nails popped and fell pinging like hard rain to the pavement below.

By the time he got to the top, Chase was sitting on the small wooden platform at the peak of the hill with her knees drawn up, staring out at the lake. Carefully, trying to make himself as light as possible, he pulled himself onto the platform and sat next to her, slowly folding his legs under himself. When he looked down at how far they'd climbed, his stomach dropped and his heart slapped at his ribs. He put his hands flat against the platform, closed his eyes, and breathed slowly through his mouth.

He whispered, to make himself lighter: "Do you know how insane this is?"

"This is excellent," she said. "Look." She was pointing at the sun dropping over the lake, at the hazy sweep of light lying on the choppy gray water, at the waves slopping against the docks of the run-down cottages, at the cars flowing sure as salmon up the highway, at the wind moving through the tops of the pines. At everything.

She squinted at him and said, "It's strange to be here with another person." She took his arm. "But nice."

From the top of The Mountain, all the dirt and damage down below looked interesting and mysterious. It was like watching a movie about a place where all the people were a little crazy but not mean, and where all the problems were caused by a goodhearted misunderstanding. A boy with a magic stone would set everything right again. And later they would all laugh.

He looked at Chase and said, "You think you'd ever want to go out with me?"

"We *are* out, dodo." She spread her arms in every direction. "You can't get any more out than this."

"I mean *out* out."

Her soft mouth went wide. She took his chin in her hand. She leaned toward him and kissed him lightly. "There," she said. "Get it? We *are* out, Nick."

REDMOND FOUND THE STOESSER HOUSE more easily than he thought he would. It was down on the flats, near the river, where all the houses were one-story cinder-block boxes covered with stucco and tricked out with a little ornamental ironwork. The place gave Redmond the chills. But then the whole town gave him chills. Crumbling factories spread out along a dirty dishrag of a river. Spring wasted its energy in a town like Esther.

The Stoesser house was peach-colored, with white trim. The stucco was cracked and had fallen away in places, showing the gray block beneath. There was no lawn, only a pad of concrete painted green, and in the center, facing the street, a small cement fawn, also green.

The venetian blinds in the front window were pretty seriously bent out of shape. Someone had used them for a ladder.

When he knocked on the door, it swung open suddenly, the length of the guy's outspread arm.

"What." The voice dead, the voice saying, I've seen and heard it all before. His mouth was too wide for his narrow face. He was rangy and wore old jeans and a blue T-shirt with a neckband so loose it showed some of his dark chest hair. He stood tensely, waiting for one good excuse to fling the door shut. Redmond would have mistaken him for the kid if not for the way the skin sagged around his eyes, the yellow of his fingers where he held his cigarette.

Stoesser put the cigarette in the corner of his mouth, narrowed his eyes, and said, "Just exactly what in the hell do you want?"

"I'm the father of the boy your son fought with," Redmond said. And then, to work himself up a little, he said, "The boy your son attacked."

"Which one?" Stoesser laughed. A bit of ash jumped off the end of his cigarette.

"The one today. At school."

Stoesser nodded. "The faggot," he said quietly. "Come on in."

In the living room, a baby stood next to a glass coffee table smeared with small wet handprints. Redmond couldn't tell if it was a boy or a girl. Its fat arms were propped against the glass, and it smiled up at him, head wobbling. Its diaper was loose and wet.

Stoesser picked a piece of tobacco off the end of his tongue. He looked hard at Redmond and yelled, "Sean! Get your ass in here."

The baby must be a boy, Redmond decided. Stoesser was the kind of guy who wouldn't let a girl live. The baby stood among the ducks and trucks and other toys scattered around, gazing up at Redmond and trying to swallow his lower lip.

The room was narrow, barely wide enough for the gold brocade sofa and brown vinyl recliner that sat next to it. At the other end of the room was a console television and a small framed painting of Jesus hanging on the wall above it. The carpet was the gray of a sewer rat but near the edges, away from the sunlight, beige. The room was too narrow, like the man's face. Redmond noticed that all the round toys — a beach ball, a grass-stained softball, a Big Wheel — had rolled to the front wall of the house. That's when he realized the room had once been the porch, was barely more than that now, its floor still sloping toward the street.

"Sean!" Stoesser called again. "Now!" The next room was a bedroom. Beyond it was the lighted doorway of the kitchen. Redmond saw the turquoise refrigerator. He heard the whine of an electric can opener. He smelled meat cooking. He wanted to be home now, fixing his dinner, not challenging some stranger under his own roof.

The baby seemed to like Redmond. He started to rock on his wobbly legs. He hummed and blew air between his closed lips until a bubble of saliva fell off his chin. He slapped the glass tabletop with his open hand, winced, smiled. He slapped it so hard Redmond thought the glass had broken. He slapped it again, laughed, shook his head, slapped it again.

It occurred to Redmond that he could leave, that he could just make a run for it. But before he did anything, Stoesser's son appeared, a kid who looked like his father but was taller, with wide, powerful shoulders. His mouth was swollen and bright purple around the split in his upper lip. Under his right eye, the skin was starting to blacken.

"Go on," Stoesser said, "say it."

At first Redmond thought Stoesser was talking to him. He had to stifle his urge to apologize.

The kid's words came grudgingly, a faint sneer hidden behind them. "I'm sorry about the fight." He held his arms straight and stiff by his sides, his fists clenching and unclenching.

After a pause Stoesser said, "And?"

"And," the kid said, wringing the word out, "it won't happen again." He exhaled sharply, angrily.

Redmond looked at Stoesser. "I thought . . ." he said, "I thought your boy jumped Nick. I didn't realize . . ." He lifted his hand toward the damaged face.

Stoesser's laugh was a single dry click deep in his throat. "You think that faggot kid of yours did this?" He took his son by the chin and turned the face back and forth. "I did this," he said proudly. "I know how to take care of my kid. Why don't you go home and take care of yours?"

Later, in the grocery store, Redmond pushed his things along the conveyor with his forearm so the girl wouldn't have to work the belt. Gallon of milk, frozen burritos, box of Kix, even two half gallons of ice cream.

She recognized him. She rang up his groceries, crossed her arms, and said, "Twenty-four seventy-eight," said it like a dare.

And Redmond dug thirty dollars out of his wallet. "Here," he said, pushing the money into her hand, bagging the groceries himself, then making for the door like a thief. She followed him, holding his change out to him, leaving a line of stunned shoppers at her register.

"It's yours," he said, backing into the gaze of the electric eye. "Keep it."

*"You think your father's tough?" Randy says to Lloyd. They're both ten,
but Randy is bigger, and mean. He's standing now, one foot on the
first step, the other on the sidewalk. He's leaning forward, licking his
lips. They glisten in the dim light. "Well?" Randy says, kicking his chin
at Lloyd. "Is he?"*

"What?"

He rolls his eyes, then makes a face. "Tough. Is he tough?"

"Pretty tough," Lloyd says. He has no idea what his father is.

*"Liar," Randy says quietly. "I'm here to tell you you're a goddamn
dirty liar."*

Lloyd just sits there.

*"I'm standing here calling you a liar, and you do nothing. I'm
calling your old man a queer, and you do nothing."*

"I'm not going to fight you, Randy."

"A liar and a coward. I think you must be queer as your old man."

"I am not."

*Randy laughs. "So I'm right? Your old man's queer?" He turns his
head to the side and spits into the yard.*

"I'm not."

*"Only one way to find out," Randy says, stepping closer. "If your
old man's tough, you should be able to take a punch. Simple." He
makes a fist and swings a few times. Jabs. Uppercuts. "One punch. Just
to see what you're made of."*

"That's stupid."

*"Sure, you think that because you're a queerbaby. You're queer as
a three-dollar bill."*

*Lloyd is stunned. In his dresser drawer he has a two-dollar bill. How
queer did that make him? The Commander had sent it to him, telling*

134

him that someday it would be worth a fortune to a collector. Lloyd feels sick to his stomach but stands up and steps forward. "Go ahead," he says, "hit me."

Randy stares thoughtfully at him, rubbing his fist along the edge of his jaw. He smiles. He's been waiting for this moment, maybe all his life.

"You know what I think?" Lloyd says, his eyes closed, his arms held wide. "I think you never saw three dollars in your whole, entire life."

A look of pain shoots through Randy's wild eyes. He blows his cheeks full of air and swings hard, his punch landing solidly in the middle of Lloyd's stomach. But Lloyd stands firm. He doesn't back off an inch. And then, with all his strength, he smiles. He's had practice with pain. Randy just stares, his mouth hanging open.

Lloyd turns and walks away slowly, out of the yard, down the sidewalk, toward home. He knows Randy will watch him all the way. He walks up his driveway, past the living room, where his mother's watching television, her gaunt face flickering in the pale-blue light. He walks past the back door, out into the backyard, where no one will see him die. As soon as he's around the corner of the house, he falls to his knees. From the moment he was hit, he hasn't been able to breathe. His head wants to explode. His heart's beating in his eyes. When he can finally breathe again, his gasps come with racking sobs. He falls onto his face, weeping into the freshly cut grass.

My dad's a war hero. A sailor. A submariner following Russian trawlers on the Black Sea.

These are the words he always tells people who ask him where his father is, words he began saying before he even knew what they meant. He's said them so often he can't remember if they're the truth, or something his mother has told him to say, or words he's picked up from Huntley and Brinkley. He says nothing about his father's late-night visits to his room. It's a secret. If he tells, everyone will know what a dirty, filthy thing he really is, and they will take his mother and father away from him. He doesn't let himself think about it. Not even on those nights when, half asleep, he feels the weight of his father on the edge of the bed, the rough grip of his father's hands. He closes his eyes and fills his mind with father, father, father.

M‌ISTAKES WERE MADE, IT'S TRUE. You couldn't live as long as he had without making a few mistakes. In some ways, as a father, he'd been a bit of a bonehead. He was prepared to admit that. But the navy had taught him some things about life. One was that your failures are often more significant — more desirable — than your successes. You can't learn from success, only from failure. He'd tell the boy that, if he got the chance. I may have failed as a father, but I was a noble failure.

He parked his camper in Redmond's driveway and walked up to the front door. He plucked the screen door open, reached inside, and knocked sharply. He stepped back and looked up the face of the house in case someone was peering from behind the curtains.

He had a lean face and close-cropped hair. The line of his mouth was so even it seemed to have been drawn with a straightedge. He wore a short-sleeved white shirt and green plaid high-water pants. He reached inside the screen door and knocked again.

It had been a long time. Years. But he was here now. That was worth something, wasn't it? Of course it was. He pulled his handkerchief out of his pocket and wiped his face. His name was written along the edge of one corner with an indelible laundry marker. Like all his handkerchiefs, like every piece of clothing he owned. Twenty years in the navy had taught him to take care of his things, to make sure what was his stayed his. And besides, it made him feel good to see his name. Redmond.

He knocked again. No answer. At first he thought it was the way the sun bounced off the house, but now he was sure he could see where two kinds of white paint had been used, the one hard and bright, the other muddy. A crooked line ran down the siding where one white stopped and the other started. It was not the way he did things, not the way things should be done.

He'd been watching the house for a week and a half now and knew that the boy was usually home in the afternoons, unless he was humping sacks of feed at Kinsey's.

It wasn't much of a farm. A few days ago, when no one was home, he walked around the place. A handful of sickly hens, a few head of neglected cattle, weedy garden patches here and there. Everything choked with weeds, nothing growing well. The disorderliness of it bothered him. Just below the house, in the paddock garden, there was a single row of corn among the vegetables, a single row of corn standing a few inches high. Cross-pollination would be impossible. Didn't the boy know that? And all those tomato sets. What was the point of that? And on the other side of the house, between the orchard and the road, some two hundred pumpkin vines. It looked like the seeds had just been thrown all over creation. Who needed that many pumpkins? And even if you did, why not do it right? Nice round mounds three feet apart, so the vines had room to spread out. There's no percentage in carelessness. That's another thing the navy had taught him. And then chasing those hens all over like that. Not good. And him from a farm family. What he ought to do is go down there and cull the flock the way his old grandma did it: grab a neck in each hand and crank.

He knocked again, stepped back. Well, no one was home. That much was clear. He went back to the camper, but as he walked around to the driver's door, something caught his eye near the corner of the barn. Someone was crouching behind the clump of rhododendron, clutching two sweaty bags of groceries. It was his boy. They stood there — the man staring into the rhododendron, the boy holding his breath, trying to disappear. And then the man did the only thing he could think to do. He waved. Lifting his hand weakly, almost apologetically, he waved. The boy dropped his grocery bags, a quart jar of jelly rolling out of one.

The first rock landed nowhere near him. The boy dug up a slab the size of a serving tray and heaved it two-handed as far as he could. It flew a few feet and then dropped to the asphalt, cracking into three pieces. The man cocked his head a little, like a dog. The boy was in the open now, scrambling for more rocks. He threw a piece of slate that sailed into the side of the camper, scarring the finish he'd worked so hard on, sanding and lacquering, sanding and lacquering. And then a nice round one that landed two or three feet from the man's right foot. Still, he didn't move.

The boy grabbed his knees, sucking wind. He pulled himself up, his face running sweat. His voice ripped: "Get — out!" He slashed at the air with his arms.

Strange boy, the man thought. This is a moment that needs managing. He looked up at the sky, at the field of new corn across the road, corn like it was meant to be — row after row of feathery shoots. Now *there* was a real farm. A rock bounced in the dirt and skipped lightly over the top of his shoe, scuffing the shine. Maybe he should come back later.

A new tack was called for. He was prepared to admit he'd failed as a father, if that's what was required. But now, with rocks flying and the boy pitching a fit, now was not the time.

He went to the door of the camper, walking slowly. He'd always been calm under fire. A rock fell with a thud on the roof. He unlocked the door and climbed inside, into the space where he'd done all his careful carpentry, the space where he'd lived for the last five years, ever since his wife had thrown him out. He felt good there, in control.

He went to the little closet and from the shelf above his hanging shirts took down the leather case containing his Navy Cross. He lifted the medal out and thought for a minute. It seemed a strange thing to do, what he was thinking. A rock hit the door of the camper with a sharp *whock*. He rubbed his hand against the ribbon, against the gold cross. He'd do it. It would be like an official calling card announcing his arrival. A blessing.

Before he could change his mind, he climbed out of the camper and went back to the house. He pinned the medal on the screen, attached it from behind with the fastener, then closed the door. A rock slapped against the side of the house. He straightened the medal and stepped back. That's the ticket, he thought. The boy'll do a bean when he sees this. It was funny. The house had received a commendation. His buddies would laugh when they heard this one, how old Tom Redmond had pinned his Navy Cross on a broken-down farmhouse with a bad paint job. A rock skittered across the face of the house.

He saluted the medal, turned smartly, and headed back to the camper. He climbed behind the wheel and fired up the engine. Was there ever anything as primitive as the internal combustion engine? A fist-size rock bounced off the top of the camper and dropped onto the hood. He put the truck in gear and drove away, thinking, My boy needs me. He just doesn't know it yet.

I N HARRISBURG, Ellen got off the bus for five minutes to stretch her legs. Almost — she nearly said "home" — almost there. When she climbed back on, she found someone in her seat, a young guy with a shaved head. She stood before him, trying to decide whether it was worth the trouble to chase him away, when he lifted his pale, untroubled face to her and held out a booklet, placed it in her hand: *He Is Loyal to You.*

"The hell he is," she said, flipping the booklet to him. At the back of the bus, the air was thick with the smell of stale cigarettes, beer, disinfectant. Better.

She thought about Nick and felt the old pain in her chest, like a rope twisted tight. How could she have left him? He was just a kid. She pressed her fist against her breastbone and took a deep, dizzying breath. She needed a drink.

There are certain conditions in life, she wrote in one of the letters to him, that you just can't endure. Sometimes you don't know what they are until those conditions change, until you have, in fact, endured them.

The problem, I think, is that I was never meant to be someone's wife or mother. And anyway, it's not like I left you in a basket on some doorstep. I stopped being with you for a while. That's all. We suffered a dislocation, a rearrangement of geography. And years from now, if you turn out to be a serial killer or a celebrity, don't blame me. I was only trying to survive.

Once, I was interviewed for a job as a cleaning woman in the burn ward of a hospital. After all the polite questions and answers, the head nurse walked me through the ward. It was full of people in agony, people whose flesh was scorched black, torn raw. The sheet under each patient was soaked red. The only ones who weren't moaning or screaming were the unconscious. But even they couldn't stop trembling.

I walked calmly through the ward, looking at everything. I needed that job badly. There was a boy about seven getting a sponge bath. His hands were two lumps in bandages. The skin of his face was stiff and brown. It made me think of an old wallet. His nurse moved slowly, gently, cleaning one inch at a time. The boy screamed at every touch. Tears ran like acid down his cheeks.

I looked at everything, nodded, allowed myself to be led deeper into the ward. At the other end the head nurse said she'd just wanted to see if the sight of so much suffering would upset me. I told her I understood. I shook her hand. The nurse said I'd be hearing from her. I said I looked forward to her call.

At the door I turned to her again. "Is there," I said, looking at the red-soaked sheets, at the boy, "is there no way to stop the bleeding?"

"Oh," the nurse said, "that isn't blood. That's Betadine, the antiseptic we use."

"Of course." I shook her hand again. On the way out I remember calculating how much money I'd take home after taxes. I even tried to figure out which bills I should pay first. As I stood outside, waiting for my bus, an old woman walked up wearing a holey sweater tied shut with twine. Its sleeves were so long she seemed to have no hands. Her stiff white hair stuck out all over.

She looked at me, her eyes jittering, and said, "Are you a dog or a cat?"

"What?"

She stepped closer. "Are you a bee or a flea?"

I backed off a step. She smelled like garbage. There was a yellow nub on the white of her right eye. "Go away."

But she came closer. She said, "Are you number one or number two?"

I thought I saw behind her eyes. The wind trapped in the empty room.

Then I lost it. I screamed, I cried, I ran and ran and ran and ran.

Nick woke up before dawn on Wednesday, the first official day of his suspension. School, not he, had been suspended, called off to give him more time with Chase. He had worked it all out last night, lying awake, looking at the moon. He'd never have to see Redmond again. He'd sleep every night, all night, in the chicken coop. It was his job to look after the chickens, so there was a good chance Redmond would never find his hiding place. It wasn't so bad once you got used to the smell. He learned to breathe lightly, off the top of his lungs, the way they do it in the movies when they pretend to be dead. He raised a pinch of his sweatshirt to his nose. Rank. He'd have to do something about that.

His muscles were sore. It hurt to raise his arms. He was sore all over, sore and cold. But it was worth it not to have to deal with Redmond. He filled the feed trough and ran some fresh water into the watering can. The chickens stretched and snapped their wings, jumping down from the perches, their claws twanging at the wire floor. They fought for space at the trough, overcome by their good luck. They were used to going hungry until Nick was home from school. Sometimes he found all of them fighting over a single worm or a dry twig they thought was a worm.

He climbed out the hole, rehooked the sheet of chicken wire, and made his way up the cold, damp hillside. It was still dark, the air blue as a bruise. Somewhere the day was gathering itself together. He eased open the old wooden trapdoor to the cellar, then eased it back down when he was inside.

When he pulled the string on the bare bulb hanging from a rafter overhead, somehow the cellar seemed even darker than outside. The dirt floor was covered with old Persian carpets, so full of rot they'd molded to the damp, lumpy ground underneath. It was not hard to imagine bodies buried under there, maybe the old man who owned the place before Teague bought it. The low rafters were full of cob-webs. The place was cold and wet, ripe with decay.

The builder hadn't bothered to dig out the whole cellar. Halfway across, on the uphill side, it stopped at a wall of earth, dead tree roots reaching out and a few hundred mostly broken clay flowerpots stacked up against it. A rotting worktable ran along the downhill wall of the cellar. Hung from hooks in the bare stone above it were the old farmer's rusty tools, ancient tools Nick didn't recognize, tools to do jobs that didn't need doing anymore, he figured — big wooden clamps, hand-crank drills, huge two-handed saws, a battered wooden mallet, a hay hook, spools of rusty baling wire, jars and jars of screws and nails, some of them half full of rusty water.

There was an old shower stall in one corner, with several gray planks leaning up against it. Moldy boxes full of papers had been stacked inside, and cobwebs hung across the opening thick as twine, but it could still be used. As he moved the boxes out, he found a copy of an old magazine called *Natural Living*, its pages so dry they cracked when he turned them and the pictures so faded the nudes looked like statues.

Teague bought the farm from an old woman whose husband had just died. A "motivated seller," he called her. Nick talked to her once while she was packing up old green glass and antique medicine bottles. She was still in the middle of moving out when Teague had them move in. She said she'd made her husband put in the shower so he wouldn't track farm dirt into the house. On the worktable was a sheet of tracing paper with an elaborate drawing of a farmer waving from his tractor, surrounded by tall corn, mountains, a sun with long arms of light reaching down to him. The drawing was so careful it might have been done by a machine. "My son is an architect," the widow said sadly. "This is the design for my husband's stone. He didn't much like farming. Still, it's a nice picture, don't you think?"

It took only a few minutes to paw away the cobwebs and move the boxes out of the stall. The water pressure was weak, but strong enough to hurt his nose when he forgot and put his face under the spray. Mostly, his face felt puffy and numb.

After his shower, he crept upstairs to his room and quietly gathered up a pile of fairly clean clothes, then took them back to the cellar. He hung them on hooks the old man probably used for his work clothes. He got dressed and kicked his dirty clothes in a dark heap under the cellar stairs. The washer and dryer were in a shed out back, so Nick would need to come into the house only to steal food. One day while Redmond unloaded trucks at Kinsey's, he'd collect enough food for a couple of weeks and hide it somewhere outside. It was not so bad when he thought about it. Like camp. Chase would never know — no one would — that he lived with animals, that he had to break into his own house just to wash his face.

He heard the quick tap of a horn from a passing car. That was their signal. By the time Chase reached the turnout down the road and doubled back, he was waiting for her.

As he climbed into the car, he handed Chase an egg.

"What's this?" She stopped the car in the middle of the road, the V-8 chugging in park.

"An egg. From one of our hens."

She hefted it, passed it from one hand to the other. "It's huge."

He'd found the biggest one for her. It was twice as big as a store egg, so big it filled her hand. She held it up to her eyes. The surface of the egg was pitted and pebbly. A ridge ran around the middle. Still warm, the egg seemed to glow, translucent, vaguely obscene. He wanted to show her miracles. He wanted to be her miracle.

She said, "There's enough cholesterol here to kill a cat. Are they all this big?"

"Sometimes bigger." He didn't tell her about the ordinary eggs he'd passed up or the one he threw into the mulch pile — almost square, faint streaks of blue in the shell, more like a chunk of plaster than an egg.

"What are we supposed to do with it?"

Nick put on a scientific voice, soft and deep. "Eggs are our friends, little lady. You're supposed to eat it. You're supposed to cook it up and eat it." He patted her shoulder. It was the first time he'd touched her that day, and his hand felt charged from the contact.

He said, "Where we going?"

She made her eyes small and shrewd and, through her wide, thin-lipped smile, said, "Top of the world, Nicky."

And then they were gone, the morning still dark and frizzy with mist, the houses asleep, only a few bathroom windows lit, and no one on the winding two-lane but guards heading out to the prison, flying past them at sixty, at seventy.

She'd brought a plastic-mesh bag with her this time, and once they made it to the top of the roller coaster, she produced a pile of fashion magazines from it. "A little mind rot is good for the soul," she said. They stretched out on the platform above the derelict amusement park while morning came up over Lake Shabby.

They flipped through the magazines. Tall, thin women with sharp faces threw themselves into painful-looking postures and angles. The look of people about to be shot: one stood with her hand held out, fingers splayed, her mouth rounded as if she were saying no, no, no, no; another was lying down with her head tipped so far back that only the point of her chin was showing; another's head lolled to the side, hair in her face, her eyes half closed, already dead.

"Will you look at that?" Chase said, pointing at the picture. "I wouldn't put an outfit like that on a dog." He didn't tell her what the picture looked like to him.

A couple of times Chase saw a model with hair she liked and twisted her own into its shape.

"What do you think of it like this?" she said. "Or is it better this way?"

"It's nice," he said, touching her hair, taking a loop of it in his hand, then letting go when he realized what he was doing. "I like it all ways."

"Sometimes I have these bad hair days? It gets so tangled I can't even pull a comb through it." She made her fingers into scissors. "Nothing to do but start chopping away."

They spent the morning like that, making fun of the pictures, looking out at the lake, at the new green coming to the grass and trees. Nick was getting used to the rickety coaster. The swaying was starting to feel natural.

She told him she lived with her mother, who was divorced. They'd moved from Binghamton six months ago. Binghamton, she used to think, was the ass-end of nowhere, but now she knew better. Her mother's old boyfriend lived here, she said. "The Boyfriend," she called him. Her mother and she were trying to pick up the pieces or find out if there were any pieces left to pick up.

"Do you like him?"

"He's OK. Sometimes he looks at me and wags his head like I'm the last one at the party and don't have enough sense to go home."

"I know what you mean," he said. "I hate that." Near the end, when he told his mother she maybe shouldn't drink so much, she said, "You don't approve? You don't like my life? Leave. You're all grown up. See if you can do any better." But then she beat him to it.

Chase was still talking about The Boyfriend. "The guy can't help it. He's a man. Men are dogs. If they can't eat it, fuck it, or roll in it, they're not interested."

"Hey, in case you haven't noticed . . ."

"Oh, you're not a man."

"Thanks a lot."

"Not yet. If you work real hard, you might avoid it altogether and turn straight into a human being." When Nick turned his face away, she stroked his forearm and said, "I'm just kidding, Nick."

"I know," he said. "I was just thinking about him, the guy my mother lives with, *lived* with. He's so . . ."

"Fucked up?"

"Yeah."

She held out her open hands. "I rest my case."

"He *is* a dog, a mad dog. He ought to be shot like one."

"Is he?"

"What?"

"Mad. Is he a mad dog or just a sick one? Some people just don't know how to act."

Nick sighted along the barrel of an imaginary rifle. "I know a guy who'd kill him just for the fun of it." He was thinking of Walter, back in the trailer court. That seemed like a long time ago. Maybe he'd go see him, find out if he'd had a chance to shoot anybody yet. For a wild moment he imagined his mother might be back there, living with Walter, shooting everything on sight.

"Oh, great!" Chase whooped. "Let's kill him and get our fat faces on tabloid TV — 'Heavy Metal made me kill my daddy!' "

"He's not my father."

She shoved him lightly. "You know what I mean." After a little, she said, "I think, when I got to a certain age, my mom didn't know what to do with me anymore. She knew how to burp me and how to change my diaper, but that was about the peak of the learning curve. From there on out, my whole existence was a problem for her. Here she is, trying to start a new life with The Boyfriend. And here I am, the leftover from her old life. I'm like an old sofa she can't get rid of. If she had the money, I think she'd rent me an apartment and say, 'Here you go, kid. Let us hear from you once in a while.' "

Nick was looking out across the lake. "My mom left her boyfriend about six months ago." Boyfriend. It seemed like such a silly word to describe the monster Redmond had become.

"What do you mean? You mean she left?"

"Yeah." He tried to sound casual, wise to the weirdness of adults. "I mean she got into the car, gave the boyfriend the finger, and left. I saw it all, and let me tell you, it was hard not to take that finger personally."

"Nick," she said, touching his arm. "Nick, you mean she left *you?* Is that what you're saying?"

"Yeah." He couldn't keep the sadness out of his voice. That night he'd watched in horror while she loaded the car, watched her lay rubber, watched her jab her arm out the window, middle finger extended, as she drove off. It couldn't be happening. It couldn't be. But it was.

Chase said, "What does the guy say about it?"

"I don't know. We don't talk about it."

"I see. The woman he lives with — your *mother* — ups and leaves, and you guys don't even talk about it?"

"Lately we don't talk about anything. That's the way we deal with things."

"Jeez Louise, your family's worse than mine."

"We're not a family. We were never a family. If we were a family, she'd never have left. We were just some people who lived together for a while. Such is life in Scaryville."

Chase said, "I know what you mean." She slapped the platform they were sitting on. "That's what I like about The Mountain. It takes you above all the insanity."

They looked out at the lake together, at the shining water, at the jagged pine trees. Nick smiled. "You like high places."

"The more higher, the more better," she said. "You hungry?" She pulled a foil-wrapped package from the bag, some macaroni salad, strawberries, a bottle of wine.

"Roast chicken," Nick said. "You're amazing." She made it by magic, out of thin air.

"It's nothing. My mom's a waitress. Sometimes they let her bring food home." She watched him slyly.

"God," he said, biting into a chicken leg, "where does she work? This is great."

"Actually," she said, passing him the wine bottle, "actually, I made the chicken. I just didn't want to take the blame if it didn't turn out."

When they finished eating, Chase said, "I feel like a stroll. Come on." She led him on a walk around the roller coaster track, her arms outstretched, her tread light as a tightrope walker's. They climbed up and down the hills. By the time they made it back around to the big hill, they were so tired and it was so steep that they had to crawl up the last ten feet. When he reached the platform, Chase was already there, drinking from a plastic water bottle. She looked relaxed. A quick jog around the block, not a five-story climb up a pile of rotten wood. She handed the bottle to Nick, but he didn't take it at first. He was memorizing the moment. No matter what happened, no matter how things changed, he'd always see her like that, her face floating above the crest of the hill, her face against blue sky.

He took the water bottle from her and said, "You think of everything, don't you."

She pulled a lacquered parasol out of the bag. Hot and tired, they stretched out in its shade and held each other. They stayed like that until the blood stopped drumming in Nick's head, until the sun went down, until the cold wind came up from the lake, until the cars out on the highway were nothing more than streaking headlights.

Later, when she drove him home, he wanted her to let him out down the road but was too embarrassed to ask. Besides, he didn't want to lose a moment with her. But he wished he knew for sure that Redmond was in the house and not prowling around outside. Chase pulled the parking brake, grabbed his shirt collar, and turned him around.

"I'll bet I know what your room looks like," she said. "I'll bet you've got a Little League trophy and a shelf full of Matchbox cars you just can't bear to give away. I wouldn't say no if you invited me in for a look."

"I don't think that's such a good idea." The lights were on in the living room, but Nick was still nervous. Redmond could be anywhere.

She smiled her taut smile. He just stared back at her.

His room. Four fifty-pound sacks of Manna Pro Egg Maker poultry feed, a sack of grit, a sack of Trip-L-Duty oyster shell, feed hopper, watering can, wire cage, twenty-four hens, perches, nesting boxes, chicken shit, a dozen nails driven deep into the door. And Fatima. Poor Fatima, too dumb to come in out of the dark.

The Commander has been restationed again, and now Lloyd and his mother are driving to their new place, a house his father picked out for them. They've been driving all night, driving all their lives. Lloyd's lying in the backseat, watching the streetlights blast past, the power lines swoop from pole to pole. Finally the car makes a sharp but slow left turn. He hears gravel popping under the tires. The car stops.

They never live on a base. In the broken-down houses and apartments his father finds for them, you can hear rats in the walls. Out in the street, the neighborhood kids show you their scars and the knives that made them.

Norfolk, Newport, San Diego, Brooklyn. So many towns Lloyd can't keep track of them all. He remembers the places by the rooms he's slept in — by their smell, by the pattern of headlights sweeping his bedroom walls at night.

When he finds his room in the new house, his mother has already spread out a sleeping bag and a sofa pillow on the floor. The room smells of Lysol and feels like an office, with its cheap wood paneling and its venetian blinds. He wriggles into the sleeping bag and props the stiff sofa pillow under his cheek. He's tired, but he has to do one more thing before he lets himself fall asleep. He dreams of a bullet tearing through his father's head, the plane skittering off a flight deck, an explosion in a submarine, the sea slick with blood. He tells himself these thoughts are dreams, because he's afraid to admit they're stories he's made up, wishes, prayers.

It will take two days for their furniture to arrive, but that's OK. He likes the sleeping bag much better than his bunk bed. Lloyd has no *brothers or sisters. His father bought the bed to prepare for the future. Night after night, Lloyd lies in the lower bunk, staring up at the bed reserved for his future brother. His brother who doesn't exist yet — who will never exist, as it turns out — but who is, the Commander says, already a better man than Lloyd will ever be.*

WEDNESDAY AFTERNOON AND STILL NO SIGN OF NICK. Just when Redmond was considering calling the police, they called him, called *on* him, actually. He was next to the paddock, sharpening the blades of his posthole diggers. What his pasture needed, he figured, was a strong, tall barbed-wire fence. The electric fence was a joke. That morning he had found three cows in the blackberry bushes on the wrong side, the fence still on, still intact, still hot. He knew this because he touched it. A white spark scorched the tip of his forefinger. He couldn't figure out how the cows had done it. They were the three cows that always stayed together, the ones Nick had named Big Mac, Quarter Pounder, and Double Cheeseburger with Fries — Double Cheese for short. The cows thought they were hiding. They stood in the bushes, tails switching, their suitcase heads jutting above the black-berries, a cloud of cowbirds swarming overhead.

He leaned his diggers upside down against the paddock fence and began to work the file over the blades. He was glad to have a tough job ahead of him. Keep his mind occupied. He'd given up on the gate. Really more of a two-man job. Digging. Now that was real work.

Cows were nothing more than eating and shitting machines. That's my most successful crop, he thought — shit. Who'm I trying to kid?

About then the police car pulled into the driveway. His first impulse was to give himself up, confess to whatever crime they accused him of, tick off the appropriate violations like items on a room-service menu. His next thought was that Nick had turned up somewhere, hurt, dead. For a wild moment, he thought he might borrow one of their guns and solve his problems by putting a bullet into the brain of every living thing on the place, starting with himself. He laughed quietly, a sound like choking, the laugh of a serial killer.

150

The female cop spoke as she walked toward him, flipping through a ratty sheaf of stapled pages until she found his name. "Mr. Redmond?" Both cops wore beige short-sleeved uniforms. They didn't look like cops at all. More like overage Scouts, except for the thirty pounds of gear hanging off their black leather belts — the web-gripped pistols, the nightsticks, the walkie-talkies, the canisters of Mace, the bullets. The woman had her hair pushed up into her cap. She looked like a barrel-chested man with a gentle face. When they reached Redmond, she stopped and waited for him to answer, but her partner walked right up next to him and looked over the fence at Redmond's garden.

"Yeah," Redmond said, confessing to the first in the long list of his crimes. "I'm Redmond."

"Lot of succulents in there," the male cop said, turning back to him, shaking his head. "Lot of succulents." He had sad, suspicious eyes, and one of his cheeks was slightly hollow and pitted.

"Yeah," Redmond said. Crime number two. One he didn't even know was a crime. That's all right. Pile it on. The crime he'd have liked to be sent away for was the murder of his father, a crime he imagined many times, especially in the last few days. But they wouldn't arrest him for that without a body and a quantity of blood.

"This property," the woman said, looking down at the pages in her hand, "is owned by a John Henry Teague?"

"That's right," Redmond said.

"We're wondering," the man said, turning to him, "if we might have a look around."

"A look around?" Redmond pictured him sniffing out succulents under the bed, in the closets. "For what?"

"Just a look around," the woman said. "You don't have any objection, do you?"

"No, I just — "

"Good," she said, rolling up the pages and tucking them into her back pocket. "We won't trouble you more than we have to." They turned and went back up to the house. In a few minutes they climbed out of the cellar and started for the barn, heads together, nodding. They went in through the big doors off the driveway, then came out the tractor shed on the downhill side of the barn, still talking, still nodding. They walked by Redmond and headed down to the edge of the pasture, to the humming strand of ineffective wire, where they stood staring at the woods below. It's strange, he thought, dragging the file over one edge of his diggers.

He'd seen the camper all over. The old blue pickup with the wooden cabin built onto the back, a panel of stained glass on the door. He'd seen his father's pale face watching from the cab, watching while he unloaded trucks for Mrs. Kinsey, watching as he left the liquor store. At night, he'd hear the camper pass outside, sometimes pausing at the house. One time he heard it stop, heard the engine shut off, the door open, footsteps against gravel, then nothing for a long while but the ticking of the hot engine.

He was sharpening the blades to make digging the postholes easier, but what he imagined as he ran the file over the arc of each blade, what he kept picturing, was standing over his father's body, the diggers in his upraised hands, plunging the keen blades down into his chest and clamping them on his fat red heart. It was all he could do to keep from falling on his knees in front of the cops, knocking his wrists together, and saying, "Take me away."

They worked their way back up the hill and stood catching their breath for a second before speaking. The man stared darkly at the garden as if Redmond should have weeded while they were gone. The woman was cradling a battered spiral-bound notepad in one hand and pinching a stub of pencil in the other. She licked the end of the pencil and said, "Any structures in the woods down there?"

"Structures? You mean houses?" Redmond laid the file on top of the fence rail. He took off his leather gloves and laid them there too.

"Houses, outbuildings, whatever."

"No, not that I know of." He looked off at the woods. "I don't get down there much." She wrote something in her pad.

"Chicken coop's all nailed shut," the man said.

"Yeah," Redmond said. "We had some trouble."

"Any other uses?" he said.

"For the chicken coop," the woman said when she saw Redmond's confused look.

"Just chickens," Redmond said.

She nodded and wrote in her pad again. She might have been totaling up her score in miniature golf.

"Who else lives here?" the man said.

"Just me. Me and the boy."

"The boy," the woman said.

"My girlfriend's son."

"You, your girlfriend, and the boy," the man said.

"No, just the boy and me. My girlfriend's . . . not here." The word sounded so tame. Girlfriend. Like something a kid in junior high would say. He needed a better word to describe what Ellen had been to him.

"She's away?" the woman said.

"Yeah, away."

"So she still lives here," the man said. "She's just away."

"Yeah, away."

"Who else?" the woman said.

"Lives here?"

They both nodded.

"That's all. Just us." Redmond liked being a suspect. "You think I buried my girlfriend in the field or something?" He laughed nervously.

Neither of them even smiled. The woman said, "Mr. Redmond, this has nothing to do with you. We're looking into Mr. Teague's business dealings."

For the first time since he'd known him, he envied Teague.

She said, "You don't have any reason to protect him, do you?"

"From what?"

No answer.

"Hey, I hardly know the guy."

Slowly she said, "So if someone else were living on the property, you'd have no reason to keep that knowledge hidden from us." They watched him closely.

"I told you, nobody but us lives here."

"But if there *were* someone else," she said, "you'd have no reason to keep that knowledge from us."

"I'd have no reason to tell you or not tell you."

The man, who'd been listening quietly, folded his hands in front of him, rubbing the flat pads of his thumbs together. "We can give you a reason to tell us, Mr. Redmond, if it comes to that. Will it come to that?"

They stared at each other like boxers before a match. Redmond's gaze broke first. He looked into the garden at the lush weeds, at the frail tomato sets, already failing.

"Do you have anything else to tell us?" the woman said, her pencil stub poised over her notepad.

The chicken coop's nailed shut because I went nuts the other day, Redmond wanted to tell them. I attacked Nick, a child, and now I have no idea where he is. For all I know, he may be down in those woods, dead. I drove Ellen away, made her so crazy she had no choice. God knows where she is. Oh, and my father's haunting me. I'm afraid we may kill each other.

"No," he said, "nothing else." His grimy work gloves lay on the fence rail, one on top of the other, lay there like severed hands. "I don't think so. No."

"Thank you for your time, Mr. Redmond," she said, flipping her notepad shut and tucking it back into her hip pocket.

"I'd take care of those succulents, if I were you," the man said as they turned away.

"There is one thing," Redmond said, turning them back with his voice. "What does it take to get a restraining order or an injunction or whatever?"

The woman reached for her notepad.

"Is it Teague?" the man said. "Is he harassing you?"

"No, no. I have a friend. Someone's been bothering him." The woman dropped her hand, left the notepad in her pocket. Redmond felt mildly insulted.

"Bothering how?" she said, mildly suspicious.

"Driving by the house."

"How often?" she said.

"Twice a day sometimes."

The man chuckled softly. "You'll never get a judge to call that harassment."

"I didn't say it was harassment. It's just something that's disturbing. He follows my friend. My friend sees him everywhere he goes."

"Look," he said, "tell your friend to call the station if something real happens."

"Something real *is* happening."

The man sighed. "I'm talking about a real live *crime*. Harassment is making anonymous phone calls, threatening somebody, stalking them — "

"Stalking — that's the one."

"Stalking means more than driving by a house a couple times a day."

"But he's everywhere."

"It's a small town, Mr. Redmond."

"You mean you're not going to do anything."

He nodded. "Show us a crime and we'll do something. We'll do something so fast it'll make your head spin." They turned back up the hill.

Redmond called out, "Anything can happen, and when it does, it will be your fault."

They kept on up the hillside, the man giving him a little backward wave.

"As long as you understand that," Redmond called after them. Anything can happen, he thought. Shoot his father during one of his nocturnal visits, drag him into the house, call him a prowler.

A few hours later, after Redmond had nearly given up on the fence idea, Teague's pickup bounced into the driveway, its fenders bulging, a load of something crashing around in the bed. He was shaking a half-empty bottle of Cuervo Gold out the window.

"I got to burn down some of these extra buildings," he yelled as he jerked to a stop and climbed out. He was wearing a shabby corduroy suit. He took a can of kerosene off the back of the truck and set it on the asphalt, kicking a rock out of his way. He reached back into the truck for another can. "You going to stand there?" he said. "Or are you going to give me a hand?"

"Burn?" Redmond yelled as he ran puffing up the hill. "Are you crazy?"

"A matter of insurance. Maybe taxes. I don't rightly remember." Teague squinted at the farm buildings. "I figure we start with the barn, then the chicken coop, then that little lean-to down in the field." He plucked another shiny red can out of the truck.

"Jack, hold up." Redmond was standing next to him now, trying to catch his breath.

"You see," Teague said, "my philosophy is, if you can't join 'em, beat 'em. If you can't beat 'em, join 'em — and then beat 'em up!" He set the can next to the ones at his feet.

"Wait a minute." Redmond grabbed his arm as he reached for another can of kerosene. "What the hell's going on? The cops were out here this morning."

"Hey, they're everywhere, man. But I'll take the cops any day over Dina. I'll take the fucking Untouchables over that bitch."

"I like Dina," Redmond said.

"Of course you like her. You didn't have to be married to her. Get this. The big dogs are howling for my blood, right? So I figure it's time one of their own bit back." He plucked at his lapels with his free hand. "This morning I dude myself up in my prom suit and go over to my old man's law office."

"You?" Redmond said. "You went to a prom?"

"Yeah," Teague said, his voice full of hurt. "Dina and me." He raised the bottle of tequila, swallowed deeply, and wiped his mouth on the sleeve of his jacket. "Anyways, I figure I'll hire the old man to get me out of this jam, right? So I do a little prodigal son jive. I mean, I'm down on my bloody, fucking knees."

"I'm sorry." Redmond laughed. "I believe pigs might fly. I believe a cow could give birth to a human baby. But I can't picture you at a prom."

Teague jerked the bottle to his mouth so fast the tequila jingled like a handful of coins. He wiped his mouth again and said, "I'm not going to dignify myself with a comment on your rudeness. You want to know what Mr. Hair-weave told me or not? He told me Dina already hired him. Can you believe that? My own father. A shitstorm's brewing, man. No doubt about it. They're going to have a heyday with me." Teague grabbed another can of kerosene off the truck and shook it, shook it so hard Redmond thought it might explode. "Are you with me or against me?"

"You're drunk."

"Of *course* I'm drunk! Who wouldn't be drunk? Besides, I'm not that drunk. I'm talking simple economics. The more you own, the more you tax. The less you got, the more you get."

"You *can't* burn the place down! I *live* here!"

He shook the can of kerosene again. "Come on, man! Dina won't be happy until she has us living in caves."

It took all Redmond's effort to work up sympathy for Teague. "Go home. Sleep it off. Tomorrow things will look better. You need the sober perspective."

"Are you kidding? If I was sober, I'd blow my brains out." He raised the bottle again and took a long drink. Then, in the quiet voice of a confession, he said, "Thing of it is, all I want is a little relief."

"From what?" Redmond said. He couldn't keep the edge out of his voice. He felt nauseous from the smell of sweat and tequila. But it was more than that. He wanted to shake Teague, slap him, tell him there were other people with problems in the world. Him, for one.

"From my life," Teague said, taking another drink. "Ever wake up and find out you're not the man you took you for?"

Redmond thought of the nights he'd spent after Ellen left, calling all their friends, calling directory assistance in every town she ever lived in, then checking out every nearby town. He wanted to find her, wanted to tell her — what? But Teague had ruined all that.

Redmond felt his jaw clench. "Here it is," he said, "the cheap play for sympathy." He stepped in closer to Teague, pinned him with his eyes. "You think I don't know what happened between you and Ellen? Between you and my wife? Because that's really what she was. And now you have the gall to come around here whining for sympathy *and* trying to burn down my house. Well, you can save your energy. You already burned it down."

"Not the house," Teague said. "Just the barn. For now."

Redmond bit his bottom lip, one of Ellen's nervous gestures. He looked Teague in the eyes, hard.

Teague dropped the can of kerosene he was holding. It hit the asphalt with a hollow gulp. "Hold up, there," he said, wagging his head at Redmond. "First off, you two never got married."

"That's not the point."

"I know, I know. But the point is, what happened, it didn't mean anything to us."

"That only makes it worse."

"Maybe so. But I'm only trying to tell you I'm not what made Ellen leave. What happened to us was like . . . an accident. That's what it was — a fender bender. And anyway, that 'marriage' was on the rocks long before I ever came into the picture."

"Before you ever came in Ellen, you mean."

Teague's face dropped into slack-mouthed shock. He took another hit of tequila and wiped his mouth. "Yow, that's disgusting. I thought *I* was low."

Redmond suddenly felt tired and cheap. What did he think he was doing? Teague was just a child, a child with dangerous appetites. "Don't pay any attention to me," Redmond said. "I'm just talking shit." Teague's frown cleared. A few words. That's all it took for him to forget an insult.

Teague shook his head. "When things are right, they're right. But when they're wrong, they're . . . not right."

"Whatever," Redmond said wearily. "Just don't burn my house down, OK?"

"To tell you the truth," Teague said, tapping a can with the toe of his work boot, "it seemed like the right idea when I bought the stuff, but now I don't know."

"That's the boy."

Teague's voice sailed to a giddy octave. "In actual fact, I've lost the will to torch."

"Now you're making sense." Redmond took him by the elbow. "How 'bout you saddle up your pony and head back to the ranch?"

He helped Teague into the truck and watched him drive off. Drunk or sober, Teague's driving was the same — all over the road and all out. Here was a guy who could wake up cold sober and still think the best way out of his troubles was burning down every piece of property he owned. In a twisted way, Redmond admired him for that, for having a clear idea of what he wanted. A wrong idea, maybe, but absolutely clear. He took the cans of kerosene to the barn, where they'd be out of the sun and safe.

Two middle-aged women sitting across the aisle, talking quietly under the twin yellow shrouds of their reading lamps, one woman's face pale as concrete, the other's so red it was as if she'd just been slapped for twenty minutes straight.

The pale woman looked over her glasses at the other and said, "After my divorce, I think I just stopped being a woman."

The red-faced woman, turning to the window, to the dark landscape flashing by, nodded and — softly, thoughtfully — said, "Some days nothing is enough." Ellen couldn't tell if she meant this as a cause for hope or despair.

Ever since Harrisburg, three hours ago, she'd had the terrible feeling that the bus was heading south, away from Esther. Hard to tell at night, but the landscape seemed rockier. There were mountains up ahead, and the road was rising to them. When she asked the driver, he said, "Yeah, we make a couple stops on the West Virginia line before heading up east." She felt battered. Riding the bus was too much like her life — one step forward, two steps back. In her seat again, she leaned against the headrest and closed her eyes, trying to forget she had a body.

In some ways, she thought, you were right about me. I am sort of crisis-driven. My emotional reflexes are quick — the smallest thing will set me off — but I have only two settings: outrage and despair.

My mother used to say I was born screaming and never stopped. The neighborhood parents were always yelling at me. But I loved it too much to quit. When I screamed, I was dangerous. Electricity flew out the ends of my hair. My body was a hot wire. Eventually, I learned to stop. If you get slapped often enough, you can learn anything. But somewhere inside me, in the locked room of myself, I was still screaming, screaming the paint off the walls, waiting for the day when the door would open. And then, stand back.

Sometimes I think my brain's been badly wired. The little things chip away at me. The tiny dot of tomato sauce on the white silk blouse. The man in the street who looks at you like he's looking down the barrel of a gun. The neighbor's parrot shrieking for a kiss. I weep over underdone steak. I guess I could send it back, but that isn't the point. I get to liking something. I get to wanting it just so. I stop hoping and start expecting. Then — bang — the world turns on me, betrays me. I mean, if life were unrelieved misery, it would be easier to take. Then you showed up. In the beginning, you made me happy. The door slowly opened. The girl was not screaming. She was only waiting. For you. But then you started leaving me, started long before you ever walked out the door.

You expected me to solve the mystery of your life, a mystery you'd given up trying to solve, a mystery you'd nearly forgotten was there. You wanted me to look at you and know things, things you never told me, things you didn't quite know yourself. And when I couldn't do that, when the months and years passed without a revelation, you lost faith in me, lost love.

I'd tease and beg and badger you into telling me what you thought and felt. You talked so slowly, afraid you'd say something I didn't want to hear. It was torture. For you. For me. Whenever I asked about your father, you never said anything, but your eyes made me think kidnapping, in some cases, is not a crime.

I know I was — am — hard to take. That I'm quick to see the insult in a fairly innocent word or act. That I insist too often. That for me every minute of every day is a test of character — a test you mostly failed. It wasn't that I wanted you to be perfect, though I probably thought I did. I only wanted a few unguarded moments from you. A little ordinary rage. A little self-pity. A little vanity. A little arrogance. I wanted you to be carried away just once by a feeling you couldn't name or control. I wanted you to take yourself by surprise.

If you'd only screamed at me now and then, we might have made things work. If you'd only said, once in a while, "Do that again and I swear to Christ I'll kill you." But you never even raised your voice to me. You think it's important to be nice to people, but you're not nice. You're dangerous. There's nothing so deadly as your desire to please.

Is this what you think? That we're all casualties? That if we stop to count up the dead, the wounded, the missing, we'll have no time for anything else? That self-pity is a thing to get past? That what looks to you like a tragic whack of fate seems perfectly fair to everybody else? That you might as well just shut up and take it?

Well, I think the grief builds up and builds up until it poisons you and everyone around you. I think if you howl out your grief, there's a chance it might go away, that you'll get it out of your system, that after a while a loved one will touch you and say, quietly, "All right, now, that's enough." A chance of that, anyway. I think you kept quiet because you were afraid you'd find out that nobody was there to touch you like that, afraid that no one would help you stop howling. I tried to touch you like that. My hands were all over you.

A Saturday in summer. Lloyd's coming home from playing football, thinking about which comic books to load into his wagon and drag to Ricky Benedetti's house for trading with the other kids from the neighborhood. It's something they do every month or so, cycling their comic books through each other's hands until they've read them all.

Comics are the only kind of books Lloyd knows about. He loves them, loves the bright slashes of color, the bubbles of words rising out of the characters' mouths, the careful boxes around each scene, the way the figures sometimes break out of their boxes and step straight into the next box. He loves the sudden breathtaking drama of a full-page drawing — Batman clinging to the side of a skyscraper as he follows a thug who thinks he's escaping, Superman in the frozen silence of his Fortress of Solitude. And he loves the back pages — the ads for X-ray glasses, for catalogues of magic tricks, for life-size cardboard submarines — all the secrets and surprises you can buy for only a few dollars.

But it isn't just the stories and the superheroes and the ads. He loves the books themselves — the cool, slick covers, the ink-soaked nubbly newsprint. He loves the feel of the books, the slap they make when he drops them on top of each other, the weight of them piled high in his wagon, the colors clashing, the pages slopping together.

He's so happy he forgets about his bruises. The ones his father gave him a few nights ago are pale yellow now, almost gone. In a little while, the ones he's just earned playing football will bloom blue as midnight in Metropolis. But he can't think of that now. He can only think of the new comic books he'll trade for, the hours of reading ahead of him.

But the Commander's waiting for him on the glassed-in back porch.

He's sitting on a stool with a sheet draped over his knees. For a second he looks like Betsy Ross sewing the flag, but then Lloyd sees the yellow stain in the sheet, his sheet, and the look on his father's face. Not a look of rage but the slow, deliberate look he gets when he has a chore to do.

The Commander says nothing as he stands up, walks to Lloyd, and leads him back to the stool, his big hand on his back. He lifts him to the stool and slowly ties the ends of the sheet around his neck so the dried yellow stain falls just below his face. He goes into the kitchen, leaving Lloyd alone for a minute to breathe in the stale scent of urine. It's no use to beg, to hide.

Now his father's back with a black leather pouch that he slowly unzips, taking out the pieces of the home barber kit, snapping the comb onto the blade, attaching the cord, plugging it in. The lethal hum of it, the hardness of it dragged across Lloyd's head, over and over, his father's hands pushing his head back and forth, the hair falling in soft clouds that stick to Lloyd's face, that tumble down the front of the stained sheet.

His friends are at the back door. Ricky, then another kid, then a few more. "What's keeping you?" they want to know. "Where're your comics?" They smile at first. Lloyd's playing some kind of game. But then, when they see Lloyd's wild red eyes, they look puzzled. Then they smile again, laughing. Finally getting the joke.

Now the comb coming off and the bare blade of the clippers cold against his scalp. The hair falling away and them watching. And when it's finished, when the clippers are turned off and laid down, the clippers and his forearm covered with loose hair, his father says the only words he will say: Take your clothes off. Lloyd shakes his head, but barely, not wanting to be slapped off the stool. And the Commander, understanding, helps him down from the stool, untying the sheet, and rips Lloyd's shirt open so the buttons bounce across the floor. He peels it off him and yanks his pants — still belted, still zippered — down his cold legs and off — underwear, pants, shoes and socks all with one swift pull.

"Look! Look!" The faces at the door laughing at the good joke. Laughing at Lloyd with his hair all matted and dirty from football on one side but shaved to the skin on the other. Laughing at him without any clothes, wearing nothing but the yellow sheet his father has wrapped around him like a diaper. Laughing when he's shoved outside, the door locking behind him. Laughing at all the times they will tell it to the other kids, the kids who didn't get to see.

And Lloyd all the time thinking, thinking. Batman could take Spider-

Man because he's smarter. And Thor could take Batman because he has the hammer. And Superman could take everybody, all of them. Except maybe Flash, who can run so fast time turns backward. Who can run back to before Superman caught him with his super punch, with his heat vision, with his X-ray eyes. Who can run even farther back. All the way to when Superman was nothing but a tiny speck of some exploding star.

THE CAMPER SAT ACROSS the highway from Kinsey's feed store, in the lot of a small shopping complex — realtor, deli, miniblind store. Redmond's father had parked it so he could see everything, waiting for his time. Two days since that little rock-throwing incident. Plenty of time for the boy to come to his senses, to see what that medal represents, to see what *he* represents.

He never claimed to be the perfect parent. Everybody makes a few boners now and then. That's what keeps things interesting. But this. This is holding a grudge. Why punish yourself? That's what he'd tell the boy, if only he could get within hailing distance. How'd everything get so cocked up?

He'd followed the boy to the feed store and watched him unload a few sacks of feed off a flatbed. Then, sure the job would take a few hours, he went off to gas stations and trailer parks, trying to get his propane tank recharged. But every place was out to cheat him. He really couldn't afford to throw his money away like that. He gave up and went back to Kinsey's. The boy was still there, but where before he was throwing sacks over his shoulder and humping them into the storeroom, now he was dragging them off the truck by the ears, his face running sweat, his orange T-shirt brown with it.

It was a good place to park the camper. No one told him to move on, he had a good view of the feed store's loading bay, and the deli was right close. He was getting to be quite the secret agent, following the boy around, staying just out of sight, seeing without being seen. He had a knack for it. A tracker, that's what he was. He'd have been a natural for the opening of the West, out there finding a pass through the Rockies, bringing law to the lawless.

The boy worked hard — he'd give him that. He was a little on the

164

wiry side but strong, the kind of man you might underestimate at first glance. Just like his dad. Here he was at fifty-eight, still strong. He could probably take the boy in a fair fight. But he already knew the boy didn't fight fair. Still, you pick your spots, you choose your time. Better now to watch and wait until his moment came. It wasn't so bad. He had his coffee. His lifeblood. Almost gone now, though. Time for a refill.

"Tom, have you drunk up all that coffee already?" She was young, not more than twenty-one, and he could tell she liked it that he let her call him Tom. He set the red plaid gallon thermos on the counter.

"I'm afraid I up and drunk it to the last drop, Miss Jenny." He found it never hurt to turn on the country-boy charm when you were talking to young girls and old women.

The deli was narrow, all white, with travel posters from around the world hung at odd angles on the walls. But it was very clean. That was the first thing he'd noticed, what drew him in. That and the cute little blond girl behind the counter. The deli didn't get many customers. The realtor from next door was in and out with each new client, buying them coffee and stale pastries. He was there now, at one of the café tables in back, flipping through a thick photo album of houses. The pages creaked as he turned them. He got all worked up over something the couple said and leaned toward them, blurting, "It's *never* not a good time to buy."

Miss Jenny shook her finger playfully. Her hair was pulled taut to her scalp on the right and hung loose and frizzy on the left. He didn't get the new styles. They always looked to him like half a hairdo, or two different hairdos knitted together. She said, "You're going to have me here for another half hour, brewing up a batch of 'java,' right?"

"I'm afraid so, ma'am," he said, smiling. Gosh, he liked women, liked everything about them, liked them in every way, shape, and form they came in.

She went to the coffeemaker and poured both pots of old coffee down the sink. Then she washed the pots and rinsed the filter baskets. He'd been coming there for days, and she knew by now just how he liked things. Clean, for one. When she was finished, she set the pots back into the machine, loaded new filters into the baskets, then opened four fresh packets of coffee.

"Air," she said, gently mocking what he told her that first day, "is the enemy of coffee." She emptied two packets into each filter, double the amount she was supposed to use — strong, the way he liked it — and punched the machine on. They both stood there for a second, watching the thin brown beads of coffee stream into the pots.

"How's your party plans going?" she said.

"I'm sorry?"

"You know, silly, your surprise for your son."

"Oh, fine. He's bound to be real surprised."

"He'll come in now and then," she said. "He's nice."

"Nice," he said. "You know, I haven't seen him in almost thirty years."

"I know," she said, making a face, "which makes you a naughty old daddy, but all that's changed now. I can feel it." She leaned over the counter. There was no sound in the place but the realtor's murmuring and the deep burble of the coffeemaker. She leaned over the counter and whispered, "Do you have a lucky star?"

" 'Fraid I don't believe in luck, good or bad."

Miss Jenny shook her head dismissively. "Silly. Didn't you ever wish on a star and it came true?"

"I can't say that I have. No."

"Well, it's a real kick in the pants when the entire universe gets together and sends a little good luck your way. My lucky star tells me what I should and shouldn't do. I pray to it every night before I go to bed. If you want, I'll let you borrow my star. If you think it'd make things go better between you and your son."

But he was remembering his son chucking rocks at him, his son wanting to see him bleed. "You know," he said, "the star you pray on died many years ago. All you're seeing when you look up there is leftover light." The pretty faded right off her face.

She thought for a second and said, "So *you* say. If that's true, tell me how it is I prayed that my dead Rabbit wouldn't cost a fortune to fix, and how it turned out to be only a dried-up gasket that needed replacing."

"You brought a rabbit back to life?" he said, making his eyes wide.

"Rabbit *car,* silly. Where have you been all your life — asleep?"

He pointed at the coffeepots, which were full now. "If I get enough of that java in me, I think I might stay awake till the cows come home."

She pulled one of the pots from under the spout. Drops of coffee fell hissing to the hot plate. She carefully poured his thermos half full. "To tell you the truth, that son of yours is a little spooky. It's his eyes. Like he's always looking for the emergency exit. I think he needs his daddy."

"Well," he said, holding his arms wide, "here he is."

The suddenness of his move made her flinch. He dropped his arms and she turned to the second pot, pouring the thick black coffee into his thermos. It took exactly two pots. They'd worked out how much the thermos held when he first visited the deli two weeks ago. He made a point of tipping her three dollars on every thermos she filled for him. He loved his coffee, drank it night and day, never let his thermos out of sight. Miss Jenny was a lifesaver.

"I'll tell you what you can ask your star for," he said. "Ask it to tell you where I can get me some propane that won't cost an arm and a leg."

"Let me see what I can do," she said. She looked up at the ceiling and arranged her face into a look of contemplation, one finger lightly touching her temple. She held the pose for a moment. "The star says that one was too easy. Mrs. Kinsey will sell you some propane, right across the road." She looked into his stunned face and said, "*Now* do you believe in my lucky star?"

"Well, I'll be dipped," he said. "I do. I most certainly do."

Mrs. Kinsey was a businesswoman who liked to be prepared. She prided herself on having everything a farmer might ask for, and lots of it. That morning a shipment of Super Fit-n-Fresh had come in, and Redmond had spent all day hauling sacks of the feed off the flatbed. His shoulders ached. His back felt broken. She needed a forklift. But if she had one, he wouldn't get as many hours of work. Besides, there wasn't enough maneuvering room in the small warehouse at the back of the store.

He built a stack about the width and length of a good-size living room, built it straight up to the rafters so there'd be room for the other feeds and fertilizers she'd ordered. He was stacking the sacks in an interlocking pattern, like baled hay. At least they wouldn't fall over. He left the front wall of the stack open and arranged a stairway of sacks to the top, but it was getting steeper and steeper, harder to drag each sack up there. Like building the goddamn pyramids. He had to take a break every twenty minutes now, just to keep from passing out.

The longer Ellen was gone, the harder it was to forget her. How could that be? It was like a piece of himself was missing, a limb he couldn't identify. And now the kid seemed to have run off too. Redmond felt like a house in flames.

What if that thug student had hurt Nick badly? What if Nick was lying dead in some ditch? But Redmond knew better, knew the kid was just lying low, probably plotting against him. And now this thing between Teague and Dina, which probably meant he'd have to move, get a real job, a real life. And then there was the old man, who'd been dogging him for days, haunting him. Driving by the house all day and night, parking across the road from Kinsey's — who knows for how long.

He was sitting over there right now in his little handyman's project, sunlight spinning off its bright finish. Redmond could handle it — he *would* handle it — even though he felt like screaming.

But during a break, while he drank from the grimy water cooler next to the doorway into the salesroom, the front door jangled open, and his father stepped in.

Redmond straightened up and hid just around the edge of the doorway, where he could still hear, still see. He wiped his mouth on the shoulder of his torn Harley T-shirt, something Teague had given him. His father was carrying a squat white tank of propane in both hands, so big and round it might have been a cartoon bomb.

"That little gal over at the deli told me you sell propane."

"You bet," Mrs. Kinsey said, leading him toward the warehouse. "I've got some full tanks in the back, if you don't mind doing an exchange." Redmond retreated. There was no place to hide. He climbed to the top of the stack of feed sacks, up among the dark rafters, where the air was gauzy with cobwebs and the beams were lined with a rubble of bat dung.

As she led his father into the warehouse, she said, "I saw that camper of yours. Planning some kind of a trip, are you?" She fingered the pearls of her necklace and gazed at the old man with a look Redmond had never seen before.

"I'm doing it. Seeing the country, looking up a few of my connections. Just gadding about."

"See America first. That's what I always say. Everybody else stopped saying it, but I still say it."

He winked at her and pointed. "I'm with you."

Her eyes flickered briefly around the warehouse. A block of late-afternoon light poured in through the loading dock, spilling across the floor.

"I've got a young man on the premises who I thought might help us, but I don't know where he is. No matter. I can fix you up."

The full tanks were lined up on a shelf next to the open cargo bay, a chain running through the top rings to keep them from being stolen. She began to try the keys on her ring in the padlock. She kept talking to him while he walked around the warehouse, inspecting the bright new tools and fat sacks of feed. Looking down from the top of the stack, Redmond felt dead, like he was looking at a world he'd left behind. The plasticized burlap sacks crackled when he moved. He tried to stay still, perching carefully on his hands and knees.

"You a swabbie?" Mrs. Kinsey asked as she tried another key in the lock.

"Yes, ma'am, I am. What gave me away?"

"My husband and I lived in Norfolk when we were first married. I got so I could tell you boys by the spring in your stride. You all walk like you're still aboard ship. I liked sailors — the uniforms, those squashy hats. I liked sailors too much for Harold's taste. During Fleet Week, he wouldn't let me out of the house, not even to go to the curb for the morning paper."

While she talked, busy with her keys, the old man kept looking around — at the barrels filled with shovels, hoes, and rakes, at the rolls of chicken wire and galvanized fencing, at the sacks of dry dog food stacked against the wall, at the wooden shelves piled high with coiled hoses and baling wire, jugs of broadleaf killer and liquid fertilizer, saw blades, tack.

The old man's voice came booming up into the rafters, louder than it needed to be for Mrs. Kinsey to hear. "I've been in the navy all my life. At least, that's how it feels." He was talking as he looked over the hunting knives and deer drags. "A twenty-year man and then some. Snuck in when I was sixteen. Thought the world war wouldn't wait for me to grow up, so I lied to the recruiter. I don't think I fooled him much. I was a green country kid, still wet behind the ears."

Mrs. Kinsey said, "Grew up in a hurry, I'll bet."

"Crackers! You said it."

Redmond's father used to write home from overseas. One day when she was at work, Redmond found them in his mother's dresser under a pile of sweaters — a stack of airmail envelopes wrapped tightly in rubber bands. He read and reread them all. Each was written on pale-blue tissue paper in a tightly controlled hand, printed really, printed so carefully that the letters seemed typeset. No blots. No cross-outs. Just the regular, orderly flow of letters along dead-even invisible lines. He read the letters so often he'd memorized parts of them.

In one his father told about a time when a water spout appeared off the port bow — a column of water that seemed to rise straight up out of the sea to twice the height of the ship. "I was in the presence of the Lord," he wrote.

In another he sent a recipe for "Al'bam'" barbecued chicken, "originated by gourmet Captain Hilbert Thompson, USN."

In another he described the crew's ritual for crossing the equator, a game really, that had to do with getting naked, painting their faces, and chasing each other around.

Only one letter had anything in it about Lloyd and his mother. "I guess I'll close this thing down for now," he wrote. "You ask do I love you and the boy. What a strange question. Don't you know the answer by now? Your husband, Tom."

As he grew up, Redmond kept going back to the letters. He thought if he could find the right way to read them, he'd be able to see his father's true face. In the books he liked, the real messages were always written in invisible ink. But no matter how he read the letters, his father always sounded like no more than a big-eyed Boy Scout. Not like a husband writing to his wife, a father to a son. Not like the monster Redmond knew him to be.

The monster was standing at the foot of Redmond's monument of cattle feed. It was strange to be standing so high above him, to look down at him like that. Redmond saw the pale disk of his scalp through his crew cut, a few moles, even a small silver flash of scar tissue. From up there, his head seemed like an egg he could reach down and crush.

His father's voice rose and fell over the shape of a familiar story. "Went through the whole war with nary a scratch. On the day the armistice was signed, I tripped over a steel stake, removing some skin from the right foot. The scar matches one on the left foot I got in a corncrib back when I was a monkey. I guess a sailor has to keep his balance, even in scars." He was still standing in front of the stacked feed sacks. His eyes climbed a step, two steps, then stopped.

There was a moment when Redmond was sure he was about to look up at him, about to scorch him with his gaze. But then Mrs. Kinsey said, "Here it is." Redmond heard the snick of the padlock opening and then the rattle of the chain. "Hey, sailor, do you think you could change these tanks for me?"

Without turning to her or raising his eyes, he slowly saluted. "Aye, aye, ma'am." Redmond realized then that his father didn't look up because he didn't need to. He knew Redmond was up there, crouching like a goat, watching. And he wanted Redmond to know he knew.

As he lifted down the full tank, he said, "The really remarkable thing is that in all my time in the navy, I never met a sailor I didn't like. Never met a man who cheated on his wife or stole or took drugs or drank too much, nor nothing. Finest bunch of fellows you'd ever care to meet."

O N THE STEREO, Springsteen was wailing about Rosalita come out tonight, the music so loud it was like wind. That's what Teague needed, a sweet gypsy angel to take him someplace he'd never been. Yeah. But he knew it was no good. He'd already been everywhere he wanted to be, and it was always the same old shit. You never get free. Like the man said, wherever you go, there you are. Right between the rock and the hard place.

It was late and the music was loud, but Teague didn't care. His neighbors wouldn't know what to do with a quiet night. Hating him gave them a reason to live. He was as good as a life-support system for some of those old geezers. Besides, he was halfway through the bottle of Cuervo he'd been carrying around all day and didn't care about nothing.

He was sitting in his bedroom, at a drafting table one of his tenants had given him instead of a security deposit. He liked the shiny green graph paper tacked to its surface. He liked its wide sloping top. Every piece of paper he put on it had to be weighted down, though, or it slid onto the floor. There was only one sheet of paper on it now, many more torn up and crumpled at his feet, the one on the table held down by a cloth-covered ball, pink and yellow, so soft it sat there like a rotten tomato. Dina had given it to him, tossed it to him as she was leaving. "Here," she said. "If you miss me, squeeze this." She could be mean when she wanted to be. But he got to like the thing. He squeezed it when he was nervous, bounced it off the walls when he was mad. And by God, it *did* feel like a tit.

If he had any balls, he'd have gone ahead and torched the farm, torched every property he owned. See how Dina and her goons go about investigating a heap of smoldering ashes. But no, Redmond had to talk him out of it. Some goddamn nerve.

Teague had made several false starts with the letter. First he wrote "To My Tenants," and then crossed out "Tenants" and wrote in "Friends," then crossed that out, too, and wrote "To My Tenants, My Friends," but that was all. He didn't know what to say because he didn't know what to do. He'd thought maybe writing a letter would help him decide. He drew in a thick black dash after "Friends" and had another drink.

"To My Tenants, My Friends — "

Bug water usually inspired him, but not tonight. The room was too cold. That was the problem. Too cold to think. The lumber he'd picked up at Redmond's was piled against the wall near his wood burner, chunks of four-by-four that barely fit into the stove, but he worked one into it and got a fire going. Pretty soon the room was nice and warm. He took another swallow of tequila, looked at the words he had so far, and picked up his pen again.

> To My Tenants, My Friends —
>
>   The Esther Township Zoning Commission has seen fit to place SEVERE CONSTRAINTS on my livelihood by limiting the manner in which I administrate my properties. I'm writing to WARN you that, as a result, SERIOUS AND PERMANENT CHANGES will soon occur in your living arrangements.

"Yes!" he said, spinning around on his chair. "Dad, you ain't the only son-of-a-bitch who can talk like a lawyer." He picked up the paper and his bottle and walked around the room, reading what he'd written, holding it at arm's length, reciting it aloud. He had a knack for this bullshit. He almost called up his father to read it to him. The room was getting really warm now. It made him sleepy. He sat down and kept writing.

> For many years, providing DECENT housing for DECENT people has been my goal in life. Now my GOOD NAME is being dragged through the mud by CERTAIN MEMBERS of the zoning board. I am being described as a SLUMLORD, and you, my tenants, are being asked to put your rent into an escrow account until this matter is resolved. Because of this ILLEGAL AND UNWARRANTED ACTION, I have had to notify my creditors that they can expect DELAYS of some payments and SUSPENSION of other payments.

In addition, I must warn you that it will be IMPOSSIBLE to provide the same first-quality service on the upkeep of your living unit that you have been used to.

"Oh, baby." He was on a roll. Nothing to it. He boosted the volume on the Boss and took another hit of tequila. The bass shook the air. He felt it in the pit of his stomach. He was dizzy with it. "It's too hot for headwork!" He opened the window but jumped back when he saw a black flash falling to the ground outside. "Holy shit!" Another black flash dropped past the window. He turned down the music and thought he heard something like the sound of muffled footsteps. There it was. A dull thump. Then another. One of his wussy neighbors had maybe called the cops. But nobody came to the door. Another thump. At least it wasn't so hot now, with the window open. He turned up the music and kept writing.

I may not be the smartest kid on the block, but I am a part of this community and a HUMAN BEING WITH RIGHTS. I was here before the BUREAUCRATS, and I'll be here LONG after they're GONE.

"Law school," he said. "I should just dump the whole fucking mess in Dina's lap and go to law school." He picked up his ball, leaned back in his chair, and bounced it off the ceiling. Something made him get up and turn off the music. The sound was still there. Thump. Thump, thump. What the fuck?

He banged out through the kitchen door, still in his bare feet, and cursed at the sharp stones in the side yard. It was late. The night sky should have been good and black, but it was red as a welt. The city lights, Teague figured, reflecting off the low, hunkering clouds. His neighbors' houses were dark except for the porch and deck lights. It hurt his pride to see that they could sleep with all the music he'd been pumping out. Thump, thump. Over there, near the pine tree.

The ground beneath the tree was littered with small dark lumps. He poked one with his toe, rolled it over. Still warm. Another fell a few inches away, hitting the ground with a soft thud. Birds. Grackles. The ground was covered with them. Smoke from the wood burner's vent in the side of the house drifted lazily through the branches of the tree. It seemed to get hung up on the needles. More birds were falling, thumping onto the hard-packed dirt of the yard.

The air smelled like cough syrup. That's when he remembered about the wood, about what they treated it with to make it last forever.

Arsenic. Poison. He could've fucking killed himself. The wood burner was old. He'd picked it up cheap because it'd fallen off some truck. It leaked like a son-of-a-bitch. He could've died without even knowing it. But he didn't. He didn't die. He let out a little bark of joy as he walked away from the falling birds, back to the house. At the kitchen door, he turned to the silent houses around him and yelled, "I didn't die!"

Back inside, the whole house smelled like cough syrup. He wedged another piece of poisoned lumber into the wood burner. Why not? He was blessed. He sat at his drafting table and took another hit of tequila. It was time to kick out the jams. Time to crank it up and wring it out. Time to lock and load. Time to give 'em hell and take no prisoners. He picked up his pen.

Thus have I come to the UNAVOIDABLE CONCLUSION that DRAS-TIC emergencies require DRASTIC ACTIONS. Therefore, as of today, I declare that I shall take NO FOOD — except for water, coffee, and the occasional cigar — until a.) all parties recognize my ENTITLEMENTS or b.) I am dead.

It's up to you, people. Which is it to be?

Later, at about three in the morning, as Teague was drawing up his mailing list, with the phrase "TEN COPIES" written so furiously after Dina's name that his pen tore the paper, there was a knock at his door. It couldn't be an angry neighbor. He'd turned the stereo off an hour ago. Still, he flung the door open, ready for a fight.

Ellen Loomis was standing there. "I saw your lights. Figured you were up. You don't happen to have a spare room I can borrow for a couple days, do you?"

MAYBE MY NOSE ISN'T BROKEN AFTER ALL, Nick thought. There was a maroon scab the size of a fingernail paring at the bridge, and a sickly yellow bruise on the side, but the pain was mostly gone now, if he didn't move his face too much.

He hadn't told Chase yet, but he'd come to the conclusion that with less than three weeks left, there was really no point in his going back to school. He'd also concluded that he was in love. There'd been girls he'd ached for, girls he walked near just to see how they smelled, just to hear how their clothes rubbed against their skin. But he'd never really been in love. He knew it was possible, though. He believed the songs on the radio, that if you looked hard enough you could find someone who'd lie for you, die for you, never let you go. Someone who'd even skip school for you. Someone who could wake you from a screaming nightmare by whispering your name. Chase was that person.

They spent the last day of Nick's suspension the way they spent the first two — under Chase's parasol on top of the roller coaster. He was amazed at how easy it was to be around her, at how he never got bored or scared. They read the *National Enquirer* to each other, ate a pasta salad Chase had made, and played thought games like "If you could kill anyone and get away with it, who would it be?" The list was too long, they both decided.

Now they were napping under the parchment-colored light of the parasol. He pretended to sleep, keeping himself calm by counting. Last night he'd begun to count by tens. It was taking too long to get to a million. He wanted to be there. He wanted something to cut through his life like a sharp knife. He knew he couldn't stay in the

176

chicken coop much longer, that he'd somehow have to face Redmond. As he lay there pretending to sleep, he started counting by hundreds.

They weren't even touching, but he felt her energy, like an electrical charge. How could she sleep? He couldn't. She was constantly stirring up his insides. She was wearing a black T-shirt that said "Regarde-moi dans les yeux" and stone-washed jeans with little denim bows on the back pockets — her fem-butt pants, she called them.

"Your three favorite words," Chase said, sitting up suddenly and reaching for her mesh bag.

"What do you mean? Like — "

She clapped her hand over his mouth. "It's a thought game, doofus." She tore slips of paper from the *Enquirer,* handed him one, then dug two golf pencils out of her mesh bag. "Write," she said.

Nick sat up. They turned their backs to each other and stared out at the sky and the blowing treetops as they thought.

"OK," she said. "Now fold your paper so only the third favorite word shows." He handed her his folded paper and she compared them. "The point of the game is not to match words but just see how they go together." She read their third favorite words. His was "snow," hers was "boogie."

"Snow boogie," she said. "I like that. Now the second favorite. 'Dark,' " she read from his paper. "And mine is 'gro-light.' Do they go together?"

"Yeah," Nick said. "Let me read the first most favorite." She handed him the torn pieces of paper. "Yours," he said as he unfolded it, "is 'Nick.' " He looked at her. Those eyes. "What a coincidence," he said, showing her his paper.

" 'Chase,' " she read. "Chase and Nick — I think they go together just fine." They hugged each other. Then she pounded his back lightly and laughed. He squeezed her and rubbed his face in her thick hair, laughing until his eyes watered and a stab of pain pierced his forehead.

"Hey, wait a minute," she said, looking at her watch. It was about suppertime. "I think we can still make it, but we'll have to hurry."

"Where?" He was ready for anything. Everything seemed new when he was around her. Everything they did together had never been done before. Every word they spoke had never been spoken before. They were driving on a long road, and every turn brought them face-to-face with signs and wonders.

She drove fast around the back of the lake, stopping at a small white house with peeling paint that sat on a quarter acre of asphalt next to a gas station. Out front, at the edge of the road, was an orange neon sign in the shape of an open hand. Under it, the words "Reader and Advisor" blinked uncertainly.

They walked straight into the house, through the dark front room and into the middle room, where the lights were on. An older woman with short black hair was sitting on the floor behind a coffee table, with a teenage boy and girl sitting on each side of her. Plates of tuna fish sandwiches and potato chips sat in front of them. "Wheel of Fortune" was on TV. The kids looked like they were about thirteen or fourteen. Neither one looked up as Nick and Chase walked in on them.

The woman's eyes opened wide, and she struggled to get up. There wasn't much space between the coffee table and the sofa behind her.

"Just a sec," she said and went into the kitchen. They heard water running. On TV a woman was staring blankly at a partially exposed puzzle.

Chase said, *"The Way We Were."* The boy looked up, a wing of dark black hair hanging in his eyes. "The answer," she said. "It's *The Way We Were*. You know, Barbra Streisand? Robert Redford?" But the boy looked back at her with a pitying gaze that said she wasn't getting the point, wasn't getting it at all.

The old woman came in from the kitchen, all business now. She was wearing a yellow silk scarf knotted tightly at the back of her head and several cut-glass necklaces that hung over her heavy bosom. On her left wrist, forty or fifty silver bangles chimed lightly when she moved her arm. She led Nick and Chase into the front room, but stopped partway in.

"Girl first," she said, pushing Nick gently back into the middle room. He stood in the doorway and pretended to watch TV while he listened to the fortune-teller.

They sat in two small stuffed chairs. The old woman leaned forward and unfolded Chase's palm, staring at it closely. She took a breath and said, "You like to cook and sew. The boy you are with, you think he does not love you, but he does. That will be five dollars."

"Wheel of Fortune" was ending. The girl on the floor stretched and looked up at Nick. The muscles around her eyes were tight from hours of TV. With a tired voice, she said, "We're going next door to the gas station to put sugar in the tank. You can come, if you want."

"No," Nick said. "No, thanks."

"Boy," the old woman said, taking a pinch of Nick's sleeve and tugging him into the living room. Chase let her fingers graze his arm as she passed him. She was about to burst into laughter.

The old woman unfolded Nick's hand, stroked it a few times, pursed her lips, and shook her head. "You like football and fast cars. The girl you are with, you think she does not love you, but she does. That will be five dollars."

They were a half mile down the road before they dared to laugh, slapping the sides of the car, bouncing in their seats.

"Are you happy?" he yelled into the wind.

"Shut up," she said, laughing, slapping at him. "Just you shut up now."

It was dark by the time Chase drove up to the farm. She parked at the far end of the frontage, pulling around behind a rhododendron bush on the other side of the barn.

"How 'bout I get to see that room of yours now?"

"I don't think that's a good idea," Nick said, not looking at her. "Redmond — the boyfriend — and I are fighting. I try not to go in there."

"Into your own room?"

"Into the house at all."

"Nick," she said. She took a piece of his hair in her hand and tugged lightly. "Nick, I want to *be* with you, you know?"

"Yeah?"

"Yeah." She smiled and drew her hand down the side of his face.

Chase grabbed her mesh bag, and Nick led her to the barn, opening the little walk-through door inside the big door. The hinges creaked and the whole door shook. The barn was old. They never really used it, except to put up some hay and bed down the cows at night. It was already very dark inside, even though the cracked walls were streaked with late-afternoon light. Nick fumbled for the flashlight they kept on the framing beside the door.

He stroked the light over everything. Rotten harnesses and rusty chains hung from the hand-hewn beams. The upper story of the right side was piled high with last year's hay. On the upper story of the left side were coils of old fencing and rolls of tar paper, stacks of gray lumber, hundreds of old medicine bottles, a worn-out sofa, and antique farming tools — rusty hooks and curled claws that looked like instruments of torture.

He pointed the light to the hay on the right side. "I was thinking it might be nice up there, except there'll probably be rats and bees, and it's really not as soft as it looks. It's like lying down on a bed of nails."

Chase sniffed. "Plus what's that smell?"

"That's the cows," he said, stepping over to the hinged wooden feed flap and lowering it. In the dark stable below they saw cows butting their heads together, trying to get at the hay they thought was coming.

Nick didn't want to disappoint them. He forked some down from the loft above, shoving it through the flap to the cows. Other cows appeared, pushing out their heads, mouths reaching like hands for the falling hay. A noisy stream of pee hit the wet muck of the stable floor.

"Do you want to see our owl?" He played the flashlight up to the rafters. On a crossbeam at the back of the barn stood an owl the size of a small child. Its back was to them, feathers speckled gray, white, and black. As they watched, the owl turned its head completely around so that its white, heart-shaped face was looking down at them, its dark eyes shining, staring into the light.

"He's a true hunter. He only kills to eat. He's waiting until it's dark enough to kill." The owl's eyes glistened, unblinking.

Chase said, "I think he doesn't want us here."

Nick pulled her closer to him. "It's OK," he said. "It's good luck to have an owl in your barn." He thought this was true, hoped it was.

He led her through the barn, under the owl's perch, down the back steps, and out through the tractor shed. They were in the lane now that ran to the field below. "Watch your step." He led her over the ruts and around the cow flop, some of it fresh and steaming, some of it so old it was as dry and white as paper.

They walked past the paddock garden, the mulch pile, the chicken coop, the small patch of corn. He unlatched the wooden gate to the pasture and unhooked the electric fence, holding it high for her to walk under, then reconnecting it. He led her all the way to the bottom of the field. They ducked under the wire and climbed the stone wall on the other side, loose rocks clacking together as they climbed. Hunters must have pulled the rocks apart looking for a rabbit.

Once they were over the wall, they made their way through a stretch of marshy ground, clouds of gnats rising from the waist-high grass as they passed. Nick knelt and found some dock and winter cress. He made her taste the tender leaves. He found wild onions and strawberries. By the time they crossed through the long grass, their pant legs were wet to the knee.

Now they were in the woods, where everything changed — the light, the sounds, the sights, the smells. Even the smallest sound carried loudly through the trees. Everything was lit with a grainy light.

"Are we safe down here?" Chase asked.

And Nick, glad now to get back at her for scaring him that first day at the roller coaster, said, "Safe? When are you ever safe? If you're talking about the mountain lion that wanders around these woods, well, sure, it's a little dangerous. But he's as scared of us as we are of him." He was trying to be funny, but he scared himself. Many of the local farmers had seen the mountain lion, had taken a few shots at it, or at least they said they had. Sometimes at night Nick thought he heard its half-human cry as it prowled the shallow crease between the hills.

Chase was shivering. She leaned up to his ear and said, "God, I *love* this."

He led her deeper into the woods. The wind worked the leaves one way and then another. It blew the light from branch to branch. The leaves at the tops of the trees were a brilliant green, still lit by the falling sun, but down below, where the sun barely hit now, they were dark, almost black in places. Then the breeze blew, and the leaves stood straight up. Someone had flipped a switch, turning everything green and bright.

Nick was looking for a special place. One evening just after they moved to the farm, he watched deer head down a path beside the farm. A few nights later he found the field where they slept and took them a salt lick, but there was no sign of them. After setting it down, he turned to go, and there they were. Five deer almost close enough to touch. They stared at him in the falling light. He said, "Hello." At the sound of his voice, they bolted, leaving him alone in the field. He nearly broke into tears.

Up ahead the trees cleared, allowing a sweep of long grass. He led her over a fallen tree, its rust-colored pulpwood gone soft as felt. They crossed an apron of pine needles and through a border of cool, wet ferns into the clearing. The ground was soft and gave a little with each step, like skin. The sun was falling behind the trees, and shadows were taking shape behind the farthest trunks. The clearing was still bright, though, and he led her into the middle of it. But he couldn't find what he was looking for.

"You were kidding about the mountain lion, right?"

He said, "See how the land slopes down into the woods? This place may not look like much more than a crease in the ground, but they say it's connected to a chain of valleys that lead all the way up into Maine." Teague called it "the hollow." He said things happened there. What things? Nick asked him. It ain't safe to say. More of his lies, but Nick believed him, for some reason.

Then he saw it. "Look — " He pointed to a place where the long grass had been pressed into a kind of bowl. He knelt down. "It's one of the beds where the deer sleep."

"Cool."

"Yeah, except sometimes a hunter will lie in here and just wait for the deer to come to him."

She shook her head. "That's sick."

"The land's posted, but it doesn't do any good. So, what with the hunters and the mountain lion down here, the retired state trooper next door shoots at anything that moves." It was true. He was playing with her, but it was true.

Chase took his hand and stepped into the deer bed. When she turned to him, he held the sides of her head and kissed her on the mouth. She pulled him closer. They lay down like that, kissing, holding each other, rocking back and forth.

There was a dry snap from somewhere back among the trees. "Jesus God," she said. "What was that?" They held each other, still, listening. They heard it again. The sound of a small twig snapping underfoot.

"Wait, wait," Nick said, though Chase hadn't made a move. He raised his head above the long grass. The weeds had already grown thick as cornstalks and sent out strange alien flowers. He peered around them. He was starting to scare himself. There was still light left in the clearing, but back among the trees, where the shadows were forming, it was hard to see. Quietly, he reached for the heavy flashlight, glad he'd thought to bring it. He held it with both hands and waited until he heard the dry snap again, then shot its beam at the sound.

"Fatima!" he said, straightening up and playing the light into the trees.

"Is it the mountain lion?" She held her mesh bag in front of her, looking scared and excited.

"Come and see." She crawled over next to him.

Stepping delicately from behind a tree, the turkey turned her face into the light, her chest puffed out and her fan of feathers spread wide.

"She's ours," Nick said. "Fatima. She's kind of a pet. How'd she get out of the pen? How'd she get all the way down here?" The turkey looked from one edge of the clearing to the other, her faded red comb and wattle dangling loosely as her head swung from side to side. She turned her dark, glassy eyes on Nick and Chase. She knew exactly what was going on, and she did not approve.

"Look at her," Nick said, laughing. "She's like a pile of dirty laundry with legs."

Chase straightened up. "No, she's the queen of the forest. Like Titania in *Midsummer Night's Dream*. Nothing will harm us while she's around. Not even that old mountain lion." At that, Fatima turned and stepped back into the darkness.

And then they were on the ground again, kissing, their legs wrapping around each other, their hands in each other's hair. He dropped the flashlight and it rolled away, shining uselessly across the flattened grass. She hooked her leg behind his and pried off his shoe with her foot. He kissed her hard. His nose hurt, but he didn't care. She undid two of the buttons on his shirt and slid her hand inside. He ran his hand up the back of her leg and flicked the denim bows on her pockets. She undid two more buttons. He pulled her T-shirt loose and peeled it over her head. She undid the last of his buttons and opened his shirt back and down off his arms.

And then they were naked, lying against each other. And then, without even trying, he was inside her, moving against her, kissing her so hard their teeth clicked and his nose began to throb.

Breathless, she said, "What shall we name it?"

The hum of her voice against his mouth made him smile. He kissed her again.

"The baby," she said, pulling away, breathless but holding on to her thought. She ran her hand down his chest. "Did you bring anything?"

"Yeah. I mean — you mean a thing? No. Oh, God. I didn't — "

Shyly, she reached into her mesh bag and pulled out a small white paper bag. When she turned it upside down, a blue package of condoms and a curled receipt fell onto the grass. She took the package in both hands, opened it, and tore off one of the foil pouches. As Nick took it from her, she said, "I'm not a tramp. I just pay attention in health class. Do you think I'm a tramp?"

"Of course not," he said. "I think you're incredible."

"Me, too. I mean you." She touched his chest.

And then he was inside her again, holding her close. He'd never felt so safe. He heard a sound, a low moan, and it was a second before he realized that it had come from him. He looked down at Chase as they rocked against each other. Her cheeks were dusted lightly red, her mouth was open, and her lips were wet. She looked back at him and brushed the damp hair away from his eyes. Her breathing was sharp, sudden, driving. She swallowed once and whispered between breaths, "So . . . good," then pulled him tightly to her.

After a while they were quiet. He lay beside her, his right leg over hers, his head on her shoulder. A breeze blew the smell of the woods to them, the smell of things growing and of something wilder. It could have been them, the thick scent of sex on their hands, their faces, all over, the wildness of it. She hummed softly, a sound he felt more than heard.

The deer, Nick thought, might never come back to this spot when they smelled human, but they could just make another bed. The clearing was big enough. And maybe they'd come back anyway. Maybe. He was tired. The deer would have to take care of themselves. He wanted to sleep. He'd never felt so tired.

Chase made sure she wouldn't wake him, then slipped her shoulder from under his head. The woods were getting darker, cooler. The stars were beginning to show. She reached for her bag, pulling out a thin Mexican blanket — pink, red, and blue. She covered them both, then rolled onto her side and watched Nick sleep while the night took shape above them.

He had a good face, even with his swollen nose. He was lying on his arm now, his mouth slightly open, his eyes doing REMs like they learned about in biology. She'd wake him soon. The deer would be coming, and he wouldn't want to scare them.

She was worried about Nick. Up on The Mountain he told her he'd never been baptized. She was a Catholic, once upon a time. When she was a kid she used to like the robes and censer and singing, but that was a long time ago. She hadn't been inside a church in years. Still . . . not baptized. Didn't they send you to limbo for that?

And then an idea came to her, in case God was busy or forgetful or up to his old tricks. She thought about it for a while before doing it. Nick wouldn't approve — she knew that — but then he'd never find out. She wasn't even sure how to do it right, didn't even know the right words. But what about long ago, when women had babies far away from churches and priests and when they knew their babies were dying and knew they had to do something to save the baby's immortal soul? They must have done something, said something, and it must have counted. No way it couldn't have.

When she was sure she wouldn't wake him, she wet her thumb four times and touched his forehead, each cheek, his chin. As she touched him, she whispered, "Dearly beloved . . . this is my body . . . this is my blood . . . this is my letter to the world that never wrote to me. . . ."

T
EAGUE'S HOUSE WAS A MESS, as she knew it would be. More than a mess, really. Greasy fast-food cartons and wrappers tossed into the corners. Stacks of old newspapers and magazines everywhere. A fire-trap. The downstairs smelled faintly of almonds and ripe garbage. But the shock on his face when she showed up, feeling tired and wanting only sleep, was worth whatever hassle she'd have to put up with. Even his eyes, the way they pawed at her.

"Don't get any ideas," she said as she walked past him. "I'm only looking for a place to crash."

"Right, right." It was his got-to-remember-to-be-legal voice.

She went up to his spare room and pulled out the sofa bed. The mattress was thin. The steel bar under it pressed painfully against her ribs. She was too tired to care. As soon as she made up the bed, she took her clothes off and slid under the covers. Teague walked into the room.

She pulled the covers up around her neck and shook her head. "No way," she said. "Get out."

But he stayed in the doorway, looking down at a sheet of paper. "Don't get your blood in a flood. Just tell me what you think of this."

When he finished reading his letter, she said, "You've got a sense of drama, Titty, I'll give you that."

"Yeah," he said happily as he left the room. "Yeah, I do, don't I."

Spare room. She had to laugh. Everything about the room was spare. The walls and ceiling were barely covered with jagged pieces of un-painted Sheetrock. Holes had been cut where the switches and outlets were supposed to go. A cluster of bare wires fingered stiffly out of each one. From the corner of her eye she saw sparks jump, blue light in the darkness.

She was tired, but she couldn't sleep. She told herself she'd hole up at Teague's for a while, until she was stronger. She'd take plenty of time to think out what she was going to say. It was harder than she'd thought, this coming back, if that's what it was she was doing.

"Nick," she said.

He was just a kid, but he could take care of himself. That's what she'd told herself for the past six months, what she'd written in the unmailed letters to him. But what had she actually said to him? Anything? They must have talked the night she left. They must have. She just couldn't remember it. And there was the phone call a few weeks later, but what did they talk about? She couldn't remember that either. How could she have left him?

They used to get along so well, she and Nick. But ever since he'd turned into a teenager, he'd become distant, critical. Sometimes at night, when she was having a few, she caught him staring at her like she was a bug in a jar. And sometimes she found him sitting with his fingertips pressed together, his lips moving, silently counting out her crimes. Just like Redmond. They were alike — quick to judge, in love with their misery. Men. She hated them all.

And then there was Teague. She slept with him once. Once was enough. It happened the last time Redmond left her, angrily stuffing everything he owned into a duffel bag and walking off down the highway because he'd let the battery go dry in his Pinto. Dina had just walked out on Teague. Mutual self-pity brought them together. They got drunk, went to bed. Fucked, really. The purest definition of the word. A loveless screw.

Dina was right. Sex, for him, seemed like an ordeal, like something he had to prove to himself. He huffed and puffed over her. It was work for him. But she'd had worse.

She wanted him to understand — wanted herself to understand — why she came to him. Back then, sleeping with him was better than suffering over Redmond. She went to Teague for the same reason she sometimes ate an entire half gallon of ice cream, hating every bite, hating herself, but eating it anyway, until there was nothing left but a trickle of melted vanilla running down her wrist. She ate it because it was there and because, bad as it was, there were worse things she could be doing to herself.

"This will never happen again," she told Teague when they finished, when he rolled off her, sweating, reaching for his tequila.

And Teague, laughing hoarsely: "Yeah, but do you love me?"

Redmond stayed away six weeks that time. His shortest road trip ever. And of course she let him come back. What did Nick make of all this? She never wondered before now. He probably hated her. Everything he thought he could depend on, shot to hell.

It was the summer she turned sixteen that she learned to doubt what she thought she knew about the world. Mary Rose Becker, Joyce Driesen, and she were riding in the back of Joyce's brother's pickup. They were coming home from a party, driving the back roads between the farms, doing seventy-five, doing ninety. They were all drunk, they wanted to stay that way, and speed, speed, speed helped. That and the bottle of 240 rum they were passing around. They told jokes, laughed. Everything seemed so funny.

That's the way it went for a while — drinking, laughing at everything, driving fast between the dark fields, the black sky full of stars. It made her feel so good she leaned back against the hay bale and closed her eyes. They must have thought she'd passed out. Joyce took a long pull at the bottle and crawled over to her. Ellen watched through her eyelashes — Joyce staring into her face from two inches away.

"Bitch," Joyce said softly. She was so close Ellen felt her breath on her face. "You bitch," Joyce said again, a little louder. "You think you're better than us. You think you're such hot shit." She said other things, working herself up. In a minute she was screaming at Ellen, slapping her. Through it all, Ellen lay there like she was unconscious, just taking it.

For years she wondered why Joyce did that. Which Joyce was the true one — the one who passed notes to her in homeroom and let her borrow her cashmere sweater, or the one who hated her guts? And Mary Rose. Why did she sit there while Joyce hurt her like that? But lately she was wondering more about herself, about why she just lay there while Joyce slapped her and slapped her and slapped her.

"N O SENSE GIVING UP ALL YOUR STUFF." That's all Chase said when Nick told her he wasn't going back to school. And she was right. He didn't want to leave behind his good notebook, his calculator, his gym stuff, the old necktie and sport coat he'd stolen from Redmond for dress-up days. Early Saturday, they decided, would be the best time to clear out his locker. Maybe the building would be open for the cleaning staff.

The sky was gray. Rain was coming. They drove the Mustang up the back road of the school grounds so they'd be less likely to be seen. They pulled right up to the front of the building. When Chase shut off the engine, they heard the shouts, grunts, and whistles of football practice floating up from the playing field just below the school. Coach Carlino liked to get an early start on the football season, even though it was unsanctioned. Since the school had gone to three state championships, no one complained. Besides, he hated the off-season. No one to scream at but his wife.

"Bummer," Chase said, kicking the main doors. The school wasn't only closed. A heavy padlock and chain had been wrapped through the door handles. The steel jangled coldly with the force of her kick.

They stood there for a second, not knowing what to do, too worked up to do nothing. From the playing field, they heard shoulder pads clacking together, a voice bawling, "Come *on*, girls! Not like *that! Not* like *that!*"

Nick walked to the edge of the parking lot and looked down the slope at next year's football team, about twenty guys. Some of them were scrimmaging. A few others were running furiously for ten yards, stopping short, then running backward for ten yards. A thin guy, his gear clapping against his shoulders with every step, loped lazily around the field, his limp hands bouncing in front of him like paws.

Nick's mouth went dry. "Look," he said, kicking his chin at the coach. Carlino stood in the middle of the team, wearing a maroon windbreaker, waving his arms like a man having a seizure.

As they watched, Carlino whistled a kid over. It was Sean Stoesser. He gave him a wad of keys and pointed to a car standing in the driveway next to the field — a yellow Duster with black pinstripes, pointed downhill, its nose low to the ground.

Stoesser ran to the car, his jersey flapping loosely from his shoulder pads. He unlocked the driver's door, folded the seat forward, and fished up a clipboard from the backseat.

As he backed out of the car, he dropped the keys. When he bent to pick them up, he dropped the clipboard too.

"*Now,* Sean!" Carlino yelled.

Stoesser scooped up keys and clipboard and ran back to the coach, leaving the door slightly open.

Chase turned to Nick and tapped his shoulder with her fist. "Boy, this just might be your lucky day."

Nick was staring at the coach. "Lucky day," he said flatly. "Right." He still felt Carlino pinning his arms back while Stoesser lined up his last punch.

"Come on," she said, grabbing his arm and heading across the parking lot, toward the top of the driveway. She led him down a drainage ditch that ran along the driveway's far side. "Stay low," she said, crouching so her head was at the level of the pavement. "I don't think they can see us, but no sense taking chances."

"What?" Nick said. "Taking chances for what?"

She led him over the tangled roots and weeds and past a rusty shopping cart, two bald tires, a pile of swollen, wet yearbooks thick with mold. Out on the field, the team was doing something that required them to grunt and clap in unison.

When they got as far as the car, Chase climbed onto the roadway, keeping the Duster between herself and anyone who might be looking up from the field.

"What are we doing?" Nick said as he followed her, frog-stepping across the driveway so no one would see him.

Chase peered over the hood. Carlino was still busy with the team. He had them standing in a ragged line, arms out, jittering from foot to foot, like dancing on hot coals. When Carlino blew his whistle, they fell down, rolled to the right, and scrambled back to their feet, back on those coals. When he blew the whistle again, they fell the other way. Chase slipped back to the driver's door and pulled it open slowly.

"Are you crazy?" Nick whispered as he scooted back to her. "We can't steal his car."

"Not steal," Chase said with a smirk.

The Duster had a black leather interior that smelled of cigarettes. A pair of fuzzy dice hung from the mirror. The leather-covered steering wheel was held in place with a lock bar.

Carlino had left the car in neutral. Chase reached in and popped the emergency brake. The car seemed to shift its weight downhill an inch or so, but nothing else happened.

"What are you *doing*?" Nick said. "Are you insane?"

Chase wagged her finger at him. "Never underestimate the lasting value of a little temporary insanity."

"Yeah," Nick said, considering. "Yeah, but — "

She grabbed him by the sleeve and dragged him to the back of the car. On her knees, she said, "Go like this," and set her shoulder against the bumper. Nick did the same. They pushed. Nothing. Down on the field, Carlino blew his whistle sharply, watching the players roll one way and then the other.

"No good," Chase said, twisting her back against the bumper. "Try this." When Nick was in position, she said, "Ready, set, go."

They pushed hard, legs straining, their backs against the trunk and their feet on the ground. The car began to move. First two or three inches, then four inches, and then it began to move slowly downhill by itself, Chase and Nick slipping to the ground as it rolled away from them. By the time they stood up, the car was already halfway downhill and picking up speed. The road across the bottom of the school grounds was a two-lane that no one but students and teachers used. Across the road was a fringe of scrappy trees. Beyond that, nothing but gray sky. And below it, the county landfill.

The thin guy doing laps stopped running and pointed at the car. "Coach!" he yelled. "Coach!"

The car was bouncing and rolling at a good twenty miles an hour now, already two-thirds of the way down the hill. In one fluid movement, Carlino looked up, dropped his clipboard, and ran toward the car with outstretched arms, a cry wobbling in his throat.

By the time he reached the driveway, the car was crossing the road. Its nose dipped over the embankment on the other side, its tail rose, and then the whole car sank out of sight. They heard the sound of shrubbery being torn from the ground, small trees snapping, and then a metallic whump as the car hit bottom. A slow plume of dust rose above the trees. When he reached the spot where the car had gone over, Carlino fell to his knees with an agonized moan and tried to unscrew his head.

Nick said, "This is truly outrageous," his voice soaring with admiration.

"That's what I call a touch of ugly fun."

The team had reached Carlino now and were helping him up, leading him back across the road. Following close behind him, one guy made a diving motion with his hand and pantomimed an explosion, fingers splayed, hands spreading wide. The two players with him doubled over in silent laughter.

Carlino stopped in the middle of the road and stared at Stoesser. "You!" he yelled.

Nick and Chase scrambled closer along the drainage ditch on the other side of the driveway. They didn't want to miss any of this.

Stoesser had followed the others and was standing in the road, his helmet in one hand. "What?" he said. "What?"

Carlino lunged for him, grabbing the neck of his jersey and pulling at it until Stoesser's face was a few inches from his own. "You wrecked my car, you son-of-a-bitch!" He yanked him back and forth. "You faggot!" He swung him in a full circle.

Stoesser's helmet went flying. Nick and Chase were close enough to hear his cleated shoes clatter like ice skates on the hard roadway. Every time Carlino jerked him back and forth, his feet whipped out from under him. And everyone laughed. They hooted. They howled. Everyone.

Then Carlino pulled Stoesser up short and cocked his arm, ready to punch him. But Stoesser grabbed the coach by the windbreaker, twisting the maroon cloth tightly in his fists, and slowly forced the smaller man down. No one moved. No one breathed.

"You little fuck," Carlino said hoarsely. "You retarded little fuck." Stoesser kept forcing him down, pressing him to the ground. Carlino clawed at his shoulder pads. "Little-dick, Jew-boy fuck."

But then one of the players saw Chase and Nick standing in the ditch, watching everything. "Hey," he said. "Hey, look!"

No one paid attention. Carlino was slapping at Stoesser's arms now, still hissing at him. Stoesser, his fists full of the coach's windbreaker, forced him down on one knee and kept pushing.

"Really!" the kid yelled, pulling them apart. "Look!"

Stoesser shoved Carlino backward onto the ground and stepped away.

Carlino struggled to his feet. A small patch of road grit was stuck to the knee of his chinos. He brushed at it without taking his eyes off Stoesser. Quietly he said, "You're dead, prick. You know that? Dead."

Stoesser just glared at him.

"Dang it!" the kid yelled, pointing uphill. "Them! They did it!"

Carlino looked uphill, trying to see what the kid was pointing at, not getting it. All at once it hit him. "I know that kid," he said. "I *know* him." And then he began to run.

Nick grabbed Chase's arm. "Let's get out of here!" They climbed out of the ditch and ran up the driveway, the football team swarming after them, cleats skittering against pavement. All except Stoesser, who headed slowly back across the field, leaving his helmet in the road, where it lay like a prehistoric egg.

"*I know you!*" Carlino bellowed as he followed his team up the hill. "*I know you!*"

At the top, Nick and Chase jumped into the Mustang, and she gunned the engine to life. But then she just sat there, staring at the head of the driveway, waiting, listening to the team closing in, to Carlino's yell, the V-8 throbbing calmly.

Nick's foot jammed an imaginary gas pedal to the floor. "Don't you think we ought to haul ass?"

Chase sat hunched over the steering wheel. "In a sec."

When Carlino charged to the top of the driveway, Chase shoved the car into gear and gunned it. The fat tires shrieked, she popped the brake, and the car took off, heading for him.

Nick stood up on the seat, bracing himself against the top of the windshield. As the car bore down on Carlino, he sang, "The *hills* are a-*liiive* with the sound of *muuusic!*" Carlino dove aside as Chase swung the Mustang into the driveway, roaring downhill, football players leaping into the ditch.

At the bottom of the hill, the car fishtailed into the road. Chase wrestled it right and straight-legged the gas, her head thrown back, laughing, yelling, "Did you see that? Did you *see* that?" And then, with one eye on the road and one wild eye on Nick: "Feel my heart! Go on! Feel it!"

THE CALL CAME around nine o'clock Saturday morning. Teague's voice was shrill with desperation. At first Redmond didn't even recognize it as his.

"Bring two bills to the police station. Dina's gone and got me arrested." No *hello*. No *how about helping me out of a jam?*

"Even if I could afford it," Redmond said, "why should I help you?"

"They give you one phone call in this place. Are you telling me I wasted mine?"

"Teague, don't — "

"For the sake of our friendship," Teague pleaded. When Redmond said nothing, he added, "and because the longer my ass is in jail, the sooner Dina and her stooges will toss you into the street."

"I'm not one of your illegals. She can't do that."

Now it was Teague's turn to be silent.

"Can she?"

Teague's voice was quiet, appalled. "They dragged me away in *hand*-cuffs, for Christ's sake. Ain't that the olive in the shit martini?" And then, before Redmond could say another word, he hung up.

Two hundred dollars. Redmond didn't have that kind of money. He turned up a few dollars when he ransacked the house. Why was he trying to help Teague, a guy who spent his whole life being bailed out by one friend or another? A guy who might get him thrown off the farm? A guy who maybe broke up what he and Ellen had? Call it what it was, a marriage. Jail was the best place for a loser like Teague.

Then he thought of Mrs. Kinsey. She'd be at the store by now. She could afford a small loan. Dina probably couldn't make him move, but he didn't want to chance it. If he had to leave the farm, Ellen would never find him. He'd never realized how strongly he wanted that, how much he ached for it — to be found.

"What if I marry a sailor, Lloyd?" Mrs. Kinsey said when he got her on the phone. "What would you think of that?"

Redmond couldn't speak.

"Oh, never mind. It's just a thought." She actually sounded girlish. "But this man has come in a couple times lately. I think he's maybe taking a shine to me. Looks like he's planning to do a little hunting, though I think that might have been his excuse to come in and chat with me. Oh dear, listen how this old woman goes on."

"Hunting?" he said.

Mrs. Kinsey was still talking. "He bought Thinsulate gloves and boots, camo coveralls, disposable heat packs, a climbing tree stand."

"I have to go now."

"But — "

"I have to go." He hung up, grabbed his jacket, and headed for the car. What was the old man up to?

A block from the police station, he stopped at an ATM and played it like a gambler. One hundred? Insufficient funds. Eighty? Insufficient funds. Finally it gave him twenty dollars, leaving $3.74 in his account. Something, anyway. But why bother? Teague always had money when he was after pleasure — a new truck, a new drug, a quick trip to Atlantic City. It was the cost of living he couldn't afford.

Teague was the only prisoner in the police lockup, a pale-green room in the basement that had been outfitted with four cells. He was still wearing the shabby corduroy suit he'd worn out to the farm. He looked shocked when he saw Redmond standing on the other side of the bars, saying, "I've got thirty-four dollars and change. That's all I could come up with."

"No problem," Teague said as he stepped up to the bars. He glanced quickly down the hall, toward the door. "Don't worry about it. I shouldn't have called." He reached through the bars, grabbed Redmond's hand, and pumped it. "Thanks for coming, buddy, but I'll be fine. You go on home." His eyes kept swinging to the door.

Redmond pulled his hand away. "What, are you just going to stay in jail?" It was the first time Redmond had ever seen Teague nervous. His smile was like a grimace. Redmond shook his head and said, "What's going on here?"

The door at the end of the hall opened, and Teague said, "Well, well, look what the cat dragged in," said it before he could even see who was coming.

A bored-looking cop entered the room, carrying half a ham sandwich in his left hand. In his right he thumbed through a bristling key ring. Ellen walked in behind him. When she saw Redmond, her jaw stiffened. She nodded slightly, barely moving her head.

Redmond took a step backward. It was like seeing someone you thought was dead. He couldn't help staring. He said, "What are *you* doing here?"

"Bailing out our little friend," she said, her voice a monotone. She turned to Teague. "You didn't tell me he would be here."

"I had to have backup. I didn't know which one of you would come through for me."

Redmond said, "You said they only give you one call."

"Yeah, but I'm kind of a regular around here."

The cop unlocked Teague's cell and pulled the door open with the little finger of the hand that held the sandwich. Teague stared with longing after the sandwich, then stepped into the hallway, looking nervously between Redmond and Ellen. "Can you believe it? I'm up late last night, figuring out the solution to my Dina problem, when this one breezes in."

Redmond and Ellen stared at each other like boxers before a match. Redmond said, "You've been hiding out with him this whole time, haven't you."

"With him?" She laughed once, a sound like a cough, then turned to leave the room. "You got to be kidding."

"Hey," Teague said, following them to the door. "I have feelings too." Then to Redmond he said, "You want to hear my tale of woe?"

Redmond answered by flipping the door shut on Teague, who stepped aside, letting the door clang behind him.

"I'm driving downtown when I see Dina having lunch in the California Connection, that open-air place I call The Californication. You two listening?"

They were not listening. They were watching each other like wary animals. Ellen chewed on the corner of her mouth. Redmond's gaze was distant, clinical.

"Something just came over me. Make a long story short, I backed my pickup against her table and blew out my carbon deposits. You should have seen the exhaust! Anyway, you want to hear the solution to my Dina problem?"

Ellen turned slowly and headed for the door. Redmond followed.

"Hunger strike," Teague said, trailing after them. "No food until my demands are met. A little coffee now and then, a cigar, but that's all."

Teague's pickup was parked in the station lot among a row of black-and-white squad cars. On the creased back bumper was a sticker that read "Work is for Jerks." He opened the driver's door and pulled a bottle of tequila out from under the seat.

Redmond and Ellen stood looking off in different directions. He didn't know whether to slap her or fall at her feet. Teague hopped up onto the hood and took a drink, setting the bottle between his legs, where it stood like some kind of alien genitalia. He said, "This hunger strike's a real rush."

Redmond said, "Who you kidding?"

"No shit, man. All my senses are cranked way up. I haven't felt like this since the last time I did cocaine."

"Let me get this straight. You came up with this plan last night?"

"Yeah."

"It's now" — he checked his watch — "eleven in the morning. So far, starving yourself amounts to missing breakfast."

"But I'm *hun*gry!" Teague cried out.

Redmond pointed at the tequila. "What about that?"

Teague's face filled with pain. "Booze ain't food. Is it?"

Redmond said, "You keep drinking that stuff without eating anything, you'll really mess yourself up."

"Hey, the fatty tissue of my skin has soaked up so many psychotropics over the years, all I have to do is sweat and I get the screaming meemies."

"Go ahead, joke, but you've got a bad bottle problem."

Ellen's mouth was a hard, thin line. She wanted to say something cold and final, break something.

"It's not the bottle I have a problem with," Teague said. "It's what's in*side* the bottle." He took a quick sip. "That and Dina. But I'll show her. I'll be the most miserable, hard-driving, godawful, son-of-a-bitching nightmare that woman ever had."

Redmond laughed without opening his mouth. He said, "By starving yourself to death."

"Yeah," Teague said, his glance sliding uncertainly between Redmond and Ellen.

"Brilliant," Redmond said.

After another jolt of tequila, Teague said, "Don't you think I — "

"Tell your little jokes," Redmond said. "Play your little games. Just leave me out of it from now on."

"No bullshit, man," Teague said, shaking his head. "I'm right here on the hairy edge."

"Teague, you were *built* for bullshit."

"Give it a rest," Ellen said. "Both of you." The sky was getting ready for rain. Sunlight fell coldly on the police station parking lot. She chewed on the corner of her mouth and looked at Teague's truck, at the traffic in the street, at anything but Redmond, who watched her from the corner of his eyes. It was strange being around her again. Like she was a ghost who'd come back to haunt him. Like she might disappear if he blinked hard.

Teague was still at it. "I dropped by City Hall this morning and delivered my ultimatum. I may die, but at least I'll have my dignity, you know?"

Redmond threw a hard look at him. "Dignity? What would *you* know about dignity?"

Teague drew his lips into a knot and then said, "There have been a few episodes of excess in my life." He nodded. "I accept that."

Redmond felt rage swelling inside him, a rage, he knew, that had nothing to do with Teague. He said, "You're a user, Teague."

Teague went on like a talk show guest. "I've always lived my life two steps over the line. I tell myself, 'Try to be legal. Got to remember to be legal.' But my philosophy has always been 'Just say now.' "

"A user and a loser," Redmond said. He wanted to hurt someone or be hurt. He wanted blood.

"But can I help it if opportunities fall my way? I'm a victim of my own good luck. I ask myself, Does that make me a bad person? And I answer myself, Fuck, no."

"Take it from me," Redmond said. "You're a bad person. You've been getting away with murder your whole life, and now it's time for a little justice."

"Justice? This zoning hoo-ha isn't about justice. Dina didn't mind living off my illegal rents when we were married. This is about revenge."

"Yeah, the whole city government is helping her get back at you."

Teague's eyes went wide. "I wouldn't put it past her. She's been living her whole sorry-ass life like she's a poor, pitiful creature in the cold, cold world. I hate that. I hate how she blames everybody else for her troubles."

Redmond felt loose, on fire, capable of anything.

"I mean," Teague went on, "everything's supposed to be *my* fault or *daddy's* fault or *mommy's* fault. It's like she's the only victim in the world, and the rest of us are all criminals. Hell, I may be a royal fuck-up, but you know what? I blame nobody but myself. It's my way. Now take my hunger strike — "

"You're talking to yourself, Teague. If you want to die, die, but don't advertise. Just get it over with."

"You know," Teague said, completely calm, "you're a bit of an asshole. I never would have guessed."

Ellen turned on Redmond, her eyes flashing: "Why don't you just leave him alone?"

Before he could stop himself, Redmond said, "Why don't you just go back where you came from?"

Teague said, "Here we go. My belly button tells me to disappear, but this could be better than TV wrestling." He took another drink.

Redmond turned away from Ellen and stepped in closer to Teague. His chest was at the level of Teague's knees. He said, "You know, I used to have a cat that liked to kill birds. Every morning for months I woke up with a mangled bird in my bed, the cat sneering up at me."

"What's that supposed to mean?" Teague said.

Ellen let out a sharp breath between her teeth. "I didn't come back for this crap."

Go away, he wanted to tell her, you're dead. "Why *did* you come back?" he said, without taking his eyes off Teague.

"No, really," Teague said, "what's that supposed to mean?"

"Not for this," Ellen said, the words twisting out of her.

Redmond bounced the end of his finger off Teague's chest.

"Hey!" Teague yelled.

"What it means," Redmond said, grabbing a handful of Teague's shirt and shooting a quick look at Ellen, "is that you're just showing off what you caught and killed."

Teague tried to pry Redmond's fingers off his shirt. "Like hell," he said, stringing the word out. "I never killed nothing."

Ellen's voice was a taut wire. "Leave. Him. Alone."

Redmond let go of Teague's shirt and turned to her. "Didn't you get in enough licks before you left? I know how you feel about me. I don't need to be reminded."

"*I* need to be reminded," she said, before she quite realized what she was saying.

"Yak, yak, yak," Teague said. "You're just exercising your attitudes. Somebody slap somebody."

Redmond shot him a burning look that shut him up.

A cop came out of the station just as Teague raised the bottle of tequila to his mouth again. Teague swallowed noisily, then slowly lowered the bottle into the crook of his arm, his eyes on the cop, who watched him warily as he went to a car at the end of the line. The cop stood there in the open door, watching Teague across the roofs of the squad cars.

A slow drag of dark clouds had moved in from the west, turning the air cold. Ellen shivered. "I want to see Nick. I want to see Nick now."

Somewhere in the neighborhood, a crew of roofers was at work. Their hammering sounded like popcorn cooking. Redmond said, "I don't know where Nick is."

"You *don't know?*"

It was all too much. When he closed his eyes to stop his head from spinning, he thought he felt the earth wobbling on its rusty axis.

"*You're* the one who walked out on him," he said, opening his eyes, stepping forward, leading with his chin. "For six months you don't care if he's dead or alive, but now all of a sudden — "

Ellen cut the air between them with a quick slice of her hand. "I walked out on *you,* pal, not him." And then, to herself, she said, "Christ, I need a drink."

"That's it, that's it," Teague said. "You're getting there. You'll be whacking each other over the head in a minute." A sad look crossed his face. "I'm going to miss this kind of thing after I starve to death." He held his bottle out to Ellen, but she batted his arm away.

"Lloyd," she said with a slow, tight sigh. "I don't want to fight. I didn't come back here to blame you or beg you for anything. I just want to move on."

The roofers were still hammering. There must have been a hundred of them, whacking, whacking. Why wouldn't they stop? He wanted to tell her about the hours he spent trying to track her down, about the map book next to their bed, about the corner of Pennsylvania whirling with check marks. But the hammering. He felt it on the backs of his eyes.

He said, "Where did you go?" his voice softer now.

She seemed to see him for the first time. "I don't know where I am anymore, and I'm starting to realize that's the story of my life. I never know where I am until it's too late to do me any good."

"Yeah," Redmond said, though he didn't exactly know what she meant.

"I just want to see my son." The words made a great space open up between them. He saw it in her eyes.

Redmond shook his head slowly. He couldn't help himself: "You never loved me."

She stepped back, her arms going stiff by her sides, her gray eyes cold as ashes. "You stupid bastard."

He kept shaking his head. "Never love," he said. He smiled when he said it. It sounded like advice.

"All I ever *did* was love you," she said. "I *trusted* you. But that wasn't good enough for you, was it. You had to go and ruin everything, leaving every time I turned around. It was the only goddamn thing you were good at."

"I always came back," he said.

"You always came back. Was that the best you could do? Was that the best? . . . Pathetic."

"I never left you for somebody else," he said, nodding in Teague's direction. "And I always came back."

The cop down the line reset his cap, stepped away from the car, and started toward them. He was about forty yards away.

"What?" Ellen yelled at the cop, her hands balled into fists. "What is it *now?*"

The cop stopped walking and stared at her.

"Jesus Christ," Ellen hissed. She grabbed the tequila from Teague and shook it in the air. "Is this what you want?" She gave it another shake. "Is this what you're worried about?"

"Careful with that," Teague said, reaching after it.

She reared back and flung the bottle toward the cop. It turned over once in the air, tequila spraying behind it, then shattered on the pavement. The sound was hard and bright, like a bitter laugh.

The cop just stood there with his mouth hanging open. His shoes and pant legs were wet with tequila.

"Come on, Titty," Ellen said, walking to the passenger door of the truck.

Teague slid off the hood and looked sadly at Redmond. "Thing of it is, Dina started out loving me for all my little weirdnesses." He shook his head. "And then later it was those same weirdnesses that tore us apart. Isn't that the wicked way love works?"

Ellen popped open the door and said, "Shut up and get in the goddamn truck."

The Commander with his big square hands, coming home. The big hands squared off. The arms like turned oak. The body lanky, relaxed, ready for anything. The face oddly placid. His shirt still ironed hard and smooth as steel plating. The agony of that ironed shirt. The slow malice of his eyes. The this-is-going-to-hurt-me-more. His mother disappearing into the kitchen, into the backyard, out by the back fence, twisting a damp dish towel in her hands, listening, listening to the blue jays, to the obscene chatter of the squirrels.

And the Commander laying his big hands on Lloyd's shoulders, leading him into the bathroom. The solemn ritual beginning. Lloyd, not needing to be told, dropping his pants, skinning down his underwear, leaning over the edge of the claw-foot tub, staring into the blinding white. And then the whip-slick sound of the Commander's belt sliding out. The creak of leather as he wraps a loop around his hand. Lloyd's face hanging over the blinding curve of white. His hands flat against the cool inside of the tub, the feel of soap scum, the cascade of rust below the faucet. The Commander moving into position, drawing his arm back, the slow, satisfied intake of his breath.

And then it begins. The edge of the tub pushing at Lloyd's ribs. The belt burning. The birds screaming in the trees. The belt burning. The white of the tub turning in on itself, sucking at him. The belt burning. The muscles in his legs jumping. The belt burning. And then his father's voice close to his ear: "You think you're so tough? Because I can make you cry good, boy." The belt burning. The cry caught in Lloyd's throat, held there like a ball of hot glass in his throat. And then his father's voice again, calm, very close: "If you cry, I will have to hit you harder. Is that what you want? Is it?"

And then the Commander dragging him to the toilet and tying him to it with his belt, the same belt used for the beating, running its tongue through the buckle and snapping the loop tight on one wrist, then wrapping the loose end around the commode and tying it to his other wrist. Leaving him like that, cheek pressed against the cold belly of the toilet. Leaving him like that and going out to the kitchen for supper. And Lloyd too scared to move, lying there on the bathroom floor, too scared of what might happen if the belt comes undone, too scared to care about the pain, the steady fire in his back, his legs. Lying quietly, except for the short, caught, painful breaths. Knowing it isn't over, that his father is listening, that if he cries even now, his father will be on him again.

The smell of meat cooking. The sound of plates and bowls set on the table. The Commander reading from the fat Bible, the words murmured, rolled around on the tongue, repeated. The silence of his mother. The sound of his father cutting the meat, the orderly, measured clack of knife against plate. The cold white belly of the toilet. The light falling.

And then the cymbal clang of the neighbor's garbage can lid. The yelling of kids let loose after supper. The clatter of dishes laid in the hissing sink. The light falling and falling. The knock and rumble of pots and pans under water. The silence of his mother. The cool white and yellow tiles on the bathroom floor, the thin beads of grout holding them all together, cracked and yellow around the base of the toilet. The thinning angle of sunlight falling through the bathroom window.

Squawking TV voices in the living room, the stutter of false laughter. The sound of mothers calling their kids in for the night, each name getting two notes — the first high, the second low. Kids calling back, begging, whining. Darkness moving hard and thick through the bathroom window. His cheek numb against the cold tiles, his arms taut and aching, his hands flexing like strange birds, the finger joints creaking faintly as the hands open and close, open and close.

REDMOND PULLED INTO THE DRIVEWAY so fast he didn't notice the camper until the Pinto bounced up against its bumper, cracking a headlight. He let the car drift backward to the road. He had a strong urge to leave, to hide, to get the hell away, but he set the brake and climbed out slowly. It was the truck he'd seen following him for days. Maybe years, for all he knew. His father's truck, parked big as day right next to the house, the blue pickup with the handcrafted cabin built onto the back, a carpenter's dream. The camper door was closed. Everything was quiet, except for the mocking whistle of some bird and the distant grumble and clink of a tractor.

"You in there!" Redmond yelled. A startled squirrel scrabbled up the black walnut tree in front of the house. "You come out here!"

No response.

He peered into the louvered side windows, but they were clamped tight and curtained. The camper was tall and overhung each side of the truck by a foot. It stretched over the cab in front, propped on each side with metal struts bolted to the body of the truck. It was finished with many coats of gleaming polyurethane, which made the wood glow warmly. The joints of the box were braced all around with brown metal corner rails that lipped a neat half inch from under the corner molding meant to mask it. In contrast to the natural grain of the wood, the brown piping made the whole thing look less like a camper and more like a magician's trunk, where a man climbs in and a tiger leaps out.

He moved cautiously toward the camper door. There was a small dent in the wood where one of his rocks had hit. He laid his ear against the door, just below the panel of stained glass set in the center. The finish was like silk. When he heard no sound from inside, he set his foot on the bumper and rocked the truck as hard as he could, but the shocks were firm and the truck only shuddered slightly. He listened again. Nothing. He snatched open the door. When no one shot at him or kicked him, he climbed inside.

The camper's interior was as carefully contrived as a ship's cabin. There were cupboards, drawers, shelves, and cubicles everywhere, all of it built with lightly oiled birch, the pale wood making the space seem larger. The surfaces had been finished so thoroughly that when he stroked a cupboard door, he thought for a second that he was touching skin.

Every square inch had been designed and built to make the best use of space. And all of it so cunningly crafted, like the workings of a watch. Near the door, next to a narrow closet with shirts and slacks hung against the wall, was a two-foot-square built-in bench. When he lifted the hinged lid and unfolded the front flaps, he saw a small chemical toilet. Further down, the toy-size sink with its gooseneck faucet, fed from a ten-gallon jug in the cupboard above, might have come from a kid's playroom. The sleeping area, its foam pad fitting the space exactly, was in the alcove that extended over the cab. Everything necessary was at hand or a half step away. He'd never been as close to his father as he was now.

Sometimes, when Redmond was a little kid, his father called home from a foreign port. His mother, after a few minutes of whispering, with her face turned to the wall: "Do you want to say hello to your son?" And always the tension, the silence hanging in the air before she handed the phone to him.

But even these brief nervous conversations stopped one day when Lloyd said, " 'Member we went to the circus that time and the lady went in the elephant's mouth?"

"Yes."

"She went right inside the elephant's mouth?"

"Yes, yes."

"That happened back when you were alive."

Nothing from his father, just the thin sputter of the long distance line. And then, "You think you can get to me, boy? Better men than you have tried. They couldn't. Neither can you. Now put your mother back on."

Surrounded by his father's careful craftsmanship, Redmond felt a chill. It must be like living in a well-appointed coffin.

On the lowered table flap sat an empty coffee mug, the residue as hard and shiny as shellac. His father, he remembered, drank coffee night and day. Even at the supper table he sat with his red plaid torpedo of coffee at his feet. He never went anywhere without his thermos.

Next to the coffee mug was an open book. It had come from a bookshelf built into the wall at eye level. A hinged rail along the front kept the books from falling out when the truck was in motion. There were nearly as many books as the shelf would hold — sailing manuals, crossword puzzle books, three Jack London novels, and an empty space wide enough for the book lying on the table.

It was a battered old copy of the Scouting *Handbook for Boys,* with a split binding. Passages throughout the book were bracketed or underlined with a shaky, thick-pointed pencil. The first underlining was in Chapter One: *The Scout Handclasp is made with the left hand, the hand nearest the heart, the hand of friendship.* Later, in the chapter on first aid, there was a penciled star next to *Don't use a tourniquet if you can help it!* And under the section heading "What to Do if Lost," the earnest hand had underlined *The best thing, of course, is not to get lost.*

He had the feeling he was finally seeing into his father's true self — the desperate need to be prepared, to find out how the world works, to uncover the secret order of the universe. But then a small square of white paper fell out of the book. Something was wrong. Written on it with the same blunt pencil, and in a childlike scrawl, were the words "My average step is: 2 ft." And below that, "Date: 1/7/61."

He flipped to the front of the book. Across from the ad for bike tires, above the boldfaced command to BE FIRST CLASS!, and inside the outline of an unrolled parchment scroll, he saw his own name written out in bloated script: "Lloyd Redmond." The book was his, from his days in Troop 98. Only then, when he saw his name, did he remember the nights and weekends he spent studying the manual, preparing for every emergency.

The first page of Chapter Thirteen, "Tracking and Stalking," a chapter Redmond had never studied, was folded sharply. Still, it was as marked up as the other chapters, but with a black felt-tipped pen in dead-even straight lines. The opening paragraph was underlined:

If you have ever tried to track and stalk wild animals, you know that it takes real skill and a good knowledge of woodlore. Animals are always on the alert and their keen senses of smell, hearing or sight warn them of danger long before you see them. But with a little preparation and practice, any Scout can learn to follow animals and get close enough to them to find out how they live.

A neat black star was drawn on the page illustrating how to mark a trail with sticks, grass, and rocks.

A good way to practice observation is to follow trail markers set out by another Scout. Success in stalking depends upon how well you can hide yourself and how quietly you can move. He closed the book and slid it back into its place on the shelf.

Outside, he stood between the house and barn, where the grass was mostly dead, nothing but tall clumps of weeds here and there. The air was damp and chilly, the sky the color of a scar. He heard the creak of grackles and blue jays echoing up and down the hill. In the run, the chickens were squalling and chasing each other in crazy circles. Probably hadn't been fed for days.

The first marker was a pattern of rocks laid out on a bare patch of ground, right there between the house and the barn, a wide wedge pointing downhill. And further below, he saw where a log had been dragged through the long grass. A "whiffle-poof," according to his book. The trail snaked down the yard, the field, over the stone wall, all the way to the edge of the woods, and probably beyond. Definitely beyond. So this was the way it would be. Well, he'd need a weapon. That much was clear.

"**S**O MANY SURPRISES, AND THE DAY NOT HALF OVER ," Teague said, pulling away from the liquor store, his fresh bottle of Jose Cuervo propped between his legs. He swung right onto Market, making the pickup's fat tires shriek.

Ellen, her arm stiff against the dashboard and her right foot jabbing at the floor, said, "You ever think of using the brakes once in a while?"

"That's a good way to wear them out."

"What — using them?"

"Right."

"Titty, you wear *me* out."

"No," he said, glancing at her, "no, I don't. I'd like to, but I don't." He checked for cops, took a sip of tequila, then wedged the bottle between his legs again.

He shot into the Public Square turnaround, a corkscrew that required lots of lane changing. He always thought of the square as the perfumed armpit of the valley. The boutiques and bistros, the flower bed planted in the shape of a keystone, the Tinkertoy canopy built over the sidewalks to make the downtown seem more like the mall. Such crap. He swam the pickup back and forth, trying to get into people's business. Cars jerked out of the way. Horns flared. He was starting to feel better. This was the kind of conflict he understood.

Ellen had always told herself she wasn't an alcoholic if she could wait until five o'clock. But one hit of tequila didn't count, did it? She needed a drink badly. She had too many thoughts. Her head was too crowded — the things she'd done, should have done, could have done.

"Hey," Teague said, "you know those dead birds of mine? I'm thinking I might dress them out like game birds and sell them to a restaurant. What do you think?"

"They've been *poisoned,* Titty. Don't you think you're in enough trouble as it is?"

"Yeah, I guess so."

They doubled back on Market, driving in silence toward the bridge, past the old mansions that once belonged to the robber barons who'd carved out the heart of the valley — coal, money, blood — and then left it to rot. Now the mansions were occupied by lawyers, real estate people, public relations firms. In Teague's mind, nothing much had changed.

"White food," he said dreamily. "That's what I could go for right now. My favorite. Vanilla ice cream with real whipped cream, a big plate of fettuccine Alfredo." He stared through the windshield as if he could see the food laid out on the flatbed truck he was bearing down on.

"Yeah," Ellen said, "I know what you mean. Fluffy mashed potatoes, a hunk of French bread, steel-cut oatmeal cooked the night before in a double boiler."

"Clam chowder," he said, "vanilla fudge — "

"Vanilla *anything.*"

"Yeah." His voice was full of desire. He shook his head and slapped the steering wheel. "Are you trying to screw up my hunger strike?" He offered her the tequila.

"Just one," she said, "for fellowship." She had a small sip and shuddered. "I forgot how much I hate this stuff."

"Say, here's a thought," he said as he took back the bottle. "How 'bout we have ourselves a great big breakfast, then drive to Atlantic City? We'll bet everything we've got on one turn of the roulette wheel."

Ellen laughed. "Titty, you're a real piece of work, you know that?"

"The spot I'm in, it makes about as much sense as anything else."

Ellen nodded. "I suppose."

Teague let a moment pass, then, slowly, said, "I guess I'm asking you to try your luck with me."

"I can't leave town right now, Jack. I just got here. There are things I have to work out."

"Maybe I'm not making myself clear." He offered her the bottle again, but this time she didn't take it. "What I'm saying is, well, I'm available. That is, if you're in the market." He looked at her as he said this, didn't take his eyes off her, even when a driver to his left stabbed the horn at him.

When he saw her face fill with worry, he laughed, but only after a moment. He looked out his window and flipped off the driver, then jerked his truck into the guy's lane. Rubber squealed against asphalt.

Ellen looked over her shoulder and saw a teenager in a battered Bel Air falling behind them.

The older she got, the more complicated life seemed. Her life. Her bad intentions never let her go, and her good ones were never good enough. She used to think she was getting better as she got older, but now she thought she was only getting better at the things that were bad for her.

Teague was looking at her. "Hell," he said, "don't take it so personal. I had to take a shot, didn't I?"

Ellen said, "You're hungry, Jack. And you're desperate. You don't want me. What you need is a nice meal and a good night's sleep."

He smiled sadly. "You're probably right."

They cleared the downtown area and hit the avenue, where Teague opened it up. He wanted to get home so he wouldn't miss the phone call he was sure Dina would make, begging him to give up his hunger strike.

Ellen said, "Nobody's going to take this hunger strike seriously."

"Maybe you're right," Teague said. "Maybe I'm just jumping to confusions." He changed lanes again, cutting off a little blue compact that looked like it had been squeezed from a tube. "Much as I hate to admit it, I miss old Dina."

"You should have thought of that before you jumped into the sack with every woman you laid eyes on."

"Yeah, but I think what really sent Dina around the twist was the idea of her toothbrush in all those strangers' mouths."

"No, Titty, I don't think that was it."

"Well, thing of it is, after she left, my sex drive sort of went for a walk and never came back."

Her first impulse was to kid him, but when she saw the sad look in his eye, she said, "Sounds like true love to me."

He shook his head. "Hell of a thing." He looked at her again. "You know, what I said back there, about us going to A.C. — I didn't mean anything by it."

"No problem."

"I guess I just wanted to make sure it wasn't me you came back for." He was watching her face closely.

"How do you know I didn't?" *How do I know I didn't?*

"I figure if you were coming back for me, my door wouldn't be the first one you knocked on."

She thought about it and said, "You know, Titty, you're not as stupid as you look."

He smiled, toasted her with his bottle.

A newspaper filler in Ellen's purse explained that in Japanese, the root word for "crisis" is the same as the one for "opportunity." Since leaving Redmond, she'd hoped this was true, had taken consolation in it. Of course, even if it was true, the reverse was also true. Every crisis an opportunity, every opportunity a crisis. Still.

She tried to lay it out scientifically. The basic problem of her life was this: the one person who made her sick with despair was the one person she couldn't do without. Whose idea of love was that? She felt him in her heart, a sharp jab every time she tried to move.

Teague was driving all out. To keep her heart from climbing her throat, Ellen closed her eyes and talked to Redmond in her mind, the conversation she could never have with him face-to-face.

I think you wanted desperately to be loved but didn't think you deserved it, so you reached out to me and then turned away when I responded. How could you be with a woman who loved what you hated — yourself? But you stayed with me, sort of. Were you doing a favor for this poor soul who had the bad taste to love such an inappropriate man?

And you? What did you want?

Not all that much. Not really.

Right.

You're saying I went too far?

Obviously.

My demands were non-negotiable, it's true. I wanted you. The you I thought you thought you were, not the you you settled for.

And?

And a few other things, I guess. If a man looked at me funny, I wanted you to tear his throat out. I wanted you to be willing to kill for me, willing, if not to die, then at least to take a bullet for me. At the very least, I wanted you to take my side in every argument. I wanted brute loyalty.

You wanted me to see you standing over a dead child with a smoking gun in your hand and say, Some kids can be a real pain in the ass.

You're saying I expected too much.

Damn straight.

I also wanted oak floors, white walls, a brown leather chair, the right music, the right light, a window with an uncorrupted view. I wanted money in my pocket and glide in my stride. I wanted brilliant mornings after nights of deep sleep. I wanted nonstop, incandescent sex. I wanted to rip and romp till daylight. I wanted *Linda Ronstadt's Greatest Hits.* I wanted a '63 Jaguar, deep green. I wanted a little more kindness, a little more patience, a little more time. I wanted wholeheartedness. I wanted a pair of leather boots with silver filigree on the toes. I wanted you in me and in me and in me. I wanted to feel your last breath on my cheek, and I wanted it to carry my name. I wanted your head in a box under the bed. I wanted you to touch me right there without my having to ask. I wanted to be the moonlight falling on your sleeping face. I wanted to be the bullet burrowing into your brain.

And now?

Now, when I think about it, I'd trade all my demands for this: you, right where you stand.

Ellen opened her eyes. The pickup seemed to be banging itself to pieces. Teague was hunched over the wheel, wrenching it left and right, jamming the gas pedal through the floor.

She said, "You think you could drive me out to the farm, Jack?" But then she saw that he'd already pulled onto Buda Road, heading for the farm, all the while chanting, "Dina, Dina, Dina, Dina."

REDMOND WENT THROUGH THE BARN, into the shed out back, and climbed onto the tractor. He held a can of Teague's kerosene steady in front of him with one hand and fired up the engine with the other. Finding the Scout manual was like finding something his father had stolen from him. Not the book so much as his desires, his dreams, even his fears.

He fiddled with the accelerator, trying to get the engine to even out. Lucky he hadn't thrown away his father's little gift. He found it where he'd thrown it, where it belonged, in the junk drawer. Now it was in the pocket of his work shirt.

More clouds had piled up since he'd left the police station. Nearly noon and not enough sun to turn off the sensor for the yard lights. The sky felt like a heavy weight. He was being propelled now by some force outside himself, some old pain that had finally taken shape. With a little nursing, the engine started running smoothly. He eased into gear and yanked the metal wand of the accelerator. The tractor bucked once, almost throwing him, and lurched out of the shed.

The first rule of stalking is to move slowly and silently. Any quick or jerky movement usually frightens the animal you are stalking. Any broken twigs or rustle of leaves gives you away, so do not make a sound.

The wooden gate broke into several pieces when he drove against it. He crossed the yard, swinging the tractor downhill, the back tires sliding, tearing through the grass as he turned. He drove through a garden patch, the tires churning up dirt, weeds, and the luminous green blades of new growth.

He followed his father's trail, a six-inch furrow of flattened grass snaking down the field. He drove the tractor so the small front tires were on either side of it. The wet field glistened. Not even enough sun to burn off the dew or the mist hanging in the pines below.

At the top of the field, the single strand of electric fence crackled, stretched, and snapped when the tractor grill hit it. He didn't care. He headed straight downhill, picking up speed. Too much speed. When he touched the brakes, the tractor seemed to go faster. He stood on them. Nothing.

He shot past the lean-to they'd built for the cattle. Inside, a cow raised her head when he jounced past, but then went back to butting the flea bag. The cows wandering along the fence line, looking for a break into the wild berries, didn't notice him jumping on the brakes.

The tractor lunged down the rough field, jolting over the ruts. His teeth cracked together. He could hardly steer. He was afraid to turn, afraid the tractor might roll over on him.

A cow stood in his way, tearing up mouthfuls of damp, tender grass. When Redmond screamed, she raised her head, her runny eyes swarming with flies, flies clinging to the leathery lids. He stood up on the old iron stirrups and shook the can of kerosene at her. She took a few tentative steps toward the tractor, slow and stiff-legged, her knobby head plowing the air. She was expecting the feed bucket. Just as the tractor clattered past, she jumped away, moaning angrily.

At the bottom of the field, the tractor popped the wire and plowed into the stone wall, throwing him to the other side, knocking the wind out of him. The engine belched once and died. He struggled to his feet, ribs aching. The wall was now a tumble of rocks, but the tractor didn't have a scratch. When he bent over for the kerosene, he nearly passed out.

A few years ago, one of Teague's tenants paid his overdue rent with a couple hundred pine trees. They planted them here, at the edge of the woods, hoping to sell them as Christmas trees when they were grown. Another of Teague's plans that never took shape. Now the trees were crowding each other, killing each other off. The lower branches were brown and skeletal.

Overhead, the sky hung in thick, damp folds. He followed the trail to the trees, stepping over his father's abandoned marker, a log tied to a length of baling wire.

When he walked in among the pines, the air turned from gray to blue-black. Nesting birds snapped their wings angrily as he passed below. Standing in his path was a tall fern that had been stripped to a green wand. The trail was straight ahead. Someone with a hammer was standing just behind him, someone who turned when he turned, always out of sight. The kerosene sloshed quietly in its can.

Many outdoorsmen have a definite way of "looking." As they walk along, their eyes move in semi-circular rings in front of them.

Soon the pines gave way to the real woods — oak, birch, and taller, older evergreens. Gypsy moths had come through ten years before, eating everything in sight. The trees had mostly come back by now, but many were still bare, standing gray and gaunt, with lots of deadfall to climb over or around. Some of the fallen trees were so rotten they crumbled under his weight, soft red pulp and wood dust spilling onto the ground, insects rising in sudden clouds. He found a branch broken in the direction of one turn. Farther along, he found a small rock balanced on a larger one. He was on the right track.

It was lighter in the real woods, or maybe his eyes had adjusted. Every sound seemed too loud — birds scavenging through the leaf mold, water burbling in the creek up ahead, the uprush of leaves in the light breeze.

He came to a field of long, swirling grass, a gathering place for deer. There were several paths where the grass had been trampled flat. He chose the one that looked freshest. It could have been a new deer path or the place where his father had passed. When he parted the grass, he saw heel marks in the damp ground. He followed them to a deer bed, where he found a bright-blue condom wrapper. There were two small depressions on the ground, side by side. Before he could resist the urge, he bent down and touched them, ran his fingertips over them. They were damp with dew. The imprint of knees. He stood up in disgust. He pictured his father and Mrs. Kinsey rolling naked through the grass. The pigs. He spilled a ribbon of kerosene on the place and dropped a match, turning his back on the flames and heading down the field.

On the other side of the clearing, the ground dropped gently through the trees to the small creek. He stopped for a handful of clear water. The banks were clay, the color of mustard. Ellen once wanted to buy a potter's wheel and haul some up to the barn, where she planned to make mugs for tourists. But no one ever drove Buda Road except the people who lived there and the guards changing shifts at the prison. The relatives of inmates drove by, but they were in no mood to buy mugs. That's how he explained it to her. She gave up the idea but never forgave him for being right. A mark had been scratched in the clay, an arrow pointing across the creek.

At all times make use of cover for concealment. Move from bush to bush, or tree to tree, or slowly through the grass. When the wind blows and rustles the grass or leaves, move on a short way, but don't move when the grass around you is motionless.

He kept losing his footing as the ground sloped more sharply downward toward the bottom of Teague's property. He held on to the tall brush as he walked, to keep from falling. The kerosene gulped at every slip. Somehow it was leaking down the sides. His fingers were slick with it. Farther on, he found another trail marker, a tall weed whose top had been tied in a knot and twisted to point downhill.

Down in the hollow it was dark and damp. The sun never shone there. Teague had never figured out a way to use this land. The ground was tangled with slimy roots, vines, and low-growing plants. The air was rank, heavy with the smell of ripe and rot. It was the smell of things long dead and of something else, something sharp and greasy, something wild that wouldn't be denied. Down there, even the leaves grew thick and lewd. A possum, pale as death, came waddling out of the underbrush and then turned, taking cover again.

In woods, walk. In shrubbery, crouch. In grass, creep.

Without warning, the ground dropped out from under him, and he fell crashing, tumbling into the hollow. He lay on his back for a few minutes, afraid to move. When he was sure nothing was broken, he climbed to his feet. Pain shot through his lower back. Sweat stung the small cuts on his face. Somehow he'd held on to the kerosene.

That's when he heard it. The wet kiss of the thermos being unscrewed. A thin trickling. He smelled coffee, like the scent of well-aged manure. And then the voice — the twangy, country-boy voice — floated down to him like a vapor from the trees above.

"Sure glad to see you. I thought you'd be here long ago. I'm 'bout down to my last drop."

Redmond froze. He couldn't tell which tree the voice was coming from. He didn't want to look up into his father's face. He stood there in the knee-high brush, not sure which way to move. He said, "What do you want?" His voice felt small, a flat croak.

"What do I want?" The voice was easy, familiar. "Just what the next fellow wants, I guess. A little understanding. A little peace of mind."

Redmond moved a few steps closer to the voice, the rubbery brush straining against his legs. "I want you to go away."

"You made that plenty clear the other day, winging those rocks at me. And I will go. I'll pull up anchor just as soon as we have a few words together, if that's what you want."

"We don't have anything to say to each other." Redmond stared into the trees, afraid he couldn't say these things if he were looking into his father's eyes.

"*I* have a few things to say to you, things it's taken me quite some time to figure out."

The hollow, Redmond knew, was an old streambed. Somewhere below the thickly matted vines and wet black roots, it was still running. He thought he could feel it, the water moving underground.

"We all make mistakes," his father went on. "Isn't any man alive who can claim he's never made a mistake. A fellow can have the best of intentions, try to do right, and years later he finds out he had the wrong fix on things. That goes for me, and it goes for you too. You see what I'm saying."

Redmond looked around without turning his head. He couldn't help it, he had to see his father's face. Something had chewed up the trunk of a fir tree near him. He opened his eyes wider, careful not to tip his head back, and then he saw him, halfway up the tree, sitting on the fold-down seat of a tree stand, sipping from the red cap of his thermos.

His face was pale and placid, floating among the dark pine boughs and the false foliage of his camouflage suit. He was looking out into the trees, talking to himself. His legs were crossed, one foot resting on the metal step attached below the seat. Redmond had seen hunters buying tree stands at Mrs. Kinsey's, but he'd never seen one work. It was magic, a miracle of clamps and springs, his father lounging in midair.

"One time," his father said, "out in the desert, we were testing a new missile. We tested and tested and never seemed to get it right. It just would not hit the durn target. Finally they called me on the carpet. I was sure I was going to get my head handed to me. But you know what they said? They said they were glad we were making mistakes. They said our failures meant we were trying for more than we knew we could achieve. I learned something that day."

Redmond had moved slowly through the brush, toward the voice, to a spot below his father's tree, where the old man could see everything. The ground was level there and covered with half-decayed leaf scrap.

His father kept talking. "I don't know, though. Lately, to tell you the God's honest truth, I have not been all that shipshape. This old sea dog has seen better days. Excuse my language, sir, but lately I've had my balls to the wall."

"I learned some things from your mistakes too," Redmond said. He touched the front of his shirt pocket.

"Let's see," the old man said quietly, not listening. "What can I tell you about the continuing saga of Thomas Redmond, USN? I stayed with the navy and saw the world several times over. I've seen and done a few things in my time. I slept with cannibals in the jungle and watched a prostitute eat her purse in the Casbah. I fished bodies out of the bay with a grappling hook in the Dominican Republic. But maybe the strangest thing I've experienced is how your mother ran out on me."

Redmond dropped his hand. So she'd finally left, had finally broken her years of silence. But not always so silent, Redmond remembered. Sometimes she'd break into wild, reckless weeping. When he asked what was wrong, standing there bruised and aching from his latest beating, she shook him off. Soon he stopped asking, stopped noticing.

"Just packed her bags and left. Yes, she did. I don't mind telling you your mother is a very troubled woman. I have come to think of that marriage as one of my mistakes, actually. I have yet to see the wisdom of that mistake, to be quite honest. The woman told people she was afraid for her life around me."

Redmond recalled little of his childhood. Only bits and pieces, things he mostly tried not to think about. But he remembered the nights after his father finally untied him from the toilet and sent him to bed supperless. How his mother appeared with a paper plate of leftovers — a greasy slab of meat loaf, a cold chicken leg, whatever. How he ate in the dark, in bed, tearing at the food while his mother kept watch. "Hurry," she whispered, straining for the sound of his father waking. He switched the kerosene from one hand to the other.

"It's been a hard year for me. My golly, you don't know the half of it." He poured himself more coffee. "Would you like to know the real trouble? The days of open-ended R and D are over. That's the real trouble. I feel like a cowboy living in a world of vegetarians. It's quite a shock to get to be as old as I am and discover the world doesn't want what you've got to give. It's distressing. Pure misery. And you want to know what really gets my back up? She said I was a sickness she'd finally got over. Can you imagine? Human psychology — that's the real jungle, the last unexplored territory."

"She's right," Redmond said.

"How's that?"

"You're a disease."

His father inhaled deeply. When he began to speak, his voice was soft, musical, the play of water over stones. "You think you hate me, but that's just bull-ticky. Know how I know? If you really hated me, you wouldn't be here. But here you are. And you know why? Because when all is said and done, I'm still your father and you're still my son. A woman can maybe leave her husband, but a son — that's forever. The years don't matter. Distance doesn't matter. There's a bond of blood between us that cannot be denied. That's love, boy."

"I want you dead."

The red lid of the thermos hung limp from his father's finger. He was still staring into the trees. "I'm sure you do, sure you *think* you do. But may I tell you something? May I put just one word in your ear?" The tree stand clicked and creaked as he crossed his legs the other way. "It seems to me that any man over the age of twenty-one who still blames his parents for the way his life has turned out . . . well, crackers, that's a fellow who needs to take a long hard look in the mirror."

He remembered something else. The way his father always found him hiding in the cornfield and carried him back to the house, naked in his big hands, back to his room, where the shades had been drawn but the air was the color of fire. The way he laid him on the bed, turning him, touching him. The way he slapped him and said, "What are you scared of? Afraid people will find out what a dirty thing you are?" And then the big hands around his neck, pulling at him. "Relax, boy. It's only just a game."

The last few yards as you approach your game, you crawl on your belly.

With the side of his boot, Redmond cleared a space on the ground. He scraped away the damp leaves and the wet black rot underneath. When he had a space about two feet in diameter, he pulled the Navy Cross from his shirt pocket and held it out, draped across his fingers. He heard the steel joints of the tree climber ache as the old man tried to see what he was doing. The blue of the ribbon and the gold of the cross seemed deeper in the dark light under the trees.

The old man began to talk fast. "I've taken a gander around your spread. It needs a little looking after, if you don't mind my saying so. Garden patches need weeding, hens need culling. Those willows need cutting too. Unless a hen gets a good fourteen hours of sunlight a day, it'll take sick. Didn't you know that? One diseased animal can infect the whole flock. We could work this place together. We could put it back on its feet. I love you."

Redmond knelt down, laid the medal in the center of the cleared space, and unscrewed the cap of the kerosene.

The old man stood up in the flimsy tree stand, bending over so he could see better, bracing himself with one hand against the trunk. He spoke again, his voice harder: "I want very much to be your father and your friend. I love you."

Redmond heard the soft rattle of a woodpecker, regular as a sewing machine. A light breeze picked its way through the trees, blowing the scraps of light around. And the water. He definitely felt it moving underground, the small waters coiling and uncoiling. When he had the cap off, he dumped a good quart of kerosene over the medal.

"You're not acting right, boy. Didn't you hear your daddy say he loves you?"

Redmond struck a kitchen match and dropped it on the medal. The flames shot up with a loud rush, making him jump back. A three-foot column of flame stood before him.

The old man scrambled down the tree, dropping the last six feet. "You done it up brown now, boy," he said as he turned to Redmond. "That's my life you're burning up." The medal was a dark lump in the flames. He stepped slowly toward Redmond, who stood frozen by the old fear.

"You ain't too old to whip, if that's what you're thinking."

They both turned at the sound of something stepping delicately from the cover of the nearby brush. Fatima came slowly into the clearing, a great mass of black and white scalloped feathers, tail extended, an ancient geisha with her fans. Her wattle and comb slopped from side to side as her gaze ticked between them, her eyes shining black pellets. The old man shook his head at the turkey. "That there's one bird that needs culling."

In an even, quiet voice, Redmond said, "If you touch her, I will kill you."

His father looked stunned, but then smiled slyly. "I knew it from the beginning," he said, circling Redmond, "from the very moment you were born. I knew it'd come to this." He grabbed up the open can of kerosene. "This is what you really want, isn't it?" He shook the can, splashing his shirt a little. He shook it again. A gout of kerosene streaked the front of his shirt and pants. He held the can upside down over his head and showered himself with kerosene, never taking his eyes off Redmond. When he'd shaken out the last drop, he said, "Isn't this what you want, boy?" His face was shiny with kerosene. "Me dead?" His shirt and pants were dark with kerosene.

"You're already dead," Redmond said. "I kill you every night in my dreams."

He threw down the empty can. "That's just talk." He raised his chin toward Redmond. "Come on." His face looked pale, looked old. "Do it." He took a step forward, holding his wet arms wide, ready for an awkward embrace. "You got the matches, son. Finish the job."

Redmond heard the first fat drops of rain hitting the leaves. He wanted to turn and run, he didn't care where. He wanted to get away, away, away. But his father would never leave him alone. Redmond knew that. He'd be the wind under every door, the shadow behind every tree, every sound that had no name. He'd find him in every hiding place, in the deepest darkness, howling to him across the years.

His father's face, shiny with kerosene, hung before him, waiting. "Come on, boy," he said gently. "You need some inspiration?" He took one quick step and made a grab for Fatima's head. She ducked, her big wings beating the air, slashing at him. The old man staggered backward with a sharp cry of surprise, the bird flapping her big wings, chortling. He grabbed for her head, but she pecked at him, her wings cutting the air. He made another grab, but she dodged him again, flapping and squalling, head darting. A bright wedge of blood appeared on the old man's palm. Fatima. Too old to eat. Too full of disease. Fat, stupid Fatima.

The old man dropped his head, his breathing heavy. But then he jumped forward and kicked the bird hard in the chest.

"No!" Redmond screamed. He dove at his father, hitting him full in the chest, knocking him to the ground. Fatima's shrill warble filled the air.

The old man struggled partway up. "Here we go," he said. Redmond put his foot against his chest and shoved him down again. When he tried to get up again, Redmond dropped to his knees and slapped him, once, twice.

The old man raised his head off the ground. A bead of dark blood slid from the corner of his faint smile. A cold look crossed his face. In a fast, hissing voice, he said, "You ask me what I want. You know what I really want? I want you to let me off the hook. I want you to get out of my dreams. I love you."

Then it began. Redmond's arms churning, his fists pounding. And the old man's face — head thrown back, eyes closed, lips parted — locked in bliss.

Neither of them heard Ellen call out Redmond's name from somewhere back up the hill, calling once and from a great distance, his name no more than a sound trailing through the trees and dying on the damp ground.

NINE HUNDRED EIGHTY-EIGHT THOUSAND. *Nine hundred eighty-nine thousand.*

Nick followed Chase through her house and upstairs to her room, leaning against the wall while she packed a huge plaid suitcase. He was counting by thousands now. Chase's mother was at work. They were glad for that. They didn't want to explain themselves, not to anyone. They didn't want to be talked out of what they were doing. But what were they doing? Nick wasn't entirely sure. He knew this much: he wasn't going back to that school, and he wasn't going back home, not even for his clothes. He told himself this was because he'd had enough, but he knew the truth. He was afraid of what would happen to them when the police found out about the coach's car, and even more afraid of what Redmond would do when he found out.

Nine hundred ninety thousand.

And now Chase was packing, throwing everything she needed into a suitcase. Needed for what? They hadn't even talked about what they were going to do. Somehow without words they'd agreed that their only real choice was to leave. She threw several pairs of jeans into the suitcase, a stack of T-shirts, tank tops, books, tapes, an armload of balled-up socks, and a travel poster of the Eiffel Tower that had been hanging over her desk.

He looked around her room as she packed. It was filled with a mixture of leftover kid stuff and adult things. An old Raggedy Ann with chopped-off hair sat on the dresser next to a collection of cosmetics in black bottles and faceted jars with foreign names. She swept everything into the suitcase. It was too much trouble to leave the Raggedy Ann behind. From the shelf next to her bed, she grabbed *The Secret Garden, Diary of Anne Frank, Dark Star, Prince of Tides,* and some other books, throwing them into the suitcase. Pinned to the wall over her pink bed with its ruffled canopy were postcards and magazine pictures showing thickly muscled guys in Speedos slumping in lawn chairs, playing volleyball, diving stiff-legged into clear blue water. Nick was glad she didn't pack them.

When she was finished, she clapped the suitcase shut and lugged it downstairs, flopping it onto the kitchen table and flipping it open again.

"What's the deal?" Nick said.

"We're going to need some kitchen stuff," she said, and tossed in a small frying pan, a pot, knives and forks, two bowls, plates, cups. Then she ran back upstairs. Nick packed clothes around the breakables, putting the plates between the folds of her jeans, wrapping the cups in her T-shirts. She came back into the kitchen with two sleeping bags and a battered blue canvas tent that had been rolled up tight and tied off viciously. "My mom's boyfriend's camping stuff. It might come in handy." Nick started to close the suitcase, but Chase stopped him, digging out a tablet and two pens.

"We should write notes," she said, tearing off two sheets and handing him one. "We don't want anybody thinking we've been kidnapped or hijacked by a cult or sold into slavery or something."

She sat down and began to write. She wrote quickly, without pausing. She seemed to know exactly what she was doing and why.

Nick stared at the blank sheet in front of him. He didn't know what to write or who to write it to.

Nine hundred ninety-one thousand.

He listened to the scratch of Chase's pen. What *could* he write? And what about his mother? What if she came back? How would she find him? But he knew if she hadn't sent for him by now, she never would. And he was tired of waiting for things that never happened. So what good was it to write some stupid note she'd never get? And anyway, what words would make sense of his feelings, his leaving, his life so far?

Nine hundred ninety-two thousand.

Toward the end, when every day was filled with drunken screaming and slamming doors, he'd slip out of the house and hide in the barn, up in the hayloft. He sat out there in the sharp straw for hours, listening to birds flapping in the dark rafters, rats scuttling along the feed trough, wind hissing through the cracks. No one looked for him. No one even noticed he was gone.

Nine hundred ninety-three thousand.

Chase had covered one side of the paper and now flipped to the other. She'd planned this moment long ago, had memorized just what she wanted to say.

Almost worse than the fights, though, were the mornings after, around the kitchen table. Redmond stroked her cheek, and she looked at him tenderly. The fight had never happened, or it had somehow recharged their love. Sick. Once Nick had seen a little kid being dragged down the street, dragged by his mother, dragged so hard Nick thought the kid's arm would pop out of its socket. The kid was crying, but not so hard that he couldn't talk. He kept saying, "It don't supposed to be like this."

Nine hundred ninety-four thousand.

One night a few weeks after his mother left, while Redmond was working late at Kinsey's, the phone rang. Nick said hello, but no one answered. He listened for a few seconds. He thought he heard music in the background, distant voices.

"Mom?" he said quietly. Still no answer, but whoever it was didn't hang up either. He wanted to say the words that would bring her back to him, but all he could think of was "I made a lamp with lambs on it. I miss you."

He heard a sharp breath and then his mother's voice. She spoke slowly. She sounded sad. He could tell she'd been drinking. She said, "I think maybe I was never meant to be anybody's mother or anybody's wife."

He held the phone tight. "But you're already a mother. You're *my* mother." There was a long pause. Then he heard her sigh and say, "I'm sorry. I just can't do this anymore." Softly she hung up the phone.

Yellow paper with blue lines, a brown fleck floating near the bottom. He picked up the pen and wrote *I just can't do this anymore.* No greeting. No addressee. It sounded like a suicide note, but it would have to do. He signed it and folded the sheet in thirds.

"I'm a little scared," he said.

"Yeah," she said. "Isn't it great?" She stood both notes between the salt and pepper shakers, put the tablet and pens in the suitcase, and closed it up.

When she dragged the suitcase off the table, it hit the floor hard. "Heavy mother," she said, catching her breath. He tried to help her, but she shook her head. "Grab the other stuff," she said, backing out the kitchen door. The suitcase was so heavy she had to lug it two-handed, limping all the way to the curb.

Together they lifted it over the edge of the car and into the backseat, next to Chase's mesh bag. He wedged in the sleeping bags and the rolled-up tent. It was good they weren't stopping for his stuff. There wasn't room for it anyway.

Nine hundred ninety-five thousand.

The Mustang was old. A classic, Redmond would have called it. To Redmond, everything was a classic — black-and-white movies, square hamburgers, even Nick's old Incredible Hulk lunch box. You could probably put some roadkill in front of him and he'd find a reason to admire it. Nick would miss that about him, that and other things.

But he'd never miss the Redmond who flipped out with no warning. Once, he gathered up all the dirty dishes Nick had left lying around the house and threw them on his bed. It wasn't fair. He'd have washed them eventually.

Still, it was true — the car was a classic, even though the engine sounded like it belonged in a tank and the black vinyl dashboard had been cracked and bleached by the sun. The air felt like rain, so they raised the Mustang's top.

"I never ran away from home before," he said as he got into the car.

"Don't think of it as running away," she said, sliding into the driver's side. "Think of it as living your life."

He nodded, smiled. She was right. He kissed her. She was great. Everything was going to turn out great. She pushed her fingers into his hair and kissed him back.

Nine hundred ninety-six thousand.

They had Chase's mother's gas credit card, a little money, some canned food, not much more. They drove out of the city, past the lake, the roller coaster, the crumbling farmhouses. They drove deep into the mountains and straight on into the dark, the highway rising and falling before them. They were both afraid but said nothing. He covered her right hand with his left, rubbing the backs of her fingers lightly. The traffic whined. Headlights grew large and exploded past them.

Nine hundred ninety-seven thousand.

They were high up in the mountains now, alone on the road and far from any town.

Chase glanced at him quickly, then peered up through the windshield. "The sky's clear," she said. "There's Lyra. And the Summer Triangle. Could you put the top down?"

Nick said, "It's cold."

"Just for a little," she said. "I want to see the stars." She slowed down while he reached over and undid the catch on her side.

She said, "I wonder if it's like they say."

"What?" He was having trouble with the catch on his side.

"You know — that the stars control our lives. What do you think?"

Nine hundred ninety-eight thousand.

Did the stars make his mother leave? Did they turn Redmond into a monster? Just after they moved to the farm, his mother gave him a set of tiny fluorescent stars. He stuck them to his bedroom ceiling. He tried to follow the sky chart on the package, but all the patterns ran together — Cassiopeia, Perseus, Orion. When he was finished, he saw right away that he'd done it all wrong. His ceiling was just a jumble of light. He didn't want to tell Chase, but he was afraid the stars were nothing more than whirling balls of ash and ice and fire spinning far out of reach, and farther by the second.

Nine hundred ninety-nine thousand.

But then the catch came free and he folded the top back. There it was — the hard black sky smoky with stars, whirling with stars. It took his breath away. There were more of them than Nick had ever seen, a shining veil. They were bright and sharp, finer than dust, as big as ripe fruit. And they were numberless, numberless, numberless.

He and Chase sped under the spilling stars, calling them out when they recognized them, taking comfort from the constellations. Nick felt his old life fall away, fading into the distance like the pale city lights far behind them. He knew that no matter how fast they drove, no matter which road they took, the stars would always be there. Even during the day, when they couldn't see them, they'd still be there. That's all they could know for sure. Maybe it was enough. He held her hand tighter. If the stars did control their lives, he hoped that whatever they had in mind, good or bad, he and Chase would be in it together.

She leaned toward him, still watching the road. She said, "Where do you think we should go?"

One million.

His face felt hot. His heart was pounding in his neck.

"Everywhere."